Healing Hearts

W. Million

Stomill Books

Little Falls Series
Reading Order

Book 1 – Rival Hearts

Book 2 – Mending Hearts

Additional content: First Date Challenge by Wendy Million (novella about Kai and Mckenna who appear in Book 3)

Book 3 – Healing Hearts

Book 4 – Guarded Hearts

All books in this series have bonus content. You can check for that here: https://wendymillion.com/bonus-content/

For those who've had their heart healed in the most unexpected way

Chapter One

Trent

My phone is face up on the table when it vibrates with a message. *My Emily* is on my screen as the sender, and I'm sure Carrie, my date, has seen it when her eyebrows go up. She gives me a furtive glance, probably because she knows I don't have any sisters. We did the idle chitchat while we ordered and waited for our food to arrive. She knew who Grady, my brother, was when she asked me out.

Honestly, having a super famous brother hasn't been so bad for getting dates. Fame adjacent appeals to a surprising number of women.

We've been having an okay enough time, but I'm pretty sure no matter what Emily has said, this date is going to end early.

"Who's that?" Carrie asks, clearly trying to read whatever Emily has written.

I put down my fork and pick up my phone without letting my internal sigh out. *My Emily* has been saved as her contact for a while. We were all drinking and hanging out when my drunken self inputted it as a joke, along with *My Lila,* which turned out to be less of a joke when Lila took it a little too literally.

Thankfully, Emily has not.

"I hate to do this," I hedge as I read Emily's, clearly, drunken text message that is a mash-up of gobbledygook. She either needs to learn how to use voice-to-text better, or she really does need glasses, like I suggested last time she sent me something that almost required me to download a translation app. She claimed her incoherence was because she was speaking instead of typing—basically blaming her tech. Even I know you gotta proofread that shit before you hit send.

I check Emily's location on my phone and pull out my wallet to put some bills on the table. "I've got a friend in need."

"Is 'friend' code for girlfriend? Are you one of those guys?" Carrie glares at me, already deciding I'm guilty.

"Nah," I say. "Em's my buddy, but I do admit I have a soft spot for damsels in distress." I don't suggest we can redo our date again sometime. If a first date leads to accusatory and possessive behavior, that doesn't bode well for the casual relationships I enjoy most.

After my brother, Grady, met the last woman I went out with a handful of times, he told me that for a guy who claimed to dislike drama, I certainly liked fucking it. His comment gives me a brief moment of pause now every time I find a woman attractive or get hit on by someone. Given my history, marriage and kids isn't exactly the goal, so high-drama women in short stints is entertaining, at least. But even I know those relationships aren't sustainable long-term. That's kinda the point.

"Guys like you don't put 'my' anyone in their phone if they don't mean it," she says, rising from her seat in a huff. "Don't insult my intelligence. You're clearly lying."

"You can finish your meal," I say, gesturing to her half-eaten fish-and-chips dinner. There's no point in trying to convince her that a tattooed ex-con like me is exactly the kind of guy who'd put "my" in front of a good friend. I did it as a joke after Emily and Lila said I was the softest tough guy they'd ever met, but I kept it because the label is true. There isn't anything I wouldn't do for the Sullivan women, which included Lila until it couldn't anymore.

"You're leaving, aren't you? I'm not going to sit here and eat alone." She hitches her purse on top of her shoulder and storms out, her strong, syrupy perfume or body spray following behind her. "Worst date ever," I hear her grumble before throwing open the door to leave.

I double check the amount I put on the table, and then I toss a few more bills, just to be sure. I can hit a drive through after I pick up Em from...I scan her location. *The Flirty Englishman*...again. I know the guy and his wife who recently took over ownership of the bar—Kai and Makenna—so at least I can say a quick hello to them while I scoop up Em.

When I step outside, a blast of late-October wind hits me in the chest, and I hunch my shoulders, zipping my bomber jacket.

Once I'm in my truck, it doesn't take me long to get to *The Flirty Englishman*. It's my favorite pub and the one I introduced Em and Lila to more than a year ago when we were planning the Small-Town Saviors show, which was a benefit for my hometown of Little Falls.

At the long bar, Kai is chatting to a regular, and his wife, Mckenna, is probably supposed to be waiting tables. Instead, I can see her at Emily's table, an uncertain smile on her face. When Em gets drunk, her topics of conversation are unpredictable.

I saunter over, taking my time. Em looks fucking gorgeous with her hair in waves past her shoulders, makeup mostly still intact. She used to have the best shade of strawberry blonde before she started messing with it by adding so many highlights that's it's basically blonde. Her expression is soft with whatever story she's telling. Probably about Omar or her dad. Those always come out after a few drinks—her grief unmasked.

I slide into the seat across from Emily, and when she turns a glassy-eyed stare toward me, I grin.

"Hello, My Emily. You texted me a bunch of garbage, and I came to make sure you hadn't been kidnapped by aliens."

An answering smile spreads across Emily's face, her light brown eyes bright with a hint of mischief. "The text asked you to come get me, so I guess you must read alien."

"Seems like," I agree. "Definitely wasn't English." Turning to Mckenna, I ask, "Is the kitchen still open? I haven't really eaten yet."

"You haven't eaten?" Emily squints at her watch and then tries to get it into focus by moving it closer and further from her face. Her nose is adorably scrunched up in confusion. "Why not?"

"Well, I was eating fish and chips down the road, but then I got a distress signal and dropped everything to make sure you weren't being beamed up or the aliens weren't being abducted by *you*. Which, let's face it, is probably just as likely. You and your sister, Maggie, would love to do alien experiments."

"Oh my god," Emily wails. "I ruined your date. How could I forget you had a date?"

"If you'd been about twenty minutes earlier for this date," Mckenna says to me, "you could have ruined *her* date too. He was pretty awful, though. I think I would have had to get drunk too."

McKenna is not much of a drinker, despite being an owner of this pub, so that's saying something.

"You didn't ruin anything," I say, "and I'm sorry I didn't beam myself over here twenty minutes ago to intimidate the shit out of your internet date."

"Internet dates," Mckenna says with a shudder. "Those words are enough to inspire PTSD." She takes a deep breath. "What did you want to order?"

"Sausage and chips," I say, and then I eye Em across from me. "She needs black coffee, water, and she'll eat all my fries, I'm sure."

"I won't eat them *all*," Em says, waving me off. "I'll leave you half."

When Mckenna leaves, I focus on Emily. The last few weekends, this has become a routine. It doesn't bother me that she calls, but it's starting to feel like there might be more going on under the surface. Over the last year and a bit, she's been a casual drinker, but lately, she's turned getting drunk into her weekend profession.

"I'm starting to wonder if an alien species invaded your body, actually," I say, grabbing the glass with what's left of her shandy and tipping it back. God knows Emily doesn't need more to drink. Sprite and beer isn't my favorite combination, but Emily has taken a shine to it. "What's going on with you?"

"What do you mean?" Emily asks, her words slightly slurred.

"The last... I don't know—three, four weekends, you've gone on a date with some guy you met on the internet from Utica, gotten very drunk, and then called me."

"Shit," Emily whispers, "I knew I should have called someone else. But Maggie is out of town, Tyler has the baby, Lila moved to New York City, and my mom has Amir."

"My little buddy is sleeping over at grandma's tonight?" I ask, keeping my tone light.

"Yeah," Em says, searching the crowd, probably for Mckenna and her coffee and water. "I'm sorry I ruined your night."

"You ruined nothing. I like taking care of you, Em. I just want to understand what's going on."

"The dating pool is shallow and putrid," she says. "So stinky." She plugs her nose and groans. "But I promised my mom I'd get back out there."

"Your heart isn't in it," I say.

"It's been four years, and I don't have a clue *where* my heart is. Half of it's buried in the cemetery with Omar's name on the headstone, and the other half is dedicated to our little boy. I don't wanna *date*."

"What do you want?" I ask as Mckenna returns with water for both of us and a coffee for Emily.

She gives me a faraway stare. "I don't know. I wish I knew. I'm not really happy. I know that."

My heart gives a painful squeeze in my chest. There's no way she'd admit that if she was sober. The Sullivans are experts at pretending they're fine until all hell breaks loose.

Emily's expression and the way she said it remind me so much of her younger sister, Maggie, who wore the same helpless sadness like a cloak the night we first spoke in high school. Back then, I'd told her I could rescue her from the mean girl clique who had targeted her, and I had. I wish Emily's problem right now was as easy to solve.

"But I don't get the luxury of falling apart, because I have Amir. I won't be a mess for him, you know. I'm all he's got."

"Just so you know," I say, "you can fall apart every Saturday night, and I'll happily pick up those pieces and keep them safe."

"You'll hold them for me?' Em asks, her gaze softening.

"Until you're ready to slot them back into place."

"All right, folks, I've got sausage and chips," Mckenna says, sliding the plate in front of me and setting down a folded set of utensils.

"Oh," Em says, her eyes sparkling at the sight of food.

These dates she schedules seem to require a liquid diet—no actual food—which doesn't seem healthy.

"We're going to need a second set of cutlery," Emily says.

Mckenna pulls one out of her apron and slides it over, and when she glances at me, I wink. Mckenna laughs, and I grin. After a couple weeks of this routine, we all know our roles.

Though, Emily's confession about being unhappy, a little directionless, is new, and it's playing through my head, a movie on a loop.

Emily digs out the knife and fork from the napkin, and I slide the plate closer to her so it's more on her side of the table than mine. She cuts into the sausage and looks around for ketchup. I grab it and squirt a line on her piece.

"For the record," she says, "I actually *do* think aliens exist."

"As long as the real ones are hot, I'm happy to believe in them too," I say, picking up a fry and sticking it in my mouth. She's going to eat most of the plate, and when we leave here, she'll realize she should have brought a jacket, and I'll end up giving her mine then picking it up tomorrow. These dates are also one of the few times when Emily, who's normally extremely organized and efficient, is a bit scattered.

"I want the aliens to be intelligent," she says.

"Of course you would."

"They could come here and solve all the diseases we have." She cuts another bite of sausage, and without her asking, I apply the required amount of ketchup.

I know that's also weighing on her mind—that was last week's confession. She hasn't decided yet whether to get her son, Amir, tested for ALS, the same disease that killed her husband. When Omar died so young from it, she did a deep dive into his family history with the help of his parents, and it seems likely that other people in his mother's family had suffered from ALS, perhaps hidden or undiagnosed.

So last week when I came to rescue her, Emily made me a pros and cons list on a napkin to decide whether she wanted to get Amir's genetics checked or not. Her writing was completely unreadable, but talking out her feelings seemed to make her feel better.

I wouldn't even know how to handle that result if it didn't go the way I needed it to. Amir isn't even my son, and I know I'd be devastated for her, for him, for a life that would be cut short. We'll all die someday, but I don't think I could handle seeing the clock, watching it tick down to nothing.

"You picking Amir up in the morning from your mom?" I ask, trying to shift from the things weighing her down.

"Yeah," she says, cutting the last piece of sausage and waiting for me to put ketchup on it.

I do and then say, "There's a fall fair in Mohawk tomorrow. One of the guys at work told me they have kiddie rides with an all-you-can-ride pass on Sunday. I could meet you and Amir there?"

"Would you?" Her expression brightens. "He'd love that, and I'd love it too," she says. "You're ridiculously thoughtful sometimes."

Given how emotionally fragile Emily has been the last few weekends, I need to ramp up that quality for the next little while. Maybe I can't dig her out of her hole, but I don't mind the dirt, so I'll climb down there with her and see whether I can bring a smidge of light with me.

"Just with you," I say, offering her the last fry on the plate.

She takes it and pops it into her mouth, a hint of contentment in her expression, and as a starting place to slotting her back together, that's not so bad.

Chapter Two

Emily

"How was the fall fair yesterday?" Tyler, my older brother, asks on Monday morning. "You went with Trent?"

The second question is loaded with meaning. He's aware he can't ask more than that. From Mom to Maggie to Tyler to even Lila, who was somewhat resentful when she asked, everyone wonders if there's something going on between me and Trent.

We've been friends since last year when we all organized a fundraiser for our hometown of Little Falls. But even I can admit we've become closer since my dad's death, since Maggie and Grady got back together, since Lila left for New York City.

But there isn't anything more than friendship between us. Not even a little. He doesn't want it, and I don't want it—not that we've talked about it. No one seems to believe us. Which often makes me mad. Men and women can be friends. Even when one half of that equation is a guy who oozes charm and sex appeal.

"Yeah, we went together," I say breezily as I check that I have everything needed to look after Victoria for the morning.

Although Tyler has the money, courtesy of Victoria's famous popstar mother, Mia Malone, he hasn't hired a nanny. Instead, he's cut back his thrift store and his clothing creation business. For the hours he does work, family and friends are cobbling together a schedule. It's not ideal, but I also understand why he's doing it.

As he told me, he's not sure he'll have another chance to be a dad, so he's going to soak in every subtle change in Victoria as she grows. Paired with that is the fact that Mia is so famous, and photos of their baby are in such high demand, it's hard to know who to trust. So I get that part too. At some point, that might calm down, but so far, it hasn't. Tyler has security at the house and store now, but it's still more madness than I'd want to deal with.

My house showing schedule and my client bookings are usually reasonably flexible, so rearranging my schedule once a week during a morning or afternoon to look after Victoria at Tyler's house isn't a hardship. Amir is in school, so I get all the baby snuggles to myself. And since *I* don't know when I'll get this much baby contact again, it's a win for everyone involved.

"That's all I'm going to get—a 'yeah, we went together?'" Tyler prods.

"Heard from Mia?" I ask, giving him a pointed look.

"All right, all right." Tyler holds up his hands. "I get it. Trent, as a topic, is off limits. He's your friend, yadda, yadda, yadda."

And Mia is also off limits, but I don't point that out. She's been gone since late July, and it's now late October. At first, I thought she'd return sooner rather than later. I can't imagine leaving a child behind, despite the arrangement she made with Tyler, despite her level of fame and scrutiny. *A child.* I could never.

And I'm not as sure she *will* come back now. I imagine it's a hard pill for Tyler to swallow. Much like my friendship with Trent, whatever is or isn't happening with him and Mia is not up for discussion.

"How was your date with that doctor from Utica?" Tyler asks as he stuffs some sketches into his messenger bag. He likes to do some sewing while he's in the shop if he's not overrun with eager customers who hate his reduced hours.

"Terrible. He was arrogant and entitled. The conversation was dull. I got very drunk."

"And called Trent."

I glare at him.

"I'm just trying to figure out if Trent is actually just a friend or if he's a drunken booty call."

"We're not having sex, Tyler. And honestly, so what if we were? We're both adults."

"You've had a lot of hurt the last few years, and after what happened between Trent and Lila…"

"She misread that situation *big* time. I love Lila dearly—we grew up together. We all love her like a fourth sibling," I say, putting my hand over my heart, "but Trent honestly didn't do anything wrong. He's a flirt. We all know he's a flirt. She tried to take that seriously, and you can't. He's not boyfriend material," I say and then hold up a finger, "but he is fling material. Not that we're flinging anything around."

"Jesus, that visual," Tyler says, shielding his eyes.

"Whatever you're envisioning is your own fault," I say with a huff.

Trent *would* be very good fling material, if I was the type to have one. He's kind, surprisingly thoughtful, and offers a safe, nonjudgmental listening ear. When we were teenagers, I didn't understand what Maggie saw in him as a romantic partner—their relationship hadn't even been what we thought it was—but I understand Trent's appeal now.

The tattoos, the bad reputation, the lack of formal education are armor that he wields to keep some people at arm's length, which seems to include every woman he dates. They get so close, and then he drops them. Claims it was never serious and moves on. Any time I've tried to pry, after a few too many drinks, he'll shrug and tell me that's how he likes his women. High drama. Low stakes. No chance of someone getting the wrong idea.

Honestly, Lila probably dodged a relationship bullet in that sense. And I have no desire for his inability to commit to pierce me instead.

We're good as friends. The best. Other than Tyler, Omar, and my dad, there's never been a guy that I knew I could call—no matter the time, no matter what was happening—and have them show up for me. Only a fool would risk that kind of loyalty and caring for a brief affair.

Besides, I'm not sure if my real estate business could withstand anything more between us than close friendship. Even a fling—if I was willing to risk it—would have repercussions if it got out. Like a lot of small-town politics, real estate is dependent on reputation and connections.

Although Trent has tried to repair his status in town, make amends for his role in the drug bust that took down several kids and their families in our community, he's not back in everyone's good graces. In our small town, memories run long, and forgiveness runs short.

I would hate to be judged for something I did at nineteen for the rest of my life, but sometimes that's the way it goes. It's also part of the reason he lives in Utica, the city closest to Little Falls. A clean slate.

"None of your dates have been winners so far, huh?" Tyler checks the baby bottles and formula to make sure he's left me enough. "You've been back at it, what, a month?"

"Yeah," I say. "I don't think I want to date, to be honest. At least not from the shallow pool that seems to exist in Utica and Little Falls. Doctors and engineers and dentists and lawyers—all people who should probably be interesting to talk to or something, and they've been duds for me. I'm bored, or they're not nice, or our ideas about life don't match." I throw up my hands. "Where are the decent men with a good sense of humor? That's my Roman Empire."

Tyler chuckles. "Seems like a short enough list."

"Right? Two things. Check and check." I mimic ticking off boxes. But part of me wonders whether I'd even be interested if someone placed that exact person in front of my face. Ever since Omar died, the thought of being with anyone else—in any way, whether it be emotional or physical—just hadn't appealed to me. Still doesn't. My family wants it for me, especially my mother, but I don't yet want it for myself.

Tyler must read something in my expression because he says, "You know, there's no timeline on grief. You'd think Mom would understand that, but with Dad dying, my life in shambles, and Maggie doing long distance with Grady in New York City and beyond, I think you've inadvertently become her focus, her project. You *can* say no."

"I know," I say, and I do.

Apathy isn't a good way to go into anything, and that emotion—or maybe lack of emotion—feels like all I've been capable of for the last year since Dad died. The only thing I've truly thrown myself into in a way that is remotely positive is my friendship with Trent. Everything else has felt absurdly hard.

Even my relationship with Amir is cloudier than I'd like because I'm trying so hard to make it seem like I'm okay, his mom is okay, when I'm not sure I am. Not truly. Not completely. Not about Dad. Not about Omar...still.

"Victoria should be up soon for a bottle," Tyler says, as though I don't already know the routine. "I'll be back just after lunch." He slings his messenger bag over his shoulder and steps out the door.

Immediately, I start getting the house organized. It's the one thing that seems to keep me calm and focused. Cleaning and organizing is like meditating, or what I imagine meditating would be like if it involved a lot of moving around instead of sitting perfectly still.

I tackle the dishes, and I put in a load of laundry, and then I hear Victoria stirring on the monitor.

When I enter her bedroom and peer over the crib at her, she stares up at me until I speak. "Hey, sweetheart," I say, and she smiles, kicking her feet. I sling a burp cloth over my shoulder and lift her out, resting her against my shoulder. She snuggles in, and I breathe in her baby scent. The milky smell warms my chest, and I close my eyes, savoring the feel.

As long as I get these days with Victoria, it makes the loud ticking of my biological clock a little quieter. Even if part of me worries I'll never find someone again, that I'll never *want* to find someone again, which probably means I'll never have another child, I know I still have time. I'm only in my mid-thirties.

There's time.

And for now, this, right here, is enough.

Chapter Three
Trent

At the hardware store, Amir seems overwhelmed by choice. The aisle is dominated with materials to make a marble run—slides, tubes, levers, and pretty much everything else you could imagine. A few months ago, we made one with cardboard from the recycling bin and some tape, and ever since then, Amir has been obsessed with building a "real" one like those he's seen in online videos.

"We can build it any way you want," I say. "Your mom said we can attach it to the wall in the garage or make it free standing. If we don't like what we build, we can take it apart and try something else another day."

"What's the budget?" he asks for the second time. I'm not sure at five years old that he completely understands what a budget is or why it's important, but he must have heard his mom tell me ten times before we left the house not to "blow the budget." Emily would be the type to talk about budgets in all sorts of situations, so I'm sure the word is familiar, if not understandable.

"You can let me worry about the budget this time," I say. "It's my Christmas present to you. Just start picking things." I gesture to the basket I'm holding in my hand. "We'll figure out how to put everything together and what we want it to look like when we get you home."

He nods, a little crease of concentration forming between his eyebrows as he strolls down the aisle, arms crossed. At the shoots and slides section, he stops.

"I think I'd like some of these?" He gazes up at me hopefully, and I tip my chin for him to pick some.

And after the first slide drops into my basket, Amir relaxes, picking up other building pieces, asking questions, clearly working out in his very intelligent brain what the marble masterpiece will look like in his head. Here's hoping we can actually create it in real life. The thing I've been learning the last few months is that Amir's imagination is much greater than his skill level or what's realistic in terms of time, money, and ability. But I like his drive. The intense desire to do well, to be the best, is such a Sullivan trait.

Once Amir seems satisfied, and I'm content that Emily isn't going to want to murder me for the size or scope of the thing, we head up to the register. Stacy, the owner of the hardware store, greets us both with a smile.

As she rings up our purchases, she says, "Did you hear Bruce Mullen is looking to sell and retire in the spring?"

"No," I say.

Bruce has owned the most popular car mechanic shop in town for years. When I was a kid, we spent a lot of time there with my dad, under cars after hours. The two of them had been good friends, and Bruce has continued to be good to my mom in the years since. In my teenage years, he even offered to let me get under my mom's car and help him fix problems, but I wasn't ready then.

Sometimes I think memories of my dad are why I opted to try to get my automotive apprenticeship when I got out of jail. The scent of motor oil brings me a strange comfort, as though part of me can sink into the past, the time when I was close to my dad, without any conscious thought forming.

I also happen to be really good at fixing shit. Like an extra sense of how to diagnose a car, how to repair it, even before I hook up diagnostics or run tests. A client can describe what's happening, and even if it's not precise, I can get to the source of the problem. Just last week, my boss, Earl Runions, told me he'd never been so glad to have taken a chance on an ex-con.

I don't love the "ex-con" moniker, but I can't deny that it fits. The fact that it's still something he thinks about and comments on, even seven years after my release, is enough to make me feel sick to my stomach.

My nineteen-year-old self really didn't consider or understand all the consequences of the choices I was making.

"I've heard from a few people in town who've made the drive to Utica that you're a pretty talented mechanic," Stacy says.

Even though it's true, heat creeps up my chest and into my neck. Being told I'm good, in almost any context, makes me squirm.

"Have you thought about coming back here? Opening your own shop?" She pauses as she rings in the last item, the total appearing on the screen.

I flash my card to pay, my mind creaking to life with the implication she hasn't directly stated.

"Taking over for Bruce?" She prods when I don't react.

Having my own shop always felt like something for someday. But I don't know about coming back to Little Falls, about building a life *here*, necessarily. Last year's benefit turned a few people's opinions of me around, but I don't know if it's enough.

"I hadn't really thought about it," I lie.

"Well, you should," Stacy says. "Little Falls will be lost without Bruce. So many of the companies in town are chains now, you know? No personal touch. They'll take you for all you're worth."

I'm sure there are people in Little Falls who'd believe the same of me—that I'd cheat them somehow, be dishonest in my dealings.

"Yeah," I hedge. "I don't know. I appreciate the suggestion." I give her a little nod and pass one of the bags for the marble run to Amir.

As we walk to my truck, Amir's little hand engulfed in mine, my brain is on fire with all the ways I could not just run but improve on Bruce's current business. Stacy hit a spark, and it's ignited a wildfire.

"Did that lady say you could work in Little Falls?" Amir asks, his tone hopeful.

"Sort of," I say, opening the truck door for him. "She was suggesting I could own my own auto repair shop. Like where I work at, but it'd be mine."

"I think you should," Amir says with a grin. "I could help."

"You'd help me out?" I ask, returning his smile.

"I'm a good helper, right?"

"The best," I confirm. "Thing is..." I take a deep breath and look him in the eye. "I just don't know if it's the right thing to do. I might need to talk to your mom about it."

"She knows a lot," Amir agrees.

"She does. One of the smartest people I know." And I know she'll be honest with me about how stupid this idea is.

"Do you want to do it?" Emily asks. It's the first question she's posed since Amir and I finished the marble run and he started playing with it.

"I don't know. People don't make a lot of comments to my face anymore, but I'm not sure enough people will trust me."

"Didn't Stacy imply, and I *have* heard people say, that they drive to Utica just so you can diagnose and work on their vehicle? It might be a bit of an uphill battle, but..." Emily bites her lip and tilts her head. "You'd win them over."

I put my head down, fiddling with the screwdriver still in my hand. If I'm being completely honest, I want the shop. I want the opportunity. I want to prove to everyone in Little Falls that I'm more than what I did at nineteen. The fundraiser was supposed to do that, but it didn't convince all the people, and the event was a one-off, not sustained, easy for skeptics to miss or avoid.

This way, I'd be in their face, impossible to ignore. Definitely pros and cons to that scenario. A tough skin would be necessary.

"Do you have the money?" Em asks gently.

"I've been saving," I admit. "No idea if it'll be enough."

"I think you should go talk to Bruce, see what he's thinking, and then decide if you want to take it further. If this isn't the right fit, something else will be."

Reasonable, rational, good advice. My problem has always been that once I want something, I have a hard time veering off a path. Once the course is set, I get tunnel vision. If whatever Bruce says clicks for me, I'll want it, even if I shouldn't, even if I can't. The best thing I've ever done for myself is to stop wanting things intensely enough to make stupid decisions to get them, whether it's jobs or women or anything else. I've been coasting on the surface of what I *could* have, what I *might* want, for the last seven years, and it's kept me mostly out of trouble.

"You're a good friend, Em," I say, setting down the screwdriver on the workbench and drawing her into a hug. She comes willingly, her cheek pressed against my chest, her hands spanning my back. The scent of lemon surrounds us, and I realize she must have been cleaning while Amir and I were building.

"So are you," Emily says. "Everything you've done for me and Amir the last year has meant a lot—more than you know."

"It would be nice to be closer," I say, "though it would make it harder for me to pick your drunken ass up from *The Flirty Englishman*."

"You'd still come." She pokes my side, and I laugh.

"I would," I say. "I'd feel terrible if it turned out you really were abducted by aliens."

"They exist."

"And they're smart."

"And some of them might be hot."

"Unlikely, but sure."

Emily laughs and steps away from me, sliding me an amused glance. "I'm a firm believer that when you know what you want, you should go after it. You never know what life might have in store. Seize opportunities while you can."

For anyone else, that might be good advice, but I really don't know if it is for me. I haven't trusted myself enough to go after what I want for years.

"I'll talk to Bruce."

"You're coming to Christmas Day at my mom's, right?"

"My mom and Grady will be there, so yeah," I say with a shrug.

"Amir will be happy that his playmate will be available." She stares at her son with open affection. "He's been asking me about a brother or sister lately."

"What brought that on?" I ask.

"Victoria, I think. He likes feeling like he's a 'big brother' and he asked me when he could be one." Her lips twist and then she frowns.

"Do you want more kids?"

"Yeah," she says without hesitation. "More than anything, but I just...I don't know." She sighs and crosses her arms. "Life's all about timing."

Part of me wants to dig a little deeper, but another part of me doesn't want to think about her with anyone in that way. Picking her up every Saturday from her failed dates has become one of the highlights of my week, and I don't want to consider how I'd feel if she stopped calling.

"You'll get there," I say, slinging my arm around her shoulders and kissing her on the temple. "You're a great mom. The aliens watching over us directing traffic wouldn't waste that skill set on only one child."

She laughs and pokes me in the ribs again. "Please. Now the hot aliens are god-like?"

"They've got their eye on you and your voice-to-text skills. You can't convince me otherwise."

"Trent," Amir calls from the marble run. "I need the screwdriver. It's getting stuck here. We've gotta fix it."

I grab the screwdriver off the bench and go over to crouch down beside him, where it appears the marbles are congregating.

"Let's get 'er done, buddy," I say, settling in beside him.

When I glance over at Emily, she's watching us, affection coating her expression.

"Want to learn some new skills?" I ask her.

"Absolutely not," she says, "but feel free to teach him so I can stop calling a handyman for every little thing."

"Who are you kidding?" I ask. "You call me."

"Exactly. My handyman." She grins and then disappears back inside her house.

I watch the spot she was in for a beat before Amir tugs on my sleeve, drawing my focus back to him.

Chapter Four

Trent

Bruce finishes his brief tour of the shop and extends his hand. "I'd be pretty pleased to have Adrian's son take over the business. I still think of him often."

"Me too," I say, accepting his hand.

"There's just one thing," Bruce says, rubbing the back of his head, "and I'm not too sure how to phrase it."

I tense because I'm sure I know, and I'm tempted to assume, to make the transition easier for him.

"Not everyone in the town is going to be welcoming if you take over. I can't guarantee the business I have is the same one you will."

"That'd be true no matter who took over." No one would run things exactly like Bruce, from pricing to service. Some people will always balk at change.

"Some won't even give *you* a chance," he says.

"If I can do this, I'll throw my whole heart into it, and I might not win 'em all over, but I'll get enough. I'm confident." Or not at all confident, but I'm good at faking. False bravado works in almost any situation.

"People might even question where you got the money," Bruce hedges.

"They'll be able to follow the trail right to the bank. I'm going to talk to Warren Ferguson right after this. I don't do any of that shit anymore, Bruce. This isn't a front for anything."

"I've heard you're a good worker. You've even managed to fix some things I couldn't find or figure out over the years. The switch to more computerized components and electric cars has been a steep learning curve for me," he admits.

Whereas I've thrown myself into the changes from the minute Maggie worked her magic and secured me the apprenticeship in Utica. I might not be book smart, but I'm persistent and determined when I'm locked into something more practical, something that has a solution somewhere if only I dig long enough or deep enough.

"Earl'll miss you in Utica, if you decide to go after this."

He will, but I don't admit that out loud. There's no one else working for Earl who'll stay after hours for far longer than necessary to crack a problem. There have been some advantages in my superficial life—lots of time to get good at work. And Earl's been fair with overtime and the bonuses I deserved.

"I'll let you know when I have the finances secured. You're hoping to bow out in March?"

"I was going to put the business up for sale in March," Bruce says. "I can leave later or earlier than that if it works for you."

"I'll keep you posted," I say, shaking his hand again before leaving.

Next stop—the bank.

By the end of my day off, I've visited every bank in Little Falls, and then I even went to a few different ones in Utica that I researched online that seemed more likely to lend to me.

The only one who's offered me a loan at a rate and with terms that seemed even remotely reasonable is Warren Ferguson, and even the interest he's charging is twice what it should be. This opportunity is a year too early for my background check to be clear of my conviction.

One fucking year.

Since I'm considered high risk as an ex-con with a poor credit rating, the loan terms are shitty, and the interest rate even shittier.

Frustration eats at me as I crack a beer in my apartment.

Grady might have the cash, but I don't want to ask him. We've only just started getting closer again, and if I'm gambling on taking over the business, I can't drag him into it. Family and money rarely mix. Besides, he and Maggie are planning some big renovation of the Whittaker house to turn it into a place Maggie'd want to raise a family. That's gotta be expensive.

My phone sits beside me, but I don't know if I can pick it up, send the text I need to write.

With a deep breath, I set down my beer, and I type out exactly what I wish I didn't have to say.

Timing's not right. Good luck with the sale.

Immediately, my phone buzzes in my hand with a reply. *Sorry to hear that. Probably won't list until February or March. If anything changes, get in touch.*

I've exhausted all the legal channels to get the money together, and I'm not putting my future at risk—either through financial or legal gambles or by asking friends and family—to get my dream off the ground. Another opportunity will come up. Maybe not as perfect as this or with the memories this place has, but I can't dwell on what won't happen.

I set my phone down, take another swig of my beer, and curse my foolish youth.

Christmas at the Sullivan residence is an event with a capital E. The house is decorated as though a professional has done it. The tree alone must be fourteen feet and stretches into the vaulted ceiling. The warm wooden tones of the decor are perfect for the festive season, and the massive wooden table that sits between the open plan kitchen and living room only increases the grandeur. On a normal day, the Sullivan house is impressive, but the festive season makes it more so.

Christmas music is playing softly through the speakers around the house, and Joanna has lit candles that make the air smell like cinnamon and spice.

My mom is already here, talking to Joanna and drinking mulled wine as the two of them prep the food.

Emily told me that Lila and her family normally come to dinner too, but they decided to have their celebrations in New York. Maybe that's legitimate, since Christmas isn't a big celebration for her family. Lila told me once that she celebrated lots of American traditions with the Sullivan family growing up because it helped her feel like she fit in, but the ones she really cherished were her traditional Chinese ones.

Even still, I can't help feeling a twinge of guilt that maybe *I'm* the reason they aren't here. This is the first year the Castillo family has been invited, because of Grady and Maggie's renewed connection, and the first year Lila and her family *haven't* been here.

When I turn around, Emily and Amir are coming through the door. Em is wearing a red knit dress that hugs her frame like it was stitched with her body in mind. From just above the knee all the way to the scooped neckline, the fabric loves every curve. She makes my short-sleeved button up and jeans look sloppy—not that she'd ever say that.

Not for the first time, it strikes me how criminal it is that someone as beautiful as she is inside and out has struggled to connect with anyone since Omar died. She's the whole fucking package with a bow on top, and no one seems capable of unwrapping her or taking her home.

Maybe it really is that she doesn't want the possible heartache again. Romantic relationships *are* a gamble. Seems like the only explanation.

"Trent!" Amir cries as soon as he sees me. He races over, and I crouch to sweep him into my arms before raising him high.

He laughs, and when I settle him on my side, still in my arms, his grin is contagious.

"Did Santa come to your house too?" he asks.

"All I got was a lump of coal," I say, feigning a grimace. "Guess I was too naughty."

"You're not too naughty," Amir says with a laugh. "Mom, Trent says he's naughty."

Emily shoots me a sly smile, and there's a small shake of her head, as though she's internally censoring herself. I flash her a cocky grin, and that only makes her small smile widen.

"I bet in certain situations, Trent is a *very* naughty boy," she says to Amir, tickling his stomach, "but he's always the best with you."

"And with you," Amir says to his mom.

"And with me," Emily agrees, and she runs her hand along my exposed bicep.

The skin-to-skin contact sizzles, as though the lightest touch from her is a brand. Normally, I ignore the sensation, pretend I don't feel the heat of attraction. She doesn't seem to, and there's no way I'd ever do anything to jeopardize my relationship with Amir, my friendship with Em. Both have become sacred in the last year, ever since her dad died.

I bear the scars of what those sorts of feelings can do to a friendship thanks to Lila. We shared a few drunken kisses, nothing serious, and when Lila pressed for more, I was honest and told her I didn't have more to give. But it definitely taught me that mixing friendship with any other feelings was a recipe for disaster.

"You spend your afternoon with Victoria yesterday?" I ask Emily.

"No," Amir says, answering for her. "Uncle Tyler canceled."

"That's true," Emily says with a slight frown. "Apparently, he's had the shop closed for the last four days."

"Is everything okay?" I ask.

"I guess so," Emily says with a shrug. "Tyler just texted the group chat and said he wanted some dedicated daddy-daughter time, and he was closing the shop early for the holidays."

The door opens, and Maggie and Grady enter with Grady's two dogs. Amir immediately wiggles out of my arms to make a break for Hite and Zeus, who are in full body wags at the sight of Amir.

"You should get him one," I say to Emily.

"A dog?" She gives me an incredulous look. "I view dogs how some people view kids—nice to take on once in a while, but not for me long term. He can get his dog fix at Maggie and Grady's house. The hair alone..."

"Fair enough," I say because I feel the same about them. "Amir gets picked up tomorrow to go to his grandparents?"

"Omar's mom flies in tomorrow, and then they'll go down to Arizona for the rest of the holidays. They also have a dog," she says with an amused look. "So he can get his fix there. Though Omar's parents have a tiny, barky thing. Then Omar's dad is flying back with Amir just before school restarts."

"You weren't tempted to go somewhere too? Or go with him?" I ask because I know how involved Emily is with Amir, how empty her house and life will feel without him for almost two weeks. On Sunday mornings, she's always at her mom's bright and early to get Amir when he's spent the night.

"Running my own business means that holidays take careful planning," she says. "It's nice for Amir to have some time with his grandparents without me. Besides, I'm sure Tyler will need help again. He won't keep the shop closed indefinitely. I'll sneak in some aunt time to get my kid fix."

Just then the door opens behind us, and the house goes unexpectedly quiet. When I turn, Tyler is framed in the entryway with Victoria's car seat in one hand and Mia Malone in his other hand. Her bodyguard, Pasha, stands behind them, huge and intimidating.

"Wow," I say. "That's an entrance."

"Oh my god," Emily says, recovering the quickest. "We're so glad you're here." She rushes toward them, drawing Mia into a hug.

And that's another reason why Em is a gem. Even though I know she's had some conflicted feelings about Mia leaving Tyler and Victoria, she doesn't hesitate to embrace Mia when she reappears.

Once Emily has Mia in her arms, the rest of the family descends, embracing Tyler and Mia, cooing over Victoria, slotting Mia right back into the family like she never left.

Soon, we're all sitting around the giant table, passing food, and sharing stories. The dogs, so well trained by Grady, are perched on the front entrance mat, even though I've seen Amir try to entice them over with bits of turkey.

"Mia and I wanted to talk to you all," Tyler says, his tone confident, but his posture definitely less so. "We both really appreciate how you've closed ranks around me and Victoria over the last five months, but I think—to make sure Mia's able to get that bond with Victoria, for us to get our feet as a family—we're going to take some space to ourselves for a little while. When I'm at the shop, Mia and Victoria will either stay home together or come with me and be in the store. We're going to try to spend as much time as possible, just the three of us."

"Of course," Joanna, Emily's mom, says. "We'll all support you in any way we can, and if that means staying out of the way, we'll do that." She glances around the table for any dissention, but I know she won't find any.

But I can tell from the slight slump to Emily's shoulders that she's processing what this will mean for her, for the connection she has with Victoria.

While I also get what Tyler wants and needs, it doesn't feel quite fair to Emily, Maggie, and Joanna, who've poured so much from their own wells to make sure Tyler's stayed full.

"Just for a while," Tyler says, trying to make eye contact with Emily. Maybe he's not as unaware as I thought.

"I'm really happy for you all," Emily says, raising her glass. "A toast. To Tyler, Mia, and Victoria and their first Christmas as a family."

We all raise our glasses in unison, clinking them together, and I make a note to check in on Emily a lot during the next couple of weeks while Amir is away and her time isn't filled as she expected.

Chapter Five

Emily

M y house has never been so clean. One of the things you never realize about having a child until it's happened to you is how they leave tiny tornadoes of things around the house—garbage, toys, dishes, crafts. The cleanup is never ending until they're out of the house and you miss it—all of it.

Despite what I told Trent, the holiday season is typically slower in real estate too. I could have gone somewhere, but with Lila in a funk, Maggie connected at the hip to Grady, and most of my other friends married or coupled up, my best option would have been to venture off alone. Given the mood I've been in lately, that holds zero appeal.

But so does sitting in my house on my own.

"Where does this go?" I ask Maggie, popping out of her backroom at the pharmacy.

"Are you sure Tyler wouldn't appreciate the organizational help at his store?" Maggie asks from where she's filling prescriptions at the high counter.

"He needs it," I agree, "but he and Mia asked for privacy. I can't show up there and ask for the keys."

"You could," Maggie says. "I'm sure he'd love it."

Except, I don't actually *want* to be alone. At Tyler's store, it would be just me and my thoughts as I rearranged clothing racks and put new product out. Like most of us in the family, he has specific expectations around his business. He has a structure about how things are priced that I've never bothered to learn. Whereas here, I can stock Maggie's shelves at the back—it's mostly pairing like with like. Things that expire sooner up front. Easy.

"What about this?" I ask, holding up some sort of asthma apparatus.

"All right," Maggie says, scribbling something on a notepad and then turning to me in obvious exasperation. "What is going on?"

"What do you mean?"

"You've been here for three days."

"I know."

"Is it because Amir is with his grandparents? Can't you go stage a house?"

"That's all done," I say with a shrug. "I don't even have a listing to help declutter right now."

"I don't need you decluttering here either," Maggie says, sweeping her hand around the store. "I actually hire people to check expiry dates and stock shelves and all the things you're doing." She scans me from head to toe and then narrows her eyes. "Why don't you schedule some dates on that app you're using? Get out. Meet some people."

"No," I say with a shake of my head. "I think I'm done with all that."

"Mom will be all over you."

"I'm aware," I say with a huff. "But I hate it. I hate everything about it. All I do is have terrible conversations, get very drunk, and call Trent for rescue. Rinse. Repeat."

"He is good at rescuing. Rescued me a time or two," Maggie says, and I can tell she wants to say something else.

"That's all it is."

"Have you just been dating to make Mom happy then? I thought maybe you'd turned a corner?" Maggie leans back against the counter and crosses her arms.

"There are no corners," I say. "It's just a long road of grief. The terrain isn't so rough anymore—at least not with Omar's loss—but I've got no desire to detour anywhere else or set a course for a new romantic relationship. I don't think I want that."

"So were you just dating to make Mom happy?"

"I don't know," I say. "Maybe." I take a deep breath. "But I also think I want more kids, and that's impossible without a partner."

"Not impossible," Maggie scoffs. "There's adoption. Better yet, sperm banks exist. Just get some donor sperm. My friend Gwen, you know the really flighty one from Michigan? Her sister used a donor and had a little boy. I think her sister lives in England now. But you could totally do it on your own, if that's what you want."

"Oh," I say, breathing out the word. For whatever reason, it's a solution that hadn't occurred to me. "I guess I could, couldn't I?"

"If you really don't see yourself meeting another man, wanting another partner, but you know you want another kid, then yes, of course you can. Your life is already set up as a single parent. And obviously, we'd all help in whatever way we could."

Maggie must see the hope and indecision written on my face because she says, "Come look." She does a search on her computer, and up pops databases for browsing donors. "You'd want a fertility clinic to figure out what type of treatment you'd need with the donor sperm, and I don't know how much, if anything, your insurance will cover, but it's definitely doable." She turns a little toward me. "You still have the money Mom gave us from Dad's life insurance? This might be a good way to spend it."

I did have that money. Tyler had used his for his store, and I think to pay his staff while he went on tour with Mia. Maggie had used hers to expand the pharmacy, and mine had sat in the bank, neglected, not even invested. As though I set it there, hoping Dad would come back to claim it.

I watch as she clicks a few buttons and has one of the databases up to search. She makes some selections on the filters, and then a list appears. With her finger on the mouse, she scrolls down. "Lots of choices."

"Yeah, that's..." My mind is a bit boggled by the sudden possibility, and for the first time in months, hope is stirring in my chest. *A baby.*

"You know, this seems like something you'd probably like to do in the privacy of your own home," Maggie says when I try to co-opt the mouse.

"Right," I say with a little laugh. "You're probably right."

Already, I'm thinking about spreadsheets, pros and cons lists, genetics, and about a million other variables that I'll need to investigate.

Indecision strikes when I back away from the computer. "Do you really think this is a good idea, though? I wouldn't know the person."

"You'd know all the important bits—genetic information like height, eye and hair color, diseases, and so forth. You'll know more medical information about this anonymous person than you ever would about some guy you met on a dating app."

"I guess that's true..." I say, but inside there's still some sort of barrier to the idea that I can't name. "I wouldn't have to worry, like I do with Amir."

Maggie stares at me for a beat, as though she's mentally preparing herself. "Have you decided whether you'll get him tested?"

"No," I admit. "On the one hand, it could be a tremendous relief. On the other, every time I look at him, I might see what's to come. Watching what happened to Omar…I've never felt so helpless." There are no words to articulate his physical collapse, to explain what it felt like to know he understood what was happening, even when communication became impossible. Awful. It was awful, and I wouldn't wish it on my worst enemy, let alone two of the most important people in my life.

"Do you want one of us to get the testing done? Check the results?"

"I don't know if that would be any better," I say. "I think I need to do it, but I just can't quite bring myself to do it yet."

"Whatever the outcome, you know we're all here for you. We'll be there for Amir, too." Maggie draws me into a hug, and I squeeze her tight.

Over her shoulder, I see the screen of donor information, and I vow that I'll at least investigate it. If I was willing to go on all these awkward dates in a bid to get what I think my heart really desires, I'd be silly not to look into this too.

"And if you pick a donor," Maggie says, a smile in her voice, "I want the details."

"Once I've made a decision," I say, "you'll be the first person I call."

Chapter Six

Trent

I trudge through the snow to Emily's front door, and I grab the shovel off her porch. I scoop up the snow and throw it to the side, creating a path. After I've cleared a decent walkway, I knock on the door.

It's New Year's Eve, and I'm supposed to be back in Utica in an hour to meet my date at a bar downtown for some big bash. With this weather, I should probably be leaving now to stand a chance of getting there on time, but after helping Grady with an electrical issue with his truck, I figured I'd check on Em before heading back out of town.

I knock again and stomp my feet against the cold. When she opens the door, the wind swirls tendrils of her hair not caught in her ponytail around her shoulders. Her brown eyes are alight with surprise.

"Trent! I thought you had somewhere to be tonight?"

"I gotta head out in a minute, but I just wanted to make sure everything's good at your place? There's a storm coming."

Her two-story house is one of the older ones in town and prone to all sorts of finicky issues that crop up out of nowhere.

"Yeah, everything's fine," she says, glancing behind her.

Then I hear the incessant beep.

"Em," I say, stepping around her into the house. "It'll take me two seconds to change those batteries."

"Oh, you don't need to," she says, rushing to the kitchen table in the middle of the room and gathering some papers. "I was just in the zone, and I was ignoring it. But I can get to it."

I toe out of my boots and go to where I stashed batteries last time I was here and one of her smoke detectors started acting up. "Just because Amir isn't here doesn't mean you can neglect your own safety."

"It just started, I swear."

"Uh huh," I say, and I go to the closet to get out the little step stool. "You working on a real estate deal?" I ask, nodding at the spreadsheets and checklists she's got beside her computer. She has a knack for becoming laser focused and ignoring everything else around her. I can be the same way when I'm troubleshooting a car, so I'm not one to give her shit for it.

Her chest flushes, and the color rises into her cheeks. I cock my head, curious.

"Please tell me you're not making spreadsheets and checklists about one of those app dates you went on."

I grab the screwdriver I leave handy in the same closet and climb the small ladder to unscrew the smoke detector while I wait for her to answer. When she doesn't, I glance at her over my shoulder. "What are you up to, Em?"

"It's private," she says, tugging down her sweater and hiding her hands in the sleeves.

"O-kay," I say, drawing out the word. I can count on one finger—this one—the number of times Em has outright refused to tell me something.

"It's just..." She shakes her head and avoids my gaze. "Private."

"That's fine," I say, removing the old batteries and slotting in new ones. "You don't have to tell me anything. I'm not prying." I screw everything back together and step down off the ladder.

As I'm putting everything away, I try to keep my curiosity in check, but I'm wracking my brain trying to come up with something that'd be private but would obviously require the research of spreadsheets and checklists.

Oh shit. I hope she didn't get bad news about Amir. Maybe she *did* get him tested.

"Is everything..." I run my hand over the top of my head and scan her for signs of trouble. "Is everything okay?"

"Yeah," she says. "Yeah. Totally fine. I promise."

"As fine as that smoke detector was?"

"The smoke detector actually was fine," she says with a hint of a smile, "just complaining a lot. But I'm good at tuning that out."

"Apparently," I say.

"I would have dealt with it eventually," she says.

"Now you don't have to. Your handyman came to the rescue just in time."

"I was definitely in mortal danger."

"Imminent mortal danger," I agree, and we're now standing close enough that I could reach out and tuck one of the tendrils of her hair behind her ear. She looks cute when she's out of sorts, but it's definitely unusual.

"My hero," she whispers, looking up at me.

"You got a reward for me?"

"Is that why heroes do heroic things? For the reward?"

"Some heroes are altruistic. That's not me," I say, and all I can think about is how soft her lips would feel under mine, which is all kinds of wrong. But the thought is there, insistent.

"You're one of those morally gray heroes, are you?"

"I don't have a clue what you're talking about, and it's pretty fucking sexy," I say, biting my lip. "I love it when you go all book smart on me."

She laughs and pushes my chest, making me take a step back. "You're terrible."

Emily's phone on the table chimes at the same time the phone in my pocket vibrates. I take it out and frown at the display.

"Fuck," I mutter. "They're closing all the roads in the county. I better get going."

"If they're closing the roads, you can't drive on them, Trent. If you get in an accident, that's an insurance nightmare. Just stay here. I have a spare room."

I bite the inside of my cheek, indecisive, and scroll through all the weather alerts. "It's not going to let up, though, Em. I could be stuck here a while."

"I'm sure we can find some way to fill the time," she says with a shrug.

And I really wish I hated all the dirty places my mind goes, but I'm used to having these thoughts about Emily and not following through. It's become almost like second nature—think incredibly dirty, friendship-destroying thoughts, act on exactly zero of them.

Just then, as though to remind me that I shouldn't be having any of these thoughts about My Emily, a text rolls in from tonight's date, asking whether I'm on the road.

Immediately, I write back that I'm stuck in Little Falls with the road closures. She texts *Boo!!* and then probably blocks me. I've been out with her a couple times, and she's become progressively more unhinged. It's possible she'll show up in Little Falls looking for me. Might be for the best that I'm not keeping this date tonight.

"You all right over there?" Em asks, nodding at my phone.

"Just canceling my date."

"Violet getting a little violent?"

"Potentially," I say with a little laugh. "She's probably calling me an asshole to all her friends right now."

"Maybe you should start dating a different sort of woman," she suggests.

"What would be the fun in that?"

"You know there's nothing wrong with engaging in a serious, committed relationship."

"I find that to be a very interesting comment coming from you," I say, dropping my phone back into my pocket and taking off my coat to hang it over a kitchen chair.

"Hey, I've done serious and committed."

"Me too," I say.

"No, you have not."

"I have."

"Name one person."

"Your sister."

"We both know that's total bullshit." She laughs.

"I was seriously committed to that lie for a whole year. That's impressive. You have to admit that."

"I admit nothing," she says.

That's fair. I'm glossing over the wide-reaching consequences of that lie, so it's probably best if we leave it there.

"You didn't book yourself a hot date for tonight? Amir's gone for almost two weeks, and you're not taking advantage of the empty house?"

"I've decided the dating game is not for me. Deleted my profile yesterday."

"I'm going to have my Saturday nights back? No more drunken phone calls? That's disappointing."

"I'm sure you'll survive."

"Survive but not thrive," I say. "*The Flirty Englishman*'s profits will be down. No more shandies. No more late-night shared meals. They're going to call begging you to resume dating."

"The food and the shandies were the only positives of my weekly dating nightmares."

"Ugh. You wound me," I say, splaying a hand over my heart. "I don't rank?"

"Over the shandy, but perhaps not the food," she says, rubbing her fingers along her chin as though seriously contemplating it.

"I won't tell Kai you're downgrading his shandy."

"Only to upgrade you. Really, you should approve of that rather than ratting me out."

"It's New Year's Eve, Sullivan. I was supposed to be getting drunk off my face and making out with a hot woman. While I do have a hot woman still," I say, gesturing to her, "I do not have the beer."

"I don't have beer," Emily says, a slight flush to her cheeks. "But I do have a bottle of wine and another one of champagne."

"You have champagne?" I follow her to the fridge. "What are we celebrating, My Emily?"

She has the door open, and I'm peering over the side. When she glances up, our faces are too close, reminding me of all those thoughts I try to keep at bay whenever we're in close proximity. I love that sometimes she smells like lemon when she's been cleaning, and sometimes, like now, she smells like peaches. I just want to take a bite. It's especially hard when she returns my flirty banter, as though she enjoys it too.

"Seems like getting drunk on fancy shit and playing a few rounds of strip poker might be in order," I say, my voice huskier than it should be.

"No one is stripping," she says.

"I'll happily strip for you. Wouldn't be the first time." I start to pull on the back of my shirt, and she grabs my wrist.

"Trent." She gives me the same look she gives to Amir when he's on the verge of getting himself in trouble. Even that's a fucking turn on, and it really shouldn't be. Why do I like being scolded by her?

Flirty banter fucks me. Her getting impatient with my flirty banter fucks me even more.

"You want me back in line," I say, dropping my hand.

"Please," she says, grabbing the bottle of wine from the fridge instead of the champagne. "If this is your starting place tonight, we may not survive the storm."

"What's that supposed to mean?" I ask, genuinely curious.

"I know not to take you seriously, but sometimes you push it just a bit too far." She cracks the top off the white wine bottle, and I realize it's not that fancy. No need for a corkscrew.

Rather than digging into her comment, I ignore it. Partly because my flirting is semi-serious. She's one of my favorite people to talk to, to hang out with. Being around her is one of the easiest, most natural relationships in my life. I might not be able to say exactly how or when that happened, but I know it's true.

But I'm also very sure that I have no intention of ruining our friend-ship, jeopardizing the relationship I've built with Amir over the last year. The kid has lost two important men in his life, and I know I've made myself a third. Having lost my father at a young age, I would never want to cause him more heartache because I followed my dick when I really needed to follow my brain.

Anything that happened between me and Em would have to be short-term and mean nothing, and I don't see how anything good comes from that.

Unlike Em, who's been drunk around me several times with no serious slips or incidents, I've been very careful *not* to be drunk around her.

"Maybe just one glass," I say. "We can watch the ball drop."

"Sounds like a responsible plan," she says, pouring us each a generous amount.

"Responsible, huh?"

"You don't like that word?"

"It's not one I've often had associated with myself."

"I think you just sell yourself short," she says, handing me a glass. "When you look in the mirror, you see the foggy haze of your past, but I see you, Trent Castillo. I see all of you. And you're pretty fucking great. Even when you're being responsible." She taps her wine glass to mine and leads the way into the living room.

I stand for a beat, watching her walk away, wondering whether I dare let her comment sink in.

Chapter Seven

Emily

When Trent saunters into the living room with his glass of wine, I have to school my outside so it doesn't show my insides. He is, probably hands down, the sexiest guy I've ever met in my life. From his short light-brown hair, tattoos, and tall, muscled stature to the natural swagger he seems to possess, he commands attention wherever he goes. Everything about him oozes charm and sex appeal, and normally I can handle that.

We've flirted many, many times before. Trent is a world-class flirt who sometimes lightly crosses boundaries in a teasing way. Which I've always been okay with before—he is who he is, and you can't take any of it seriously. Lila is proof of what happens when you don't understand that Trent doesn't mean any of it. Feelings get hurt, and they really don't need to.

But there's something about having him in my house, without the barrier of Amir or other people, that's doing wild things to my insides. Heat is pooling where it doesn't belong. Thighs are tingling in ways they shouldn't. Even his cologne is hitting in a way it normally doesn't—the dark, spicy scent with a hint of vanilla makes me want to lick it off his skin.

Maybe I need to go back to my original plan of looking for a partner to be my baby daddy, because although I was starting to believe otherwise, it doesn't appear my lady parts are completely dead yet.

"You okay?" Trent asks when he sits on the other end of the couch from me, which I'm grateful for. Far away seems like a good idea.

"Fine," I say. "Why?"

"I thought we were going to watch terrible TV and count down until the ball drops." He nods at the television. "You didn't turn it on."

"Oh, well," I say, trying to cover up the fact that I've been in here contemplating all the levels of his hotness. "I thought maybe we could play a game instead."

He raises his eyebrows and takes a suggestive sip of his drink.

"*Not* strip poker," I say.

"That's a shame. I am very good at poker."

"I don't know what that means in this context—that you're actually good at cards or you're good at stripping."

He grins but doesn't say anything, just takes another pull from his drink. My heart rate accelerates, which makes me feel ridiculous. No matter how much we've flirted before, he's never made me as discombobulated as he has tonight.

"Maybe *Ticket to Ride*?" I suggest, getting off the couch to pluck it from the little cabinet where I keep all the games Amir and I have played.

"Amir has forced that one on me before, so at least I know it," he says, scooching closer on the couch so he can reach the coffee table. "Competitive, but not in the 'I'll never speak to you again' way."

"Which is why I like it," I say. "Board games in the Sullivan family were a bloodbath."

"Castillo family too," he says. "Until my dad died, and my mom had to take on another job. Then we didn't have much family time."

I grab his hand and squeeze it, and he squeezes back. When I lost my dad a little over a year ago, I was in my thirties. I can't imagine losing that connection as a kid, or in my son's case, never having it at all.

Trent draws my hand up to his lips and kisses the back of it, as though it's the most natural thing in the world, before letting my hand go. He's typically very affectionate, but the action still makes my breath catch, and I hope it's not noticeable.

Whatever is wrong with me tonight, it has to be gone by the morning.

While we set up the game, each brush of our hands, touch of our knees, sends a jolt of electricity through me, as though he's a live wire. I've never been so hyperaware of him before, but I'm also beginning to realize we've rarely been around each other without another person as a buffer. We spend time in public or in bigger groups or with Amir, but alone in this house after a glass of wine is a whole different vibe.

"Did you want another glass of wine?" I ask once the game is set up and my nervous energy is threatening to make our friendship weird. And the last thing I want is a weird vibe to spring up between us. Trent has rapidly become one of my favorite people to spend time with, and if I ruined that because I haven't had sex in years, that would be a massive disappointment.

"No," Trent says. "Responsible, aren't I?" His lips tilt into the hint of a smile, as though he still finds the notion funny.

I scurry out of the living room and into the kitchen to press my hands into the counter, taking deep breaths. No matter what, I'm not going down Lila's path—assuming something that's not really there.

Maybe I should go on one of those apps that's just about sex. Hook up with a couple guys, get this current flushed out of my system.

But I've always been terrible at casual sex. The few times I tried it in college before I met Omar, I always felt shitty afterwards, no matter how good the guy was.

"Em, are you coming back or did you go to bed on me?" Trent calls from the living room. "We have to at least make it to midnight."

"Be right there," I say. I open the fridge, grab the wine, and tip more of the pinot grigio into my glass.

Thankfully, the second glass of wine seems to loosen me up enough that the casual touches and teasing glances Trent sends my way don't get misinterpreted as anything more than flirty friendship while we play board games, watch the ball drop, and then get ready for bed.

Once we're upstairs, I show Trent the guest bedroom, and then I make a beeline for my own room to avoid any temptation. I've just gotten into my nightgown when there's a light knock on my bedroom door.

"Em? Have you got a spare toothbrush?" Trent says through the wooden door. "I hate going to bed with gross teeth."

"Just a second," I say, and then I search my ensuite bathroom until I find a new one.

When I swing the door open, Trent is there in his boxer briefs and no shirt. Muscles ripple across tattoos. His left arm has ink, but I was never conscious of how much lived under his clothes too. He takes the toothbrush from my outstretched hand, and then I realize that, while he looks absolutely delicious, I'm wearing the equivalent of a paper bag. My nightgown is shapeless and more Mom-efficient than sexy.

"Thanks," he says, but he drags his gaze across me, and I swear heat rises between us.

He's so good at switching on the chemistry, it should be criminal. When he walks into a bar, I bet women are sucked into his field—a magnet at full strength.

"Sleep well," I say, shutting the door as fast as I can without being rude.

I collapse into bed and stare at the ceiling.

I will not ruin my friendship. I will not ruin my friendship. I will not ruin my friendship.

"Roads are still closed," Trent says when I come into the kitchen the next morning, lured by the smell of bacon.

"I know. Maggie texted me too. Online, it looks like the storm is stuck spinning its wheels here." I glance out the window, appalled by the amount of snow that's already accumulated. My snowblower is broken too.

"I made breakfast from odds and ends I found. It's in the oven. Should be ready in about ten minutes," he says, glancing at his watch.

I turn on the oven light and peer inside. "You made a breakfast casserole?"

"Easy enough," he says, pouring a coffee and adding cream and sugar to it before passing it to me.

"And you made coffee? I'm never going to let you leave." I raise my eyes to the ceiling and say, "Snow gods, keep it coming."

"Snow aliens, clearly."

"The amount of snow out there already is otherworldly. And they're calling for several more inches."

"Wind's supposed to pick up too."

"You're never going home."

"Where's your snowblower? I can battle some of it back."

"About that," I say. "When I went to use it yesterday, I discovered it wasn't working."

"I'll take a look after breakfast, see if I can get it running," he says, raising his coffee to his lips.

"I guess it's good that today is a holiday," I say sitting at the kitchen table. My laptop and all my notes are still haphazardly gathered together. It doesn't look like Trent would have looked through anything, but I'm not sure my curiosity would have survived having it here and not looking if I was him. I flip them over and tuck them more under the laptop.

"If I'm stuck here again tomorrow, I'll have to call in," Trent says.

"Hey," I say, suddenly remembering what we talked about a couple weeks ago. "Did you go see Bruce? Are you taking over his shop in the spring?"

He sets his coffee cup on the counter and turns away, opening the oven to check the food. "It's not going to happen."

"Oh," I say, deflated. "I thought for sure you'd do it. It's a great opportunity. And I'm not going to lie—I'd love to have you in town instead of half an hour away."

"Couldn't get the financing," he says, poking around the casserole with a fork.

"You said you had some money saved..."

"It's the loan," he says, finally turning to look at me. "Ex-con." He points to himself. "High interest. Shitty terms."

"At what point do they stop holding that against you?"

"Next year. The Clean Slate Act means my record gets sealed," he says. "The opportunity is a year too early."

"Let me help," I say. "I have life insurance money from my dad. I can give you the loan..." My brain is ticking through options. "Or I can buy the business, and you can do a rent-to-own sort of situation. Whatever you pay me goes to paying down the loan or paying off the business."

"No," Trent says with a sharp shake of his head.

"It's not a big deal. I can totally help you. I have the money, and I understand the real estate market. I can even just buy it and then sell it to you a year from now at the same cost."

"Em, I said no."

"But why not? You'd be amazing, and this town needs an honest, knowledgeable mechanic."

"Not everyone's going to see it that way," he says, shoving his hands into the pockets of his jeans. "Besides, I'm not mixing our friendship with a business loan. If the business goes tits up because I run it into the ground, I'm not having your money at risk. You don't get anything out of any of the deals you proposed—just me."

"I'd get to see you succeed."

"It's a no, Em," he says, and this time his tone is sharper than I've ever heard.

"Okay," I say, running my hands through my hair and turning away a little.

"I appreciate the gesture," he says, his voice gentler, "but my problems aren't yours, and I don't intend to make them yours."

"That's what friends do, Trent. They help each other." My eyes land on the papers I've shoved under my laptop, on the problem I'm having that I'm keeping from him, and I suddenly feel like a huge hypocrite. "Do you want to know what I was doing last night?"

"You said it was private," he says, leaning against the counter.

"It's private because I'm struggling, and when I'm having a hard time, it's difficult for me to admit it."

"Struggling financially?" he asks, a frown creasing his brow. "Is the real estate business not doing well? I see your signs all over town."

"No, I'm...Real estate is fine." I take a deep breath. "I've been going on all these dates because my mom convinced me I should try to get back out there. As you know, my heart hasn't been in it."

"No shit," he says with a slight grin. "Your liver probably thanks you for deciding to put an end to that."

"I think I've decided to maybe do something else instead?" I say, my tone less than confident.

"What do you mean?" Another frown.

A beat sits between us, and I'm not sure if I can get the words out. Despite all the research I've done since Maggie mentioned it, all the databases I've combed through, all the fertility clinics I've contacted, all the insurance calls I've made, I'm still not one hundred percent sure this path is the one for me.

"Maggie mentioned to me a while ago that if what I really wanted was a baby, that I could do that without having a partner."

"Adoption?" Trent asks, his expression still troubled.

"Donor sperm?" I remove the papers from under my laptop. "I've been weighing all the options. Donors. Clinics. Insurance. My finances if I were to bring a second child into the mix on my own."

Trent stares at me for a beat, and I can almost see the wheels turning. "How does that even work? Is it really a turkey baster full of sperm that you just inject up there?"

That makes me laugh, and Trent actually flushes a light pink. "Sorry," I say, trying to control my laughter. "The visual." I spin my index finger at the side of my head. "Not quite. It's a syringe and a long tube, and they basically deliver the sperm as close to the egg as they can. Or at least, that's what the internet tells me. I haven't met with anyone yet."

His brow is furrowed, and I can tell there's something else he wants to say, but he's holding it back.

"Do you want me to show you?" I ask.

The timer goes off for breakfast, and Trent pulls out the casserole, dishing up plates for both of us and bringing mine over.

He takes the seat beside me, and our knees graze. He nods at the computer as he takes a forkful of hashbrowns, egg, bacon, cheese, and whatever else he found in my fridge to mix with it. "Show me."

For the next hour, I take Trent through the databases, search functions, and fertility treatment options.

"Seemed weird to me at first," Trent says as he cleans up the dishes, "but I can see how you'd like the idea."

"What do you mean?" I ask, taking the dishes from him and putting them in the dishwasher.

"With the genetic testing, you wouldn't have to worry about ending up in a situation like you've got with Amir—where you're not sure of the outcome." He glances at me after he scoops the leftover casserole into a container for the fridge. "You like certainty, and this would give you that."

"Yeah," I say, somewhat surprised that he caught all of that without me having to say any of it. "It would."

"You deserve that," he says with finality.

And I don't know why, but his comment makes me a little sad instead of happy.

"Thanks," I whisper, wishing for something I can't even name.

Chapter Eight

Trent

The day passes the way snowed-in days typically do, quick in some parts and slow in others. The slowest parts of the day were when I spent a couple of hours trying to cobble together a short-term fix for the snowblower until the roads are clear to get to the hardware store.

I finally got it going, but I know at least part of my problem is that my brain was half caught up in thinking through Em's decision to go with a sperm donor.

Despite what I said to her, and even though I know it's a solution that makes sense for her, I don't *like* it. The idea of some unknown guy getting her pregnant, the idea of watching her expand with some other guy's baby—none of it sits right with me. And I *know* that's ridiculous.

We're friends. I've got zero say in what she does with her life and certainly not with her body. So it bothers me that I'm bothered.

Get a fucking grip, Trent.

I should be happy that she's pinpointed what she wants out of life. A few months ago, I vowed that I'd do whatever I could to get her out of this slump, and now that she's found what she wants, I can't seem to make myself get fully behind it. Like all those dates she was going on that didn't seem to satisfy her, this solution doesn't seem like quite the right fit either. At least to me.

I really hope my reluctance wasn't obvious when she was telling me about it all.

I want her to be happy—whatever that looks like. And all day I've had to remind myself of that fact.

For lunch, we eat the leftover breakfast casserole while Emily combs through databases and adds to her spreadsheets. I find other odds and ends around the house to fill my time—changing light bulbs, tightening handles, fixing squeaky doors, anything to keep myself busy.

At dinner, we make food side by side, getting in each other's way, jostling shoulders and laughing while we make some stuffed chicken recipe that Em found online. It's messy as fuck but also funny as hell. The finished product looks like we dug it out of the garbage, but it tastes amazing. The cheese, tomatoes, and spinach complement each other to perfection.

"That's a winner," Emily says, pointing to the chicken and potatoes on her plate. "Though I think we also could have submitted it as a Pinterest fail."

"Does not look like the picture online," I say. "I don't know how they got all this shit to stay together in the photo. I suspect a Photoshopwin, there."

"That would make sense," Emily says, pointing her fork at me. "Do you want some wine? There's probably enough for two more glasses."

"Sure," I say. "I'll get it."

I pour us both a glass and deliver it to Em at the table. We eat in silence for a few minutes before Emily's phone rings. When she sees it's Amir, she puts him on speakerphone, and the two of us tell him about the snowstorm, about me fixing the snowblower, and he tells us about swimming in his grandparents' pool, about walking their tiny dog, about the new Lego sets they bought him.

Listening to him talk fills me up in a way I wouldn't have expected, as though some part of me has become deeply invested in his happiness too.

When my gaze connects with Em's across the table, just before the call comes to an end, I see the soft affection in her gaze.

"He's a really lucky kid," I say when Emily ends the call.

"Getting to spend the break in Arizona?"

"Having you for his mom," I say, sopping up more of the sauce with the chicken and potatoes.

She doesn't meet my gaze for a beat, and then when she does, there are tears in her eyes.

"That means a lot, you know. I've been trying so hard to keep myself together since Omar died, and then after Dad died. And if you think I'm holding it together really well, then maybe Amir does too. Maybe he doesn't realize how broken his mom is."

"Fuck, Em," I say, and the legs in my chair screech on the floor as I get to my feet and circle the table, hauling her into a tight hug. "It's okay to be a little bit broken after everything that's happened to you. And I mean it when I say you never have to hold anything together around me. Never."

"I can't even get him tested because I'm worried the result will wreck me." She cries into my shirt. "But it feels irresponsible not to know, to be aware."

"It's not irresponsible. There's no cure. Knowing or not knowing doesn't change that right now." I take a deep breath, because part of this doesn't seem like any of my business, but I hate seeing her suffer.

"Right now, it feels like he has it, doesn't it? Isn't that the weight of not knowing? Can you imagine if he doesn't? How much relief would you feel?"

"But what if he does?"

"Do you think that weight would truly be heavier than the one you're carrying right now?"

Em steps back and rubs her eyes. "If I get him tested, will you..." She takes a shaky breath, her voice thick with tears. "Will you be with me when I get the results?"

"Whenever, if ever, you decide to do it, I'll be in lockstep with you, I promise. Whatever you need, you've got me. I promise."

She flings herself at me again, and I hug her tight, breathing in the smell of peaches and the scent that's all Em just underneath.

After we clean up from dinner, Em asks if we can just watch a movie, so we go into the living room. She puts her head on my lap, and I run my fingers through her hair as we watch one of the *Fast and Furious* movies. Mindless entertainment.

When she falls asleep, I carefully scoop her into my arms, and I carry her to bed. As I'm laying her down, she wakes up, and she grips the back of my neck, clearly disoriented for a minute.

"There's just one thing that bothers me about the donor," she whispers, as though we've been having a silent conversation all day.

"What's that?"

"I'll have another kid who doesn't have a dad, and I was really hoping it would be different this time, you know? That I wouldn't have to do it alone."

I kiss her forehead and her temple. "You're not alone. You've got your family, and you've got me. I'm not going anywhere. Get some sleep."

I tuck her into bed, and she turns onto her side, her eyes closing.

At the door, I stand watching her for a beat, my heart aching for all the weights that seem to be dragging her down. I'd do anything to ease any of them if I could.

Chapter Nine
Trent

The roads are still closed, and the walkway and driveway need to be blown clear again when we wake up. I send a text to Earl, my boss, to let him know I'm still stuck in Little Falls. Luckily, I keep a spare set of clothes in my car for nights when I get so into fixing something at the shop that I stay over.

Downstairs, I've just pushed down the toaster when Emily appears. I hand her a coffee, and when the toaster pops, I put two waffles on a plate, give them a liberal douse of maple syrup, and pass her the plate.

"Used all the good stuff in the casserole yesterday," I say. "I guess I need a lesson in rationing."

She smiles and takes the plate. "Breakfast and coffee two days in a row?" She slides into one of the kitchen chairs and lets out a satisfied sigh. "Seriously, I'm kidnapping you. I'm going to tie a chain to your leg. Give you enough room to move around the house but not out the door."

"That doesn't sound psychotic at all."

"Blame the aliens. They warped my brain that one time you didn't show up when I called."

"That's slanderous chatter," I say, sliding into the seat beside her. "I've never not shown up when you told me the aliens were upon you."

"You realize from now on, all my texts are going to lead with one word: Aliens."

"And I will drop everything to appear at your side, like a good boy."

"I do love a good boy," she says.

"Good boy in the streets, naughty boy in the sheets." I waggle my eyebrows at her.

"Do not ever teach my son that rhyme," she says with a laugh. "Like, ever."

"Someone is going to have to teach him how to pick up women," I say, taking a sip of my coffee. "You want me or his friends?"

"That is many years from now," she says, "so that'll be a game day decision."

"Put me in, Coach."

"By then, we'll be old, and he'll have no desire to learn anything from either of us."

"More slander. I'll always be the cool uncle."

"You'll be someone's cool dad someday, I'm sure," she says, avoiding my eyes as she takes a drink of her coffee.

"Doubtful," I say as I cut a piece of the toaster waffle. "These aren't as terrible as I thought they'd be."

"Amir and I have tested many, many brands in our bid to find the best toaster waffle."

"I think it's a success."

"If I was a better mom, I'd be making them from scratch."

I catch her gaze and hold it. "You gotta let go of other people's expectations or stupid standards—you're enough for him, I promise."

"You've been making a lot of promises lately," she says, her tone light, but I think the meaning might be heavy.

"I was thinking about what you said last night when I carried you to bed."

"Was I talking in my sleep?"

"I don't know. Maybe." I eye her. "You said the idea of a donor didn't appeal to you as much because you'd have another kid without a dad."

She flushes, and I wonder whether she really doesn't remember saying that to me. She *had* been half-asleep.

"And I think, if that's how you really feel deep down, that maybe you should keep dating. You've still got quite a few years before you need to worry about being too old, right?"

"Too old is relative," she says. "I could freeze my eggs, get a surrogate. But I also don't want to be starting over again in ten years when Amir is fifteen. Already, if I got pregnant today, they'd be about six years apart."

"I hadn't thought of that," I admit.

"Trust me when I say that's all I've been doing lately is thinking about it. From every angle. Every scenario." She points to her computer and her stack of papers. "Pros and cons. The whole thing. I don't want to use a donor. That's not my first choice, but I don't want a relationship either. The idea of having a relationship with a man doesn't appeal to me. Not yet. There wasn't a single spark on any of those dates. Maybe that phase of my life has passed, I don't know. Maybe the donor is the lesser of two evils."

"I just want you to be happy," I say.

"I want to be happy too," she says, "and I'm trying really hard to figure out what that looks like."

The roads remain closed, but the snowfall starts to let up. I spend most of the day outside, digging Emily's car out, digging my truck out, clearing the sidewalks, and helping her elderly neighbors to get their properties clear of snow too.

When Leann Picallo comes out of her house with a shovel in hand across the street, I steer the snowblower over.

"I can get this for you," I say, even though I've heard through the town grapevine that she absolutely despises me.

She squints through the drifting snow at me, clearly not sure who's talking. "That Trent Castillo?" she calls out.

"It is," I say.

"Don't need no help from you," she says, coming down her porch stairs into almost waist deep snow with her shovel.

"I can at least have a path cleared for you in ten minutes. It's no problem with this," I say, giving the snowblower a good pat on the side.

"You know who my son is, Trent? He was one of your clients back in the day. Got hooked on meth. Still hooked on meth, as far as I know. But I don't know much since he left home when I wouldn't support his habit, when I tried to get him help. You might see what you did as harmless, but it wasn't harmless to me. Wasn't harmless to a lot of people in this town."

"I made a lot of mistakes when I was nineteen," I say, struggling to find the words. "I'm sorry your son got mixed up in those."

She ignores me and starts shoveling, but it's so ineffective that I'd laugh if I wasn't so fucking ashamed of myself. Rather than leaving her to it, I start at the end of her driveway, blowing the snow out of the way.

There's nothing I can do about what happened to her son, my part in it, but if I never start making amends, never try to help those people I hurt in some way, then I might as well have stayed in jail.

We don't speak the whole time I clean up her property, even when I'm almost on her feet as she shovels, and when I turn to leave, she goes into the house, shovel in hand.

When I come in from clearing snow from what feels like every property on the block, Emily's making dinner.

"All I had was stuff to make spaghetti. With Amir gone and so much on my mind, I think I lost track of groceries."

"Who doesn't love spaghetti?" I stomp my boots and take off my snowy jacket. "Any word on the roads?"

"Maggie has heard they might be open late tonight as long as the wind doesn't pick up."

"You okay if I stay here until then? Grady texted and said I could go over to Maggie's with them if you were tired of me."

"Is it possible for someone to get tired of you?" she asks with a hint of teasing.

"I know it seems impossible, but it's bound to happen to someone at some point."

"Not me. Not yet." She drains the spaghetti and gives me a heaping portion before dishing up her own.

We both take our plates to the table, and there's a surprising heaviness in the air. I don't know if I carried it in from my conversation with Leann or if it's been in here with Emily most of the day and I wasn't here to feel it.

"Everything okay?" I ask.

"Yeah," Emily says with a sigh. "I've just been doing a lot of thinking." She gestures to the pile of papers. "I think I just need something to take my mind off it."

"The *Fast and Furious* movie wasn't enough to keep you awake last night," I say.

"I only like the ones that have Vin Diesel in them," she says.

"Ah, that was the problem."

"And I'm a boring mom who goes to sleep early so I can get up early most days."

"You're not boring, Em. Far from it. Another movie while we wait for the roads to open or some games?"

"A movie," she says. "My brain can't brain any more than it already has."

"We can watch my favorite Christmas movie," I say as we finish our meal.

"What's that?"

Emily takes her dishes to the sink and comes back to grab mine. I lean back in my chair and take a long pull from the glass of water she gave me. "Die Hard."

"Controversial choice."

"Only for people with no taste," I say.

"I've never actually seen it," Emily admits, slotting the dishes into the dishwasher.

"Criminal," I say, rising to start the water for the dishes too big for her small dishwasher. "We'll rectify that tonight." I bump her shoulder, and she smiles at me.

"Looking forward to being schooled."

Emily's head is back in my lap, and I've got my fingers in her hair, idly playing with strands while we watch the film. Maybe it's a bit too intimate, but she doesn't protest, and I like when I can touch her without it becoming loaded with sexual tension. For whatever reason, her head in my lap and my hands in her hair is more comforting than hard-on inducing.

We're half-way through the movie when Emily takes the remote and lowers the volume.

"I've been thinking a lot about something, and I'm really nervous to talk to you about it," she says without turning to look at me.

"Okay," I say, my heart kicking. I can't imagine what she'd want to talk to me about that would make her nervous, given everything we've covered in the last year of friendship. "You can talk to me about anything. I'm not gonna judge, Em."

"Right, well, it's less about the judging and more about the freaking out," she says with a little laugh, but she's still staring at the TV rather than turning to look at me. She takes a deep breath. "I want to buy Bruce's shop and we can do a rent-to-own type of situation."

"Em—"

"Let me finish. Yesterday, one of the reasons you didn't want to do it was because you said I wouldn't get anything out of it. But what if…What if I did?"

"Like interest payments?"

"More like a deal," she says, her voice quiet. "I want a baby, and you want that shop."

I sit in stunned silence for a minute, trying to figure out whether I'm interpreting what she's saying correctly. "You want me to father your child? Is that…Is that what you're saying?"

She sits up and scoots back from me so she's sitting cross-legged on the couch facing me, but she still won't make eye contact. "I know it's a wild idea, but I think it could work. We'd both get what we want. And neither of us wants a relationship, but we get along really well. You're already so important to Amir."

I run my hands down my face, not quite sure what to say. "This isn't a small thing, Em."

"I know. I know." She sneaks a glance at me. "And you hate it. Oh, god. Please tell me I haven't ruined our friendship."

I take a beat to gather my thoughts before I respond. "I don't have any intention of having kids at all, if I'm honest. I would never want to bring a kid into the world attached to my reputation." My mind strays to Leann's reaction to me today. "It's just not in the cards for me."

"You don't have to pay for the mistakes you made at nineteen forever."

"Maybe not, but I'm nowhere near making up for what happened back then. Not even close. I've barely pounded out one dent in my reputation, you know? I can't do that to a kid." I run my hands along the top of my head and scan Em, trying to figure out whether I say more. "And even if there wasn't that, I don't want to fuck up our friendship.

I already did that with Lila by being too careless, not understanding the weight of my actions, and there's no doubt about the weight here."

"I think we'd be okay," Em says.

"Maybe we would. But if we weren't, it's not just you and me. I love your kid. The other day when we were on the phone with him, I realized that I want him in my life forever. If you and I fuck up our relationship, that's not fair to him, either. He's already lost so much."

Em finally looks at me and there are tears in her eyes. "It just seemed like the perfect solution for both of us."

"But at what cost?" I ask. "I don't jump in anymore without checking the depth. I learned my lesson there."

"I could still—I'd still do the loan, you know that, right?"

"I know, but mixing money and friendship is a bad idea too." I shake my head.

"I hope I haven't ruined anything in our friendship by asking, but I couldn't stop thinking about it. I just...I had to ask."

"You didn't ruin anything," I say. "It would take a hell of a lot more than you offering me the honor of fathering your kid to break our friendship. Truly, Em. Whoever gets to be that person for you is going to be a lucky fucker."

Her expression is sad as she stares back at me, and I get the sense she'd like to press me, see if she could use her debating skills to win me over. But I'm not going to be won—not about this.

Her phone and mine chime at the same time, and rather than dwelling on the growing awkwardness between us, I snatch my phone off the coffee table.

"Roads are open," I say. "I'll get my stuff together."

"We're okay?' Em asks, rising with me.

I drag her into a hug, and I squeeze her tight. "I'm honored you asked, Em, and I'm sorry I can't do it."

She presses her cheek against my chest, and I let myself feel it in a way that I shouldn't, let myself wish for a brief second that I could say "yes." But if I let myself sink into those thoughts, I'll be consumed with the idea of Emily being pregnant with my kid, and I can't let that notion take hold. That's a fucking dangerous path.

For me, wanting leads to foolish choices, and I'm done making those.

Chapter Ten
Emily

By the end of the first week of January, I've met with two fertility doctors at two different clinics. For whatever reason, neither of them clicked for me in a way that felt like fate or destiny stepping in. I don't know why I'm convinced it needs to feel that huge, but that's my mindset. From the minute I step into the clinic, it needs to feel right, or I'm not doing it.

I've just finished showing a house when my phone buzzes with a text.

I've got a dentist friend in Utica. Divorced. No kids—yet. Nice guy. Just starting to date again. Any interest? I can set you up.

I stare at Kelvin's message, feeling conflicted, which is all I seem to feel lately. As though I'm doing life in the dark, no path clearly lit.

The men from the app weren't working out, but maybe dating wasn't the wrong course of action. Maybe how I was meeting the men was the problem. Kelvin's typically a good judge of character, and he knows me well.

This weekend? I text back to Kelvin. *My mom takes Amir most Saturday nights, so I could make that work.*

I'll set it up. Kelvin texts back. *I'll send you the meeting details.*

We meet at a cocktail bar in downtown Utica. It's not *The Flirty English-man*, and I'm determined that I'm not going to call Trent to rescue me, regardless of how the date goes. Maybe part of my problem was that Trent's been my safety net since I started dating. Maybe I never gave any of the other men a chance.

Michael is tall with dark hair and light-blue eyes. He's conventionally handsome, and he's managed to straddle the line between casual and dressed up with his jeans and button up shirt. Once we get the small talk out of the way, he carries a conversation that doesn't feel forced. Maybe I was dating the wrong way all along.

"We could end it here," Michael says when we finish our second cocktail. "Or there's a dance club next door, if you want to extend the evening."

I can't remember the last time I went dancing, but I've also never had a guy suggest it. "Do *you* like dancing?"

"Um, actually," he says, letting out a self-conscious laugh, "last year Kelvin talked me into participating in the benefit for Little Falls."

"You were in that?" I ask, surprised. I'd been part of the organizing committee for the Small-Town Saviors fundraiser after the town flooded, but after my dad died unexpectedly, I'd stepped away near the end.

"Just part of the group number," he says, "but it sparked something in me. I've taken a few lessons since. Turns out, I like dancing."

"Let's do it," I say, hopping off the stool from the high table we've been sitting at near the window.

He takes my hand and leads me out of the cocktail bar and down the street to the dance club. As soon as we enter, I second guess my decision. The music is thumping, and it's going to be impossible to talk.

Once he leads me onto the dance floor, I realize we can use non-verbal communication instead. We move to the music together, and it's pleasant, if not electrifying. It's the first time in a long time that I've felt like a date might have even a hint of potential.

When there's a brief lull in the music, I shout to Michael that I'm going to the bathroom, and he says he'll get us drinks. He points to a spot near the bar for us to meet, and I agree before weaving my way through the crowd toward the bathroom.

I'm almost to the bathroom hallway when someone grabs my elbow, and I turn, ready to give whoever it is a piece of my mind when I'm met with a familiar face.

"Trent?" I say. "What are you doing here?"

"What are you doing here?" he asks, looking past me and then focusing on me again.

I haven't seen him drunk since Lila decided to leave town. Before things fell apart between the two of them, we all used to drink together. After their misunderstanding, he's never gotten drunk with me, and I've only just put that together now, as we stand face to face on the edge of the dance floor.

"What are you doing here?" he repeats.

"I'm on a date," I say.

"Here?" Again, his drunken gaze checks the bar. "With who?"

"A guy Kelvin set me up with," I say. "Who are you here with?" Part of me internally cringes at what he'll say, but he gestures to a few guys chatting up a group of women.

"Guys from work," he says. "I didn't know you were back dating."

"Kelvin offered, and…I took your advice, I guess."

His gaze sweeps over me, and he licks his lips. "You look fucking lethal tonight. I hope he knows how lucky he is."

"I should go," I say. "I'm supposed to meet him at the bar, and I still need to go to the bathroom."

Trent releases my arm, but I can feel him watching me, and my spine, bare in my black backless dress, is tingling as I weave the last little distance through to the bathroom.

When I come out, Trent is waiting. "Can I talk to you for a minute?"

"Right now?" I ask, uncertain. I've also had a few drinks, and red flags are being thrown left and right at Trent's behavior—I'm afraid I'm going to run them all over.

"Yeah," he says. "There's a room most people don't know about."

He doesn't wait for me to agree, but takes my hand, leading me around a corner to an area with a few high tables and one couch. As soon as we've rounded the corner, he presses me up against the wall, caging me in.

My heart thrums, but I'm not worried or anxious, I'm excited. This is such a bad idea, and I'm just buzzed enough not to care.

"What did you want to talk about?" I whisper.

"How fuckable you look in this dress, for one," he says, staring down at me. "And then how your little proposal the other day has been a complete mindfuck."

"What do you mean?" I ask, arching toward him a little.

He puts his lips right next to my ear, and I shiver. The dark, rich vanilla tones of his cologne make me feel drunker than I am.

"The idea that you want my baby inside you might just be the hottest fucking thing any woman has ever said to me," he murmurs. "And I can't stop thinking about it."

His calloused palm is on my leg, just where the short hem of my dress sits, and I'm almost desperate for him to drag it up and under, to feel how turned on I am too.

When he goes to pull away, I put my hand on the back of his neck, rise onto my toes, and kiss him. There's the briefest hesitation, where his lips don't move, and then with an audible indrawn breath of surprise, he's kissing me back. His lips slide over mine, warm and soft. His tongue dips into my mouth, and I angle my head to take him deeper. A moan of wanting escapes, and I'm not sure if it's me or him.

He squeezes my ass and brings me tight against him. His other hand slides into my hair, but it's not like when he plays with it on the couch, this is demanding, insistent, as though he's been waiting for permission to get a little rough, and I've finally given it.

This is such a bad idea, and I could not care less about the consequences as he draws back, groans, and then kisses me again. His fingers sneak up the hem of my tight dress, and I want to beg him to keep going.

A playful giggle erupts beside us, and we break apart as two girls, who were clearly looking for somewhere to talk, wander off laughing.

"Fuck," Trent says, his forehead resting against mine. "We shouldn't have done that." He steps back. "This is why I don't drink around you. I didn't mean to…" The look he gives me is tortured. "I don't want this to change things between us."

"It won't," I say quickly.

"What happened with Lila, I can't have that happen between us."

And I don't know if he means that we can't get drunk and make out or we can't have our friendship fall apart. Maybe he means both, but I'm too buzzed off the alcohol, off the kisses, to think clearly.

"It won't change anything between us," I say, but it feels like a lie.

"I gotta get out of here," he says, but he grabs the back of my neck and plants a kiss on my forehead. "I'm sorry, okay. I'm so fucking sorry."

Then he's gone, and I'm left standing in the room, feeling branded, as though he's written his name everywhere he touched, impossible for anyone else to find a corner that's not been marked by him.

Chapter Eleven
Trent

Grady's house is a mess, which I'd like to say is because of the ongoing renovations, but it was a rundown piece of shit house when he bought it. But at least he can get a mortgage, have someone loan him the money to do what he wants.

"Should have just dozed the place," I say, standing in the kitchen and surveying the missing walls. They've taken everything back to the studs. The place is an empty shell.

"Maggie has a vision," Grady says. "I'm just along for the ride."

"The Sullivan women are a force to be reckoned with," Kelvin, Grady's best friend, says, cracking a beer and passing one out of his cooler to me and one to Grady. Joanna, Emily, and Maggie, like Kelvin, have lived and worked in this town their whole lives.

All week I've been trying to pretend things are normal between me and Em, even though nothing feels normal, and we haven't been around each other in person yet to get rid of this lingering unease. Seeing each other will get us over this hump, but every time I've tried to stop in, she hasn't been home or has been too busy to meet up.

Which would feel convenient if I wasn't able to put it in perspective. There are lots of weeks when one or both of us is too busy to see the other. Doesn't mean anything.

"My friend, Michael, has been out with Emily three times now, I think," Kelvin says, squinting as though trying to remember. "Maybe four?"

"Since last week?" I say, unable to temper my outburst.

"Yeah," Kelvin says with a grin. "Must be going well, right? I had a feeling when I set them up."

That backless short black dress she'd worn to the dance club had pissed me off in the moment, and I hadn't been sure why. But later, I realized it was new. I'd never seen it before. The idea of her purchasing it with the intention of showing off her assets to this Michael guy had sparked something I did not want to examine—then or now.

I wonder if she moans for him when he kisses her like she did for me, if she arches into it, eager for more contact.

Christ. I am so fucked.

"You seen her this week?" Grady asks me before taking a sip of his beer.

"Not this week," I admit.

"If she gets serious with him, you'll be lucky to see her at all," Grady says. "Male-female friendships are hard to keep as close once you've got a significant other. Or at least that's what I've seen."

That was true for me and Maggie. It hasn't bothered me because Maggie's friendship had been drifting for years before she reconnected with Grady. Then Lila and Emily entered the picture, and I actually really loved having strong female friendships again. We could hang out, flirt, give each other advice. Uncomplicated. Or so I thought.

Then I fucked things up with Lila, and now I'm in the process of fucking things up with Emily.

I really need to stop leaping before I look.

"Amir might get a stepdad after all," Kelvin says, clinking his bottle with Grady's as though doing a "cheers," but when he tries to clink mine, I pull away to take a drink.

"Getting a bit ahead of yourself," I say, but a ball of anxiety is forming in my gut. There's no way I've spent the last year protecting and nurturing my relationship with Emily and Amir only to have it yanked out from underneath me.

"She's been on three or four dates with this guy," Grady says. "When was the last time she even went on a second date? According to Maggie, it's never happened. No guy has made it to a second date since she started dating again in October."

That is one hundred percent accurate, and I hate that he knows that, that he's rubbing it in my face without realizing he's rubbing it in my face.

"Emily and I are tight," I say. "She's not going to drop me for some guy she's been on a few dates with."

"Maybe not right now," Kelvin says, "but eventually, probably. Your partner becomes that go-to person in a crisis or when you need support. I get that you two have become close, but I think this is what she wants isn't it? A relationship."

It's not what she wants. It's what she'll settle for because she can't get what she wants. And I feel an old fire light in my belly, one I've tried so hard not to spark in the seven years I've been out of jail.

It's the kind of fire that burns shit down, where I become so laser focused on achieving something that nothing and no one can talk me out of it.

"She definitely has things she's looking to achieve," I agree and take a long drink of my beer to avoid saying something I shouldn't. Neither of these two need to know more about Emily's business than they already do.

"Wouldn't be fair for you to insert yourself if you've got no intention of being that person for her," Grady says, a clear warning in his tone.

"I wouldn't dream of it," I say. "I want Em to be happy just as much as the next person." Probably more.

I'm more nervous than I've ever been in my life—even more than when I got arrested—because I knew I was fucked then. There was no way I was going to avoid what was coming.

But this? Well, there are all kinds of ways I can fuck shit up right now. I sit in the doctor's office, my foot jiggling while I wait my turn.

This emergency appointment I asked for is bullshit, but when the receptionist said I'd have to wait two weeks to get an appointment that was a non-emergency, I lied.

It's the start of me eroding my life, my values, to go after what I want. Which should terrify me. Wanting something this much is what got me into trouble last time.

"Trent Castillo," the nurse says from the door that'll take me into the doctor's rooms.

I rise and follow her back. She records my height and weight on the way through in case the doctor has to prescribe any medication.

He won't, but whatever. I'm not going to argue when I'm here under false pretenses.

When Doctor David Rigilotto finally enters the examination room, he gives me a big smile. "Trent, it's been a while. What can I do for you today?" He slides into the wheelie chair near the desk that houses a computer, and he types in his information to pull up my file.

"I need some help with something, and I think I need a doctor to do it."

David leans back in the chair, steepling his fingers. "Tell me what you think you need."

So I do.

Chapter Twelve

Emily

It's been six weeks since I suggested Trent father my baby, and five weeks since I kissed Trent at the nightclub, and exactly zero minutes since I felt like I had my life together.

I sit outside Maggie's pharmacy in my car, contemplating all the ways in which I'm fucking up my life.

The vibe between me and Trent still isn't back to normal, and I don't know if it's because of the baby thing, the kiss thing, or the fact I've been dating the dentist for almost a month, and we've done little more than kiss. In fact, I've purposely arranged all our dates to be in public locations and to have a limited timeframe.

I have blatantly used my son to keep Michael at arm's length.

But the real problem isn't Michael or the fact I'm a mom, or even Trent. It's me. I'm the problem. Because even though I said I'd never take Trent seriously, that I'd never get in over my head with him, that I wouldn't become Lila, I can't stop thinking about that kiss. The few times Michael has kissed me, I've compared it to how I felt with Trent—which is all kinds of wrong. So, *so* wrong.

Whenever I close my eyes, Trent's lips are brushing against my earlobe, calling me fuckable, talking about putting a baby inside me. Just thinking about it is enough to get me wet. It sounds like he meant it, which is what's really screwing me up. His comments weren't fun and flirty—they were possessive, and god help me, I liked it.

It's not as though we haven't seen each other either. He's come over a few times to grab Amir and take him somewhere—to the shop to "work" on cars to the hardware store or sometimes over to Maggie and Grady's to hang out. But Trent's been very careful not to spend any alone time with me, and I haven't invited him in either, suggested he spend the day with me and Amir. We aren't yet back to normal, and I miss it, ache for our old friendship like a phantom limb.

I can't move forward with Michael until I know my feelings for Trent—sexual or otherwise—are in the rearview mirror. It's not fair to Michael to go full throttle into anything when I'm thinking about someone else so much.

In some ways, it's a relief that I'm even capable of thinking about anyone else at all. For the longest time, I thought I was doomed to pine after Omar. While what I feel for Trent isn't on the same scale as what I felt for Omar—this seems like extreme lust—I am a little happy that I can feel *something*.

If there's a positive anywhere, that's it. I'm not sexually dead.

Thankfully, when I haul myself out of the car and into Maggie's pharmacy, she doesn't have many customers. While she deals with the few people in the store, I browse the shelves, checking expiry dates.

"I have people who do that," Maggie says, her tone wry from the counter as the bells jingle on the door with Mrs. Freeman leaving.

"I like to keep busy," I say.

"I've heard you've been keeping so busy you've barely seen our dentist friend, Michael, in the last week."

"Am I the only gossip game in town?" I ask.

"In the family at the moment, yeah."

"I don't know if it's going to work out with Michael," I admit, slotting a children's aspirin back onto the shelf.

"Really?" Maggie says. "Aww. That's too bad. Kelvin was already planning the wedding."

"He just got divorced," I say. "I'm sure Michael is not in a hurry to walk down the aisle again anytime soon."

"I don't know. Kelvin said Michael told him he didn't want to be an old dad. So you had that in common."

We did. Neither of us wasted any time in getting to the heart of what we wanted. His first marriage hadn't worked out because she'd changed her mind about kids, and he definitely wanted them. In that way, we were a match. But just because two people wanted kids didn't make them long-term compatible. Dating Michael has been pleasant, and it has reminded me that there are princes who want commitment out there—not just the toads I found on my dating app, but I couldn't force a spark.

Wanted or not, I know what a spark feels like again, and I can't fake it.

"Are you going to keep dating then? Or back to a donor?" Maggie asks as she starts tidying to close up.

"Donor," I say with more decisiveness than I feel. "I had it narrowed down pretty well at the start of January, and then I got cold feet."

"You're breaking things off with Michael?"

"Tomorrow. We're meeting for coffee after he's done at work. Are you okay to watch Amir?"

"Grady can grab him from school again. He's got him right now. Grady doesn't go back to New York for another producing project until next week." Maggie checks her phone. "Would you like us to feed him?"

"Oh, I can go get..." My phone rings, and I check the display. *Mullen Mechanics* flashes as the caller.

"Just a sec," I say to Maggie as I turn away. "Emily Sullivan Real Estate," I say when I answer.

"Emily! How are you?"

"I'm good Bruce, how about you?"

"Well," he chuckles, "I don't know exactly how to do this, but I'd like to list my business and the shop in March. I'm retiring."

"Oh, that's wonderful," I say, as though I didn't already know his plan. My heart thuds at how sad Trent will be, even if he tries to hide it. I hold my hand over the phone and say to Maggie, "Can you feed Amir? I'm going to pop over to assess Mullen Mechanics."

"No problem," Maggie says. "You can pick him up when you're done."

Removing my hand from the speaker, I say, "I can pop over now and give you a preliminary estimate, if that's helpful?"

"Yes, that would be great," Bruce says.

After I've left Bruce's shop, I sit in my car, and I debate whether I should text Trent. I have some sense of how much is a fair price for Bruce's business, but things haven't been normal between me and Trent, and I don't know if a reminder of why they're not normal is a good idea.

Still, if the situation were reversed, I'd want to know that my dream business was going up for sale. Even if Trent expected it, it doesn't mean I shouldn't tell him.

Before I can second guess myself more, I fire off a text about Bruce contacting me.

I'm still happy to keep my part of the deal, if you've changed your mind and you'd like my help. I type it all as quickly as I can and hit send.

What happens next is up to Trent.

I'm not expecting a quick reply—he's been slower to respond the last few weeks, which I've tried not to worry about. One kiss, as hot as it was, isn't going to break us.

Text me when Amir's asleep, and I'll pop over.

His answer is swift and decisive, and it makes my pulse race. We haven't been alone together since the kiss. But if he's coming over to talk about the business, about a loan, maybe we'll be able to find our footing again as friends.

Amir has been asleep for thirty minutes before I even text Trent to let him know it's safe to come over. So when there's a quiet knock on my door less than fifteen minutes later, I'm surprised Trent's already here.

When he comes into the house, my throat feels tight, like all my worry and uncertainty is being held there.

He has a manilla envelope in his hand, and I wonder whether it's all his financial information so we'll know where we stand with the business.

"Should we sit down?" he asks, gesturing to the table, but he seems uncharacteristically nervous.

"Sure," I say, sliding onto the seat across from him.

He sets the envelope on the table and meets my gaze. "I know we haven't talked about anything important in weeks, and I'm sorry about that. Are you still dating the dentist?"

I swallow, and for the first time I wonder what it looks like to Trent. On a literal date with the dentist, I was practically climbing Trent in a back room. From his perspective, it must have been ridiculous that I even went on a second date, let alone a third, fourth, and fifth. Unfair as it was, I needed the buffer of Michael to not be tempted to take Trent seriously, and it hadn't really worked in the end anyway.

"I'm actually breaking things off with him tomorrow. It's not working out."

"I'm sorry about what happened in the club," he says, "that was a real dick move on my part. I knew you were there with someone…" He shakes his head, his annoyance clear.

"I kissed you, Trent. That was all me. I'm the dick."

"Sixty-forty on the dickishness," he says with a hint of a smile. "I definitely didn't say 'no.'"

In fact, he said a lot that might have driven me to kiss him. "I accept that split," I say. "Is that what you came to talk about?"

"In a way," he says, sliding the envelope toward me. "I just got all this back today, so I guess the timing is good."

"You want me to look at this?" I ask, plucking the envelope off the table.

"Yeah," he says, running a hand along the top of his head. "I'm a bit nervous about it."

With a frown, I pull out the papers, and the first one I see is STD results proclaiming Trent to be disease free. "Okay," I say with a little self-conscious laugh. The next one is a genetics test, and my breath catches in my throat, scanning it quickly before looking at the third paper—a sperm analysis. "Trent," I breathe out.

"I don't know if you still want to do it, and if you don't, that's okay. But if we do it, I wanted to give you as much peace of mind as possible. I'm not hiding anything from you. The only thing that came up on that genetic profile that the doc said might be an issue is my dyslexia."

My chest feels like it's both too big and too small for all my warring emotions. "I can't believe you did this," I whisper, my throat tight with a sob.

"I got the sense with the donor stuff that you'd feel better if you knew all this about me too. I wouldn't want to put you in the same position you're in with Amir, if I can avoid it."

I drop the papers on the table, and I cover my face as a sob escapes. Trent is around the table, hauling me into his arms, and it feels so good to be hugged by him again. I breathe in the full, dark scent of his cologne. We haven't touched in weeks, and I clutch onto him, crying into his chest, overwhelmed by happiness and relief. I don't need a donor. I don't need to keep dating men who make me feel nothing.

He smooths my hair and keeps me close as I cry, and he doesn't try to get me to stop or convince me that I shouldn't be crying. He lets me feel it all.

"We've still got some things to talk about," he says, "when you're ready."

Chapter Thirteen
Trent

After Emily stops crying, we move to the living room couch. The rest of this conversation probably isn't going to be as easy as what just happened. I'm not sure how she's going to react to my terms.

My test results are in her lap, and she keeps looking through them and then staring at me as though she's never seen me before. Which is fair—my response a few weeks ago was pretty emphatic. Does this give me a way to make sure I'm always in her life? Yes. Is that the best reason to be doing this? Maybe not, but I'm offering anyway.

"If you still want to do this, then I'm willing, obviously," I say, gesturing to the papers. "But I have some requests."

"What are those?" she asks, her voice still hoarse with emotion.

"I don't want anyone to know I'm the father," I say.

"Trent," she says, and I can hear the disappointment in that one word.

"People already think you're using a donor, and my big reason for saying no in the first place is still valid. I have a shit reputation in this town. Horrible. I'm not putting that on a kid. The Sullivan shine isn't enough to counteract it, at least not yet. If I can turn around people's opinions of me through the shop, then we can reconsider."

"We're going to have sex in secret," Emily says, her tone brimming with disbelief.

"Well, that answers another one of my questions. I wasn't sure how we'd do it, but yeah, I guess we would."

Her cheeks turn red, and she avoids eye contact. "If that's not the way *you* want to do it, then that's fine. We can use a fertility clinic instead."

"I suspect the route you had in mind would be much more fun," I say. "Not going to lie. That kiss got in my head." Really far in, so far that I'm not sure I'll ever forget it.

"For me too," she says, her voice still abnormally quiet.

There's a beat of silence between us, and then Emily squares her shoulders. "I'm not going to lie to our kid about who their dad is."

"I'll be around a lot, and he or she will know me as a person, just not as their dad," I say. "Hopefully, by the time we need to worry about telling anyone, I'll have the shop in good shape, and I'll be back in the good books of most of the town."

"I have complete faith in you, Trent, and I'm not asking this because I don't. But what if that's not what happens? What if you never convince all the people you want to convince that you're a decent, upstanding guy who made a colossal mistake at nineteen? What then?"

"Then I'd only want our child to know if it was critical."

"A dad is important. You know that." She stands up and starts pacing. "If you're not okay with our child knowing you're their dad, then I don't think we can do this. Donor sperm would honestly be easier. More straightforward."

I release a deep breath. "Fine. We can tell them when they're old enough to understand what it all means—no matter what." And then I decide to say more, "But I'm going to work really fucking hard, Em. I'm going to win people over. Until I do, I don't want anyone in this town shitting on you, giving you a hard time about your choices. I wouldn't take it well if someone hurt you." I raise my eyebrows and consider any scenario that involves negativity directed at her. "Really, really wouldn't take that well."

"For now, you want me to tell people I'm using a donor, but that donor will actually be you."

"Correct. If you want it to be."

"And you and I would be..."

"Friends with a shared goal."

"That's a very sanitized version of what we'll be doing."

"I hope so too," I say, giving her my cockiest grin. In fact, I'm hoping it's all quite dirty.

"I'll keep track of the best dates for us to be together. Anything that makes this more transactional is probably better in the long run." The crease in her brow suggests she's deep in thought.

"I just need," I say, turning serious again, "I need your guarantee that whether this works or not, we'll be okay. I don't want to ruin 'us' in this process."

"Do you want to set a timeline? Like a number of months we'll try, and if it doesn't work, I'll go to Plan B."

The responsible thing would be to say "yes." An end date makes sense so we're not tied to each other indefinitely, striving for something Emily really wants but that I might not be able to give her—despite my excellent swimmers.

"I say we just play it by ear. See how it goes. Keep the lines of communication open."

"I think we're being naïve to think we can keep this a secret," she says. "Remember the last secret you kept with a Sullivan? It didn't exactly go as expected."

"And this might not either," I admit. "But I'm willing to take the chance if you are."

"You want to go ahead with purchasing the shop?"

"And a year from now, I'll take out a loan and pay you back the price you purchased plus some sort of interest. Whatever's fair."

"You'll move back to Little Falls?" she asks.

"I'll need to look for a place to rent, but I can sleep in the shop until I've sorted that out."

"Or," Emily says, drawing out the word. "You could 'rent' from me for a few months while you get your feet under you. I have a spare room. No one would question it, since you've just made a big purchase, and it would cover our asses in terms of how we spend our time together."

"You want me to move in with you?"

"Temporarily. If a great apartment comes up or you just decide you want your own space, we can do that. But I think it might make sense at first."

I take a deep breath and consider her offer. Part of me wonders whether the storm, staying under the same roof for days, is what got us *here*, and it makes me a little nervous to consider where else the close proximity might lead us. But I can't deny that we got along well during the storm. She's easy to be around.

"I'll give my notice," I say. "We can try it, see how it goes."

"Amir will be ecstatic," Emily says, a true smile appearing for the first time since I arrived with my proposal. "Trent twenty-four-seven is his dream."

"Buy the shop, track your cycle, move in here," I say. "Nothing monumental there."

"Just a totally regular Monday afternoon."

"Jesus, Em, can you believe we're doing this?"

"No," she says with a little laugh. "I think we're so far out of our depth that we're probably already drowning and don't realize it."

"No matter what, we've got each other, right? That's not going to change."

"*I* promise," she says with a small smile, "that's not going to change."

When I stand up, Emily follows me to the door. She tries to hand me back my test results, but I shake my head. "You keep them. I did it for you."

After I've got my coat and boots back on, we examine each other for a beat.

"I don't think this is really the kind of deal we seal with a handshake," I say, searching her expression.

"No?"

"No," I say, and I slide my hand into her hair, gentle but firm, and draw her into a kiss, my heart hammering against my chest. The minute her soft, gloss-stained lips meet mine, I know I'm a fucking goner.

Just like at the club, it's as though one touch ignites a wildfire. She angles her head, deepening the kiss, and her tongue meets mine. It's impossible, but it feels like we've done this more than once before.

She presses against me, pushing me back against the door, and normally I'd laugh at how feral she seems, but fuck if I don't feel the same way, as though I could already rip her clothes off, take her here on the kitchen table, sink so deep inside no one else would ever make her feel full again.

I've never had a pregnancy kink—in fact the idea used to terrify me—but something new has been unlocked. The idea of spilling myself inside her, of knowing how much she wants it, wants me, is heady, intoxicating.

"I should go now," I murmur against her lips, and then, as I brush her hair to the side, I trail a line of kisses down her throat, "or I'm not going at all."

"You should go," she says, but her voice is breathy, and I'm not sure she means it. "We should keep this professional."

"Should we?" I ask. "What does that even mean when all I can think about is fucking you on your kitchen table?"

"I haven't slept with anyone since Omar," she says.

"What?" I say, drawing back as though she's doused me in cold water. "Really?"

"Oh god," she says, closing her eyes. "I shouldn't have told you that. Now, you're going to make a big deal out of it. I had lots of sex before Omar, okay? It's not like I'm some kind of born-again virgin. You don't need to treat me with kid gloves. It's fine. I shouldn't have even said anything."

"This feels like a big deal," I say, stepping to the side and biting the inside of my cheek.

"It's not," she says with a huff.

"No one?"

"Ugh. Okay, look, this is probably going to give you a big head or whatever, but I haven't *wanted* to sleep with anyone since Omar died. Like, I thought maybe all those feelings were just *gone*. But I'm not, apparently, dead below the waist."

"I'm oddly flattered right now that I've made your pussy purr," I say, splaying my hand across my chest. "Do you think it'll develop claws too?"

"Trent!" Emily says, but it's half-laugh, half-scold.

"In all seriousness, I know this is just a means to an end, but I really am flattered that I get to be that guy."

"Do not get weird on me," she says, giving me a light punch in the arm. "It's probably just because I trust you. I know I can trust you."

"Em, you cannot say shit like that to me and expect me to be cool about it. You're firing fucking arrows right to my heart."

"Yank out the metaphorical arrows, and let your heart harden over the next few days before we see each other. Cupid's arrows, real or pretend, are not allowed."

"Noted," I say, and I draw her back into my arms for another hug and a kiss on her forehead. "I'll be back to my flirty, hard-to-take-serious self next time you see me."

"I hope so," she says, pressing her cheek against my chest. "I've missed that guy."

I don't know if I've missed him, but I've definitely missed this—Em in my arms as that familiar little sigh of contentment escapes her.

Chapter Fourteen

Emily

Lila is home for the weekend, so we're all gathered at my mom's house for a catch up and then a multi-family dinner. Trent and I agreed to announce his purchase of Mullen Mechanics with help from "investors" tonight and to drop the potential bomb that he's going to rent my spare room while he gets his feet under him.

Now, I just have to tell everyone I've decided to go with a donor without somehow giving away the fact that none of this is exactly how it seems.

I've never liked lying, and I'm not sure if that's because I'm not good at it or because the potential for hurt seems greater.

Lila wanted some girl time before everyone got together for dinner. Maggie, Mia, Penny, my mother, and I are all gathered in the living room, sipping tea and coffee, catching up on where everyone is at.

I have no idea how much Trent has told his mom, and I almost feel more guilty putting our lie out into the world with her here.

After Mia finishes talking about the process of getting her album ready to release on or near Victoria's first birthday, Maggie shifts the attention to me.

"Have you decided what you're doing, Em? Last time you were at the pharmacy, you were talking about searching for a donor again," Maggie says.

"I've picked one, actually," I say, hoping the half-truth doesn't sound stilted.

"What?!" Maggie says, shooting forward on the couch. "And you didn't show me?"

"Or me," Lila says. "I told her I wanted eyes on that shit too."

"I think," I say, choosing my words carefully, "I'd prefer to keep the specifics private."

"Which is her right," my mom says when Maggie opens her mouth to protest. "We don't need all the details to be supportive."

"I think it's really brave," Penny, Trent's mom, says. "Being a single parent is incredibly hard work."

"I have a great support system," I say, which is an easy truth. "Besides my family, your two sons have been so helpful."

"Grady loves spending time with Amir when he's not in New York City. I think he feels like he's practicing for when we have kids," Maggie says.

"I'm excited that Victoria will have at least one cousin close to her age," Mia says.

"Are you going to have more children?" Lila asks Mia, taking a sip of her coffee.

"Someday," Mia says. "But right now, we're just figuring out how to be parents, how to be a family. I didn't have the best example of either one growing up." She takes a deep breath. "Tyler's just so supportive and understanding." She glances at my mom. "Joanna, you and your husband did an amazing job raising him."

My mom preens a little bit, and her smile is wide. "I'm sure having two very opinionated sisters also helped."

"Opinionated," Maggie scoffs. "I'm sure you meant to say very involved and caring sisters."

"That's what I heard," I chime in. Maggie and I laugh.

"Anyone want some cookies?" My mother asks, standing up.

"I'll help you," Penny says, following my mom to the kitchen.

Maggie and Lila strike up a conversation about infrastructure in the town, and Mia turns to me.

"I didn't want to put you on the spot, but I also think you're brave for doing it on your own. I couldn't imagine not having Tyler."

"Sometimes life doesn't work out how we expect," I say. If I let my mind drift to losing Omar, I'll question whether I *am* doing the right thing.

"You'd rather not get married again?" Mia asks, her tone gentle but quizzical.

"I haven't really connected with anyone since Omar died," I say. "I liked being married. I liked our relationship, and maybe something like that'll be for me again one day. I don't know. For now, my focus is on having another baby, and thankfully, I don't need a man in my life to do that." The half-truth rolls out surprisingly easily.

"Pasha lost his fiancée in Russia before my mom brought him over to America to be a bodyguard on the tour. I worry about him sometimes."

"Why's that?" I ask, glancing at the hulking man standing near the door.

"Maybe I'm projecting," she says. "My therapist says I have to be careful that I don't let my feelings overrule other people's feelings. My mom did that all the time." She takes a deep breath. "Anyway, *I* think it would be lonely to be him."

"Has he told you that?" I ask.

"No." She lets out a little laugh. "He says that Tyler, me, and Victoria are all he needs. That we're like his American family."

"Maybe you are," I say.

"I think I just…" She twists her lips as though she's debating what to say. "Now that I know how good it can be, how good a *real* relationship can be, I want that for everyone." She lets out a self-deprecating laugh. "And that's definitely projecting, right? I can't want things for someone that they don't want for themselves."

For some reason, Mia's last comment bangs around in my head as though it's a new idea that's come knocking, even though it isn't. I'm proof of that very sentiment. If wanting something for someone else was enough to achieve it, my mother would have willed me into a committed, long-term relationship, likely with Michael the dentist. She was noticeably sad when I told her I didn't think that would work out, and sometimes I wonder if she's missing dad and projecting that onto me and Omar.

The front door opens, and Tyler comes in with Victoria in her car seat. Mia jumps out of her chair and rushes over to him to throw her arms around his neck and kiss him, and then she crouches to draw Victoria out of her car seat, setting her onto her hip.

Watching them makes that familiar longing spring up. But I'll have a baby again soon, and then I won't have to wish for that feeling. I'll have it.

While Mia and Tyler talk to Joanna and Penny, Grady comes in the door with his dogs. Amir will be delighted when he arrives with Trent that the dogs are here. He'll spend most of his time in the backyard playing fetch with the two of them.

I don't notice that Maggie has gone and I'm alone with Lila in the living room area until Lila speaks.

"Is Amir with Trent?"

"Yeah," I say, dragging my gaze away from the happy family scene near the front entranceway. "They spend a lot of time together."

Lila scans my expression for a beat, and a strange tension springs up that I've only ever felt between us when Trent's name is mentioned. When we talk on the phone, I don't bring him up on purpose. But now that I've made this deal with him, I have the first inkling that what we've decided might fracture my friendship with Lila. Even if I think she was naïve to have taken anything that happened with Trent seriously—and he swears it was only a few drunken kisses—she hasn't moved past it.

Of course, having now kissed Trent, I can understand how the feelings he evokes could seep in, plant a seed that's not quite real.

When Trent ushers Amir in the door, my heart kicks. There is something about his height, his broad shoulders, the short brown hair, the tattoos on his left arm, the ones that I know exist across his rippling muscles under his shirt, that have turned him into a package I never expected to find attractive.

Not that I didn't think he was good looking—you'd have to be blind not to notice—but that certainty about his appeal used to be objective. And it doesn't quite feel like that anymore.

It's not until we're all sitting around the dinner table that Trent uses his fork to tap his glass, drawing everyone's attention to him. Across the table, our gazes lock, and while I'm not sure it's a good idea for us to connect so clearly over what he's going to say, I also can't drag myself away from the happy intensity I see there.

"I have an announcement," Trent says with a broad grin. "With the help of some investors, I've purchased Mullen Mechanics. I'll be taking over at the end of March, reopening at the start of April."

Penny lets out an audible gasp, and then she scrambles out of her chair to Trent's seat, hauling him out and into her arms. I can't hear what she's saying to him, but I can see the expression on Trent's face, how moved he is by whatever she's whispering.

It causes warmth to race across my skin. Obviously it means as much to her as it does to Trent that he's on this path.

"Little Falls is lucky to have you," Tyler says.

"Well, we'll see how Little Falls feels about that," Trent says with an uneasy laugh as he slides back into his seat. "And to that end, because it's a bit of a risk, I'm giving up my apartment. I'm going to rent Em's spare room."

"Oh," my mom says. "You could have had a room here for free."

"Once the renos are done on our house," Grady says, chiming in, "you can stay there or stay at Maggie's for free too."

"Oh my god," I say, "I'm not charging him anything, okay?"

Everyone turns and stares at me like my outburst was completely inappropriate, and I flush with embarrassment. Maybe I'm a little more sensitive about what we're about to embark on than I like to believe.

"No one was judging," Maggie says. "You're doing the whole fertility treatment thing, and that's expensive. If you and Trent are happy for him to pay you rent and it helps both of you, that's fine."

"Yeah," Grady says. "I wasn't implying anything. Just trying to help him out."

"Em's been very kind," Trent says, trying to catch my eyes, but I avoid him. "I'm happy with the deal we've made."

"Well then," my mom says with more enthusiasm than is needed, "that's wonderful. Isn't that wonderful everyone?"

"We should do a toast," Mia says, raising her glass. "To new beginnings."

Everyone raises their glass, and beside me Amir whispers, "I love when we do the cheers thing." Then he stands up and goes around the table doing a "cheers" with every single person.

"Have you installed a revolving door?" Lila asks as we're shoulder to shoulder doing dishes at the double kitchen sink.

"A revolving door?" I ask, confused.

"Yeah, on the spare bedroom. One girl in. One girl out."

"Lila," I say, exasperated.

"Are you really going to be okay with him having girls over there, probably having loud sex while you're trying to sleep? Or explaining to Amir what all those noises are coming from Trent's bedroom?"

"You're making a lot of assumptions," I say.

"Have you even talked about it?"

"We're both adults, and despite what you might think right now, Trent is a reasonable human being. He's not going to put me or Amir in an awkward situation. What happened between you and him actually really bothers him."

She goes quiet and finishes the dishes without another word. Just when I think I should say something, Amir comes and tugs on my leg.

"Mom, can you go look for those Lego pieces I lost? I need them for the set."

"Which room, again?" I ask, drying my hands.

"The green room," he says. "Thanks, Mom." And then he's racing outside with Grady and the dogs.

I didn't realize I'd be looking alone.

"I can help you look," Trent says from behind me.

I give him a grateful smile, and he follows me up the stairs to the green bedroom. Once we're inside, we both fall to our hands and knees, searching under dressers, the bed, the closet.

"What exactly are we looking for?" Trent asks when we both stand up again.

"Lego pieces," I say with a shrug.

Trent opens the nightstand drawer and holds up four blocks. "Like these ones?"

"Yep," I say with a little laugh. "That seems about right." I hold out my hand and he drops them into my palm.

Before I can step away, he tucks strands of my hair behind my ear. "I saw you and Lila talking. She still think I'm the devil who emerged straight from hell?"

"She's still not over it, no," I say with a grimace. "She did sort of inadvertently bring something up that we hadn't specifically discussed..."

"What's that?" he asks.

"Other people, while we're doing this. Is it just us or...?"

"Be a bit silly for me to get tested and then sleep with someone else," he says with a chuckle. "Right?"

"Yeah, I just, I thought we should be clear."

"You and me. For however long it takes for the deal to stick."

I can't help the little laugh that escapes me at his phrasing. "Let's hope it's extra sticky."

He searches my face for a beat. "I don't know. I'm not opposed to getting in some practice before I deliver the winning shot."

Which sounds fun, in theory, and I'm sure that's what he's picturing. But for me, given what sex has meant to me in the past, what I know I get from it, need from it, "some practice" is a bit nerve wracking. The last thing I need is for this deal to slip beyond my control.

"Did you find it?" Amir says, storming into the room.

"Trent did," I say, opening my palm and showing him the pieces.

"Trent always delivers," Amir says.

He sounds so grown up that I can't help an amused smile, and I make eye contact with Trent over his head.

"That's right, buddy. You can always count on me to deliver when I'm needed." Then he winks at me and follows Amir back downstairs.

I stay behind for a beat, willing my heart to slow back down.

Chapter Fifteen
Emily

We signed all the paperwork at the bank the last week of March for Mullen Mechanics, and Trent moved all of his stuff into storage at the shop and my spare room the same week.

Bruce agreed to stay on for April to help Trent get a handle on the flow of customers, payroll, and all the bits and pieces it takes to run his own business. Trent has been working such long hours that, coupled with my usual increase of real estate business in the spring, means we've hardly seen each other.

On the wall in the kitchen, I've put a calendar where I've been tracking my cycle. Even that conversation wasn't as awkward as I expected as I took Trent through January, February, and March. I'd started tracking in the new year in case I decided to go with a donor and needed the information for the doctor, and then once Trent and I had our agreement, I kept doing it so I'd have a sense of what days were likely to be important.

But now that we're here—the important days—I'm freaking out a little. It's midweek, but I asked my mom to take Amir overnight, get him to school in the morning. I used late-night house showings as the reason, which *has* happened before in the spring when the market is hot. But I was sure she'd see right through my lie, ask me why I wasn't being honest.

I'm tempted to text Trent, but he's been so focused on the shop that I'm not even sure if he's checked the calendar, if he realized that the important days were here. What would I even say in my text? Please leave work to come home and fuck me?

Just the thought of sending that text makes my pulse do triple time and my stomach seize with nerves. There's no way I could type those words or say them out loud.

I haven't slept with anyone since Omar, and while I know the chemistry is there between Trent and me based on those two kisses, part of me is a little concerned I won't actually be able to go through with it. I'll get too in my head, and it won't feel right. That even initiating will be awkward or uncomfortable.

That maybe this month will pass us by because I won't be able to say anything if he comes home too late and hasn't checked the calendar.

But then, when my worrying is about to hit fever pitch, he comes in the door carrying a grocery bag and some flowers. He hands me the flowers, kisses me on the cheek, and asks what listing I'm trying to price.

I'm at my computer, other listings strewn around me on the kitchen table. I have an office upstairs and another one in town that I use to meet with clients, but I haven't used the one in the house since Amir was a baby. It's easier to be in the kitchen, which is where Amir frequently asks for help with things when he's home.

"This one is an older, run-down home, but in the good part of town," I say. "You bought me flowers?"

"Saw them, thought of you. Call it an impulse purchase." He glances at me over his shoulder while he unpacks groceries.

But there's something in the way he's looking at me that makes me think he knows exactly what day today is, and he's actually home right at dinner. This week, he's been dragging his ass in around midnight.

"I bought all the ingredients for that chicken mess we made during our snowed in cooking adventures," he says, holding up the chicken breasts. "If you're doing that, I'll make this."

"Do you need me to print the recipe?"

"Did it at work before I left," he says, getting out dishes, measuring cups, and a cutting board.

I'm tempted to tell him that he doesn't have to treat me like a born-again virgin, which I already said. But having him take care of me a little *is* a nice treat. The rhythm of him in my kitchen is soothing in an odd and unexpected way. It shouldn't be a surprise. One of the reasons I knew having him live here wouldn't be terrible was based on our snowed-in days together, but how natural all of this is still trips me up.

Maybe we both know exactly what's going to happen tonight, but he doesn't seem in a rush, and god knows I am really fucking nervous about going through with this, even though it was my idea, even though it's genuinely what I want.

I try to go back to price matching the house with other things that have sold in the last few months, either through my company or other realtors, but I can't focus.

Finally, I give up, and I pack everything away. Then I go over and assess where Trent is at with the recipe.

"Do you want some help?" I ask.

"There's some wine in the fridge," he says. "Bought it yesterday and stashed it in a drawer, if you want to get it out."

When I stand up to go to the fridge, Trent follows me with his gaze. "Nice dress," he says, his voice husky.

"Thanks," I say, nerves zinging down my spine. It's not the black dress from my date with Michael, which he said made me look fuckable, but it's definitely straddling the line between my normal work attire and something meant to entice. Open back, short hemline, but it's not overly tight.

In the fridge is the exact pinot grigio we had when we were snowed in, and I stare at it for a beat before unscrewing the top and pouring us both a glass. Here I thought he was so consumed by figuring out his own business that he was completely unaware of the calendar, but it turns out I was the one who got it all wrong.

"You know you don't have to do this, right?" I say, keeping my voice quiet when I pass him the glass.

"Do what?" he asks, holding my gaze over the rim of the glass.

"Wine and dine me."

"You mean before I sixty-nine you?"

"Trent!"

"I love when you say my name like that, as though you're both amused and disgusted by what I've said."

"Usually more amused," I admit.

"I know." He gives me a small grin. "That's why I like it." He casts his hand over the food he's been preparing. "And maybe none of this is for you. Maybe *I* like being wined and dined before someone sixty-nines *me*."

I can't help a laugh. "You're wining and dining yourself, then?"

"You're still *here* in the house, so not quite. And I sure as hell am not sixty-nining myself."

A beat sits between us, both of us grinning, and I become acutely aware of our flirting and our comfort with each other.

"Tonight and tomorrow are transactions, though, and I'm not sure how I feel about you turning it into something else."

"You wanted me to come home, throw you on the kitchen table, and fuck your brains out? Wake up tomorrow morning and say, 'all right, babe, get that pussy out.' That's what you wanted?"

"I wouldn't have put it like that."

"And *I* don't think you would have liked that," he says. "Beyond all this, you're my friend, Em. You're one of my best fucking friends, and there's no way in hell I'm treating you like you're disposable, like you don't matter. Maybe this is a *transaction*, but I think we'd be doing it wrong if it didn't still feel important in some way."

It's the *important* part that worries me. For me it would be that no matter how we did it. Making myself vulnerable with him in any way is going to feel like free-falling off a cliff. But I don't know what to do with my feelings if he also considers what we're doing important, as more than a deal we've struck. It can mean *something*, but not *too much*, and I have no idea how to walk that line. I'd rather stay away from that line than cross it, but I'm definitely less of a risk taker than Trent.

He leans against the counter and tugs me over so I'm standing between his legs, his hands resting gently on my hips. "You're overthinking this. At some point," he says, leaning in so his lips are close to my ear, "I will have you on that kitchen table, but it'll be because you've had the guts to ask me, maybe even beg me, to do it."

"Maybe you'll hit the bullseye on the first try," I whisper. That would be best for both of us, I think. Clean. Quick. No chance of more feelings seeping into our arrangement.

"That would be fate laughing in my face. Giving me an A+ for the first time on something I'd actually enjoy doing multiple times." He gives my ass a light pat as he steps away and continues the dinner prep.

"We haven't even done it once, so I don't know how you can say that." I pick up my wine and take a big drink for courage. "Maybe you'll be glad to hit the target the first time."

"You have been starring in multiple scenarios in my head for far, far too long. I get to admit that tonight. It's one of the only days in the month I'm allowed to cop to sexual feelings about one of my very best friends, so I'm offloading that gem to you. You're welcome."

"Multiple scenarios?"

"Oh, yes. All over this house. In your backyard. All over my shop. Just..." He grins at me. "All over."

Despite the flush across my skin, the way my thighs are tingling in anticipation, I refuse to let myself get carried away. He's a flirt. Saying these sorts of things to women is probably his modus operandi. Any woman would be thrilled to hear that the man they're about to have sex with can't stop thinking about them. He'd know that. It's part of his charm.

"I just don't think we should lose sight of *why* we're doing this," I say, but I'm not sure who I'm warning.

Trent doesn't say anything in response, he just finishes prepping the food before sliding it into the oven. Then he sets a timer, tops up his wine, and he takes a sip while eyeing me from across the kitchen. It feels like an assessing gaze, but I'm not sure what he's trying to decide.

My pulse climbs as the air grows thick around us. Part of me assumed, considering he's making dinner, that we wouldn't have sex until we went to bed, but the way he's looking at me is not remotely PG. Why am I so turned on by a look?

"You all right over there?" he asks, as though he can read my mind.

Then as he moves around the kitchen, moves around me, his hands keep grazing parts of me—a hip, the small of my back, the curve of my ass while his lips make contact with my bare shoulder or my neck or my temple. Light touches that should mean nothing—he's always been more affectionate than most—are loaded with anticipation.

My body is a lit fuse, and each point of contact carries the flame of desire closer to detonating.

And although I've also thought about having sex with Trent, a lot in the lead up to today, I haven't let my mind run wild with fantasies. I tried to keep my thoughts mostly clinical, logistical. Now that he's opened the door by admitting he's had more salacious thoughts, I can't stop thinking about all the ways and places we could have sex in the kitchen alone.

Between the touches and my out-of-control brain, I'm so turned on by the time we finish dinner that I don't want to do anything but drag him upstairs.

After we slot the last dish into the dishwasher, Trent tugs me into his body, his hand going into my hair, and he angles his head, drawing me into a deep kiss.

And I can't help the moan that escapes, the way I meet his kiss with the same pent-up desire. It's been weeks since we last kissed, and I can't believe how much I want this, how much nerves aren't even a factor. If he stopped right now, changed his mind, I'd cry about more than the loss of a potential baby.

He lifts me onto the counter to stand between my legs, and he runs a rough palm from my ankle and up to my thigh. His fingers curve around to my inner thigh, but he doesn't move them where I'm dying for them to explore—instead he kneads my flesh.

"Fuck, I love that I get to touch you like this," he says. "You have no idea how much I've thought about it."

Then he's kissing me again before I can respond or even really process what he's said. His hands are up the back of my dress, unsnapping my bra on their way to the nape of my neck, drawing me closer and tighter as he kisses me more. His thumb grazes my raised nipple, and I gasp at the contact.

He breaks the kiss to peer around the kitchen. "Are all the blinds closed?"

"I closed them all when I got home."

"In case I came home and fucked you on the table?"

"I wasn't sure how it would go," I say, but I almost can't concentrate because his hands have continued to explore my body while he's been talking. He keeps coming close to where I really, really want them without actually getting there—skimming the edge of my panties with his fingertips but not fully engaging.

"I know exactly how it's going to go," he says, giving me a wicked grin before lifting me off the counter.

I wrap my legs around his waist and my arms around his neck as he carries us out of the kitchen. He stops in the hallway and grabs a bag and a couple towels before turning into the living room.

"Here?" I say, surprised.

"Definitely here," he says, laying me on the wide couch. "One hundred percent here."

Then he's cradled between my legs, my dress around my waist, and he's back kissing me, his rough hands kneading and gently squeezing while he rocks between my thighs. He's hard against my sensitive core, and I moan at each contact.

I can't even remember the last time I was so turned on. Even getting myself off hasn't been that great the last few years, as though my brain can't find anything worth imagining.

The reality of this, though—I'll have memories, remembered sensations, for years. There's definitely something chemical between me and Trent—pheromones on overdrive.

He pulls me up, my dress goes over my head with my bra, and then I'm left in just my panties. He tugs at the back of his shirt, drawing it over his head, and I can't help scanning his muscles, the tattoos that litter his chest. I want to trace each one with my tongue, ask why he got them and what they mean.

His jeans drop to the floor, and then he's just in his boxer briefs, clearly as turned on as I am.

"I've got one rule, Em," he says, his voice husky.

I drag my gaze from his body to make eye contact. "What's that?"

"I don't get off unless you get off."

"That doesn't make practical sense," I say, quickly calculating the number of times I've orgasmed during sex. It's not nothing, but it's definitely not every time.

"I don't care about practical," he says, dropping to his knees, his fingers running along my soaked panties. "And I can definitely work with this." He tugs my panties down my legs and then spreads me wide. "You're so fucking wet for me. I can't wait to taste you."

Then his mouth is one me, and I arch my back at the contact. The last time a guy had his mouth on me was in college, and it wasn't anything like this.

Trent's tongue is magic, and suddenly his rule doesn't seem so impossible to not just reach but sustain. I have never been so sure I could come before.

When he slips two fingers inside, I cry out from the need building inside me.

"Trent," I gasp.

"That might be my new favorite way you say my name," he mutters against my thigh while his fingers work me over, and then he's back with his mouth and tongue. "I love the taste of you, and you're going to come for me, like a good fucking girl, aren't you, Em?"

Holy fuck. I don't know what he does, but my orgasm hits me like a freight train. And I absolutely cannot control not only how loud I am, but how intense it all feels. It's like he found some secret well of pent-up orgasms and set them all off at once.

He kisses his way up my body, and he buries his face in my neck while I feel like liquid, full of life and lifeless all at once.

"Trent," I say, and I can't help the amazement in my voice.

"I'm going to hate the sound of my name coming out of anyone else's mouth after this," he says, "cause that one is also a winner."

"You've had those skills this whole time?" I murmur.

He chuckles against my neck and then he smooths back my hair when he makes eye contact. "You might have been wound a bit tight."

Understatement of the year. And then it occurs to me that we haven't even done the thing we were supposed to do.

"I got off," I say, another understatement, "so now you get off."

"I didn't want to rush you," he says. "And I bought lube, but I don't think we need that."

I cover my eyes, and I laugh a little. "No, I don't think we do."

"It's flattering." He tugs my arm off my face. "I just didn't want to assume." His eye contact is intense. "Don't hide from me. You're not allowed to hide from me."

Then he sheds his boxer briefs, and my eyes widen at his length and girth. It's been a while, but he seems slightly above average. Not like "Oh my god, it'll never fit," but definitely substantial.

He sits on a towel on the couch and places another one next to him. Then he encourages me to straddle his lap, which I do. His hands go into my hair, and he says, "You can still change your mind. No hard feelings."

I wiggle against him. "Something is definitely feeling hard."

"Em." He searches my expression, not at all into my jokes.

"I want this." I lean my forehead against his. "I want you."

"I've been turned on since the minute I walked in the house tonight, so I don't know how long I'll last," he says as I guide myself down onto him. "And fuck if you don't feel amazing."

"This feels okay?" I watch his strained expression, fascinated that I'm capable of doing this to him.

"You have no idea what you do to me," he says. "How long I've thought about this." His hands span my back, drawing me tight to him so that each rise and fall brushes our bodies together, chest to chest.

The whole thing is more intimate than I ever expected given our deal, but he kisses me as though I'm all he's ever wanted, as though doing this with me is the best thing that's ever happened to him. And it makes me wish that any of those things were really true, that the feelings I'm caught up in could actually exist between us.

Then his arm is along my spine, his hand on the back of my neck, keeping us tight, and his other hand is on my hip, urging me to go faster as he kisses me deeper. He breaks the kiss to breathe against my ear, his teeth grazing my earlobe.

"Fuck, Em. You feel so good. I can't hold on much longer."

Our cheeks are pressed together, and I murmur, "I want your baby, Trent."

And he groans as I feel him pulse inside me, his hand holding me in place as he spills himself. His hands sink back into my hair, and he's kissing me, slow and deep, so gentle that it breaks my heart a little.

"You okay?" he asks, his tone hushed.

"I'm good," I say. "You?"

"As long as we survive this," he says, "I'm great."

We make eye contact, staring at each other for a long beat, and I want to reassure him, promise that this won't get out of hand, but if *this* is where we're starting, I really don't know. I just don't know if my feelings will get away from me.

Instead, I decide to take his statement in a different direction. "You're not sure you can survive another twelve hours of having sex with me?" The internet was full of strategies on when and how often we should have sex, but we agreed to keep a narrow window to start. It's easier with Amir, and it's easier with our work schedules.

Plus, I like the idea of keeping things tightly focused. If I don't get pregnant, we can try something else.

"I told Bruce I'd be late coming in tomorrow," he says. "More like sixteen hours. This cock is all yours to use as you wish."

"All mine, huh?" I say, tracing a line down his body with my finger.

"It's all yours." He runs his thumb along my cheek. "Every inch."

"There are a lot of them."

"You liked that, did you?"

"Did the job."

"We hope."

And the banter helps set my mind at ease a little. We're still just Trent and Emily. Nothing has to change.

"We're going to survive this," I say. "I'm sure of it."

Chapter Sixteen
Trent

Bruce has been working with me at the shop for three weeks, and I'm still not sure about any of his systems or ways of doing things. Rather than being fully digitized, he's still been relying on filing cabinets, paper files, and handwritten notes and calendars.

Instead of insulting him, I've been trying to grapple with his system. He even does his scheduling—holidays for staff, payroll—all by hand.

I finally broke down and installed a desktop computer at the front desk. The last few years, Bruce did most of the office management while the other guys worked on cars. But I want to be in the shop, seeing how things run, not behind a desk, hoping for the best. I know I'll need to hire someone, but I have to be sure the finances support that.

I have a laptop in my office, and I'm trying to get everything from the last three weeks loaded. With only one week left until Bruce actually retires and I take over, I need to get a handle on how *I* want to do things so the shop doesn't stall. I know clientele is already down.

Looking back at the bookings from January to the end of March, Bruce's schedule was packed. Looking ahead to May, mine is a lot less so. There are substantial gaps, and while Bruce tried to reassure me that many of those will get eaten up with oil changes people suddenly realize they need, brakes that give up, car accidents, electrical problems, and so forth, it's hard to see so much empty space.

I don't want to lay anyone off, but I also know that running this business into the ground isn't just a problem for me. Emily's put her faith and her cash behind me, and knowing the money came from her dad's life insurance policy only doubles the pressure. To me, that money would be sacred, and so I'm treating it like it is for her too.

At seven o'clock, I'm still hunting and pecking on the keyboard of the laptop when there's a knock on the frame of the office door. I look up to see Emily, and I grimace.

"Everything okay?" I ask, trying to find my place again and typing the next line.

"Amir's at jiu jitsu, so I thought I'd stop by to see how things are going. I know Bruce is done at the end of next week, and you seemed a bit stressed."

"It's just what I already told you," I say, moving the ruler down to another line on the ledger. "Everything's on paper, and I've decided I'm getting it into a computer. It just doesn't make sense to do it all by hand when there are programs that can calculate these things—payroll, taxes, all that."

"How much are you digitizing?" she asks, coming to my shoulder to peer at the laptop.

"As much as I can."

"Trent, that's going to take you forever. Why don't you hire someone?"

"Can't," I say. "Until I know I'm going to have the customers to keep this place ticking along, I need to conserve money, not spend it."

"That's very responsible," she says, and when I glance at her over my shoulder, I see the glint of teasing in her eyes.

"Happens once in a while," I say, grudgingly.

"You know," Em says, perching on the edge of my desk.

Her skirt rides up her thighs, giving me all kinds of ideas. The turn in the weather from winter to spring has meant more skirts and dresses for Em, and it's been hell on my concentration. When I drag my eyes up to hers, I realize I missed whatever she said after she sat down.

"Sorry," I say, "I missed that."

"I said," she says with a bit of a laugh, "that I could probably talk my mom, your mom, and Maggie into helping me get this all digitized for you in a weekend."

"You're really busy right now with real estate, and Maggie is always busy at the pharmacy. I couldn't ask that." I go back to hunting and pecking the keys.

"You're not asking." She rotates off the desk to wrap her arms around my neck, resting her chin on my shoulder.

The scent of peaches drifts across my senses, and my body springs to attention. Ever since we spent those sixteen hours getting to know each other on a super intimate level, I haven't been able to be around Emily in exactly the same way. I pretend like it's fine, and I don't think Em has realized that it's not *quite* fine.

Now that I know how she tastes, what she sounds like when she comes apart around me, I'm a bit fucked. My concentration around her is shot.

If I thought I fantasized about her a lot before, that was amateur hour compared to how detailed and frequent those fantasies are now. Nonstop Emily porn plays in my head whenever she enters a room or I catch a hint of either lemon or peach scents. The lemon is particularly cruel since it's such a common disinfectant. Even taking care of myself in the shower every single morning and evening isn't making it better.

"I don't even know what we're talking about right now," I say, pecking away at the keys.

"You know what we're talking about," she says, a hint of exasperation in her tone as she moves away from me.

My head clears a little, and I stare at her across the desk. Something about doing the digitization work for me.

"It's a 'no' from me," I say with a shrug.

"Maybe I'll just organize the team and do it as a surprise."

"Em," I say, a hint of warning in my tone.

"Okay, fine. Look, you've been a bit grumpy the last week or so, and I just want to help."

God, the *ways* she could help. I close my eyes and try to keep all those thoughts from forming at the front of my mind. She wants to help with the business, not my intense sexual frustration.

"Fine," I say with a deep sigh. "My mom and your mom are fine, but leave Maggie out of it."

"Sunday," Em says, heading toward the door to the office. "If you'll hang out with Amir, we'll get everything categorized and inputted for you. Just leave sticky notes on everything you need done. We'll use both computers, and I'll bring mine, and we'll get you sorted."

I sit back in my chair, and I run my hands down my face. "I appreciate you, you know that, right?"

"Yeah," she says, her gaze softening. "This is what friends do, Trent. It's okay to need help. It's okay to ask for it."

And it reminds me a little that last time I didn't ask for help, last time I didn't reach out and tell people what was going on with me, I got myself into a lot of trouble.

"Thanks," I say. "I just don't want to fuck this up, and I'm a little worried I already am."

"It's going to be a lot of learning," she says, leaning against the open door. "When I first started my own real estate business, I was overwhelmed with all the things I needed to know. But once you've got a base, it'll become easier. Part of it is that it's all on paper, and that's not one of your strengths. You're good with tech."

I get out of my chair, and even though I know it's a bad idea, I wrap her in a tight hug, and she hugs me back. I breathe in the peaches and try to keep my thoughts PG. She's good for me, and I need to stop thinking about all the ways I can fuck up either of our arrangements.

Maggie's pharmacy has a sign on the door saying that she's closed for the afternoon, which makes me suspicious that Emily didn't listen to me about who could and couldn't help.

It should annoy me that she didn't listen, but she was so excited to go in and organize my office and space that I can't drum up the negativity. She had a whole game plan mapped out on pages she wouldn't let me see before she left the house at ridiculous o'clock this morning.

If Amir hadn't woken up through some sixth sense about Emily leaving the house, I wouldn't have been up early enough to make her coffee and then the requisite thermos to take with her. Luckily, he came and got me when he saw Emily getting ready. He's been hyped up the last few days about me taking him to a local inland lake.

This afternoon we're rowing a boat and fishing, which Amir hasn't done before. I'm not a great fisherman, but the lake is stocked, so we might be lucky enough to catch something small to throw back.

By eight o'clock at night, Emily still hasn't texted to say I can come check out her handiwork, and I'm getting antsy. Amir has to go to bed soon.

There's a knock on the door, and Amir races to answer it.

"I need to open the door, buddy," I say, following behind him.

Amir peers through the side window at his level. "It's Aunt Mia's bodyguard, Pasha."

I yank open the door, heart thrumming. "Everything okay?" Pasha's normally attached to Mia, Tyler, and Victoria, not out wandering around Little Falls.

"Should be text from Emily," Pasha says, nodding at my phone in my hand. "I watch Amir while you go to shop."

And sure enough, my phone buzzes in my hand with a text from Em. They're done, and she wants me to go there. But I still text her to check that Pasha should be watching Amir.

"I could just bring him," I say to Pasha, and also to my phone as I wait for her reply.

"No distractions," Pasha says with a shrug. "She worked all day."

That she did. I ruffle Amir's head and step out into the cool spring air. "He normally goes to bed in about half an hour."

"Emily say you not be long."

"Okay," I say, feeling a bit better about leaving Amir with Pasha, who isn't a stranger but isn't far from it.

I get in my truck and navigate the familiar route to the shop. When I get there, Tyler's truck is there along with Maggie's car, my mom's car, and Joanna's car. Stepping out, I wonder whether they did more than digitize my files.

Opening the door, the lights are all off, and when I step through, the lights come on and everyone yells, "Surprise!"

I stand still for a moment and take in the new front office. It has a fresh coat of paint to cover all the scuff marks, grease, and everything else that had been left behind after years of abuse. The counter has been replaced with a black two-tiered system so we can deal with guests standing up or seated to discuss more complex cases.

The waiting room for people who have oil changes or other fixes that don't require substantial time has been upgraded with new furniture, a coffee machine, a small fridge, and other homey details.

"Em," I say, my voice rough. "You did all this?"

"We all did," Emily says, gesturing to Tyler, Joanna, Maggie, and my mom. "Grady couldn't leave New York City today, but he purchased some of the materials. Pasha came and did a lot of the grunt work of moving things around. Your mom and my mom did a lot of the book-keeping. Maggie and I installed a system for scheduling shifts, holidays, and appointments. You can sync it all to your phone. We also set up email software and had your website upgraded thanks to Mia, who had someone on her team who does that stuff already."

Even though I'm hearing that all these other people played a part in making this happen, all I see is her. I step around everyone, and I envelope her into a hug, bringing her off the ground. She squeezes me right back, and I wish I had the words to tell her how much it all means to me. Her faith in me, the time she's spent to make this place better.

It takes me longer than it should to set her down, to let her go, and then I circle around to everyone else, giving the traditional Sullivan hug.

"It's a fresh start," my mom says when I hug her. "I'll come in for the next couple of weeks to make sure you know how all the computer programs work."

"Oh, you don't have to—"

"I know that, Trent. Tech stuff comes easily to you, but I want to. We all want you to make a go of this."

"Okay," I say, and I make eye contact with Emily over my mom's head, and I hope she sees in my expression everything I don't know how to say.

The first week without Bruce is slow, and given that things were a bit slower than normal when he was still kicking around, I'm worried. Instead of keeping my worry to myself, I come home from work on time, and I eat dinner with Emily and Amir.

As soon as Amir is in bed, I pull up my appointment book on the computer, and I show her.

"You have a year, Trent," Emily says. "And you knew it would be an uphill battle at first. I would say this is normal. I get why you're anxious—I would be too—but I also think this was to be expected."

I take in what she has to say, and I try not to let my doubts win. While I took this shop on, and I want it to do well, almost more than anything, the only time I've had a real success on my own was when I was putting my skills to illegal use. It's hard to let myself lean into something real when I'm worried my drug business accomplishment, one I've become deeply ashamed of, might be the height of what I'm capable of.

"I'm a good mechanic," I say, carefully choosing my words, "but maybe I should have been happy with that."

"You're allowed to aim high," Em says, running her hand down my back in a soothing way I've seen her do with Amir. "I'm saying this with my whole chest, Trent—your past doesn't have to define your future. Yes, it still impacts it pretty significantly for the next year, but you're already building something better so that when you come out the other side, your path is set in a positive direction."

"Maybe it's too early to tell," I say. "I just...I clung on too hard to the wrong thing when I was a kid, and I took a lot of people down with me. I don't want to make that mistake again."

"I don't think you will," she says, and she leans over to kiss my temple. "You're not the same person now."

I close my eyes at the contact, relish the closeness, and I hope she's right—that I really do understand when to cut my losses to avoid taking other people down with me.

Chapter Seventeen

Trent

The next day, as though the fates heard my silent begging, I get my first client referred to me by Earl. The woman is from Utica, but Earl has replaced every electric part that his diagnostics have said is problematic, and her car is still throwing codes. He calls to tell me she's on her way to me, and that he's going to pick up the tab. I'd love to tell him I can do it for free for old times' sake, but the reality is that I can't.

When she arrives, I run my own tests. A couple of the guys who work for me, that I'm only starting to get to know, come over to watch me walk through the problem. The old joke about how many people it takes to change a lightbulb pops into my head, and I hope she doesn't think it's amateur hour over here.

It takes me almost two hours to root down to the issue, but I find it. A wire that probably wasn't attached properly at the factory. She leaves with no more codes showing, and she's happy with me and happy with Earl.

It's the first real win since I opened, and I breathe a sigh of relief. *This* is what I'm good at.

"That was impressive, man," Brett, an older mechanic who worked for Bruce for years, says at lunch. "You were like a bloodhound. Are you going to train a few of us in how to narrow that shit down?"

"I can, yeah," I say. "If anything comes in, I can work side-by-side with whoever wants to understand how I'd tackle it."

"Pencil me in for the next one," Brett says. "I wasn't sold on Bruce selling to you, but that was impressive." He wags a finger at me as he returns to his oil change.

Just after lunch, Maggie and Grady show up in separate vehicles. Maggie comes in with a broad grin, holding Grady's hand.

"We came to get our oil changed," Maggie says.

"He doesn't do that for you?" I say, nodding at Grady.

"Fuck off, man," Grady says, immediately picking up on my double meaning. "We're getting our *car* oil changed here, and then we're taking a few shots for social media. Hyping you up, as it were."

"Hiran is coming to do a story on the shop takeover, too," Maggie says. "For the local paper. Lots of people read it online or get it in print. He's getting his oil changed too."

I glance at my mom, who's been the one in charge of bookings, and she gives me a slight smile.

"Did you really want me to tell you?" she asks.

It's a fair question. I probably would have turned it all down, and I really shouldn't. The press and social media push from Maggie, from Grady, from Hiran could make a difference. I *do* need as many people as possible hyping me up, even if the notion makes me want to hide out in my office and avoid people. I can deal with negative attention—I've learned to steel myself against it—but pats on the back are tougher to take.

"Emily arranged it all," Maggie says. "Had Penny book it."

My chest goes tight and then warm at the realization that she heard me the other night, and then she immediately tried to help. "She's my best hype man," I say.

Maggie gives me a long, considering look. "Yes, she really is."

But she doesn't pry or push, and I'm grateful. I don't even know what I'd say, depending on what she asked.

Then Tyler's truck roars into the parking lot, followed by a flashy black car that I know will have Mia and her bodyguard, Pasha. Sure enough, they all climb out.

"Them too?" I ask my mom, trying to keep my grin under control.

"Them too," my mom confirms.

Mia alone could blow up my business, especially when I see several other cars pull into my parking lot, which means she called in the paps for this. It won't just be on her socials, it'll be across the interwebs. Tyler told us all once that Mia sometimes called the paparazzi on herself, depending on what she was doing, but I never quite believed it.

Mia strolls into the shop, Tyler holding her hand. Cameras click frantically behind her, but no one enters the business. Pasha stands at the door, tall and intimidating. His "don't fuck with me" face is excellent.

"I just called my favorites," Mia says, by way of explanation as she nods at the photographers outside. "The photos should sell reasonably well if I give them a bit of PDA with my pretty boy." She gives Tyler a sly grin, and it's one of the first times I've seen the confident businesswoman. Normally, she's the anxious mom around the Sullivan crowd. "Hopefully it gives you some cred and some business." She gives me a long look. "If I tell them you're my trusted mechanic, business might get a bit out of control. Do you want that or not?"

Even though I should say "yes," I hesitate. "Maybe we should see how this all comes together first?" I suggest.

"Whatever you want," Mia says. "I can pop by whenever to do a few lives as your guys work on my car." She eyes me. "Or maybe you. You'd play really well to my demographic."

Tyler tugs her into his side, and I can't help my grin. He kept the faith remarkably well in the months she was gone, so to see even a hint of jealousy from him is funny.

And then as they all spring into work, getting photos taken, having their oil changed, talking up my business to Hiran, I can't help feeling extremely lucky that I somehow stumbled into the Sullivan orbit.

When I was a cocky teen, I approached Maggie at a party and offered to change her life, and instead, she changed mine.

Em has a house showing, and I already agreed to get Amir from his after-school care. I arrive a bit early, take him to the town center, and park my truck.

"What are we doing?" Amir glances around.

"Your mom did something really nice for me today, and now I'd like to do something really nice for her." I purse my lips and stare down main street. "What do you think we could get?"

Amir frowns and taps his chin. Then he brackets his face with his hands and seems a bit stumped.

Me too, buddy. Me too.

I thought about bringing home flowers again, and she did like those last time. But it doesn't seem like enough for what she's done for me, what she continues to do for me.

"Can we drive down the road?" Amir asks. "I think I remember something."

"Okay," I say, restarting the car and driving extra slow down main street. I'm sure the cars behind me are loving my pace.

"There!" Amir says, clearly excited. "Mom went in there last weekend, and there was a book she picked up. She carried it around for a while and then put it back."

"Do you think you can remember which one?" I ask, skeptical.

"Yes," Amir says with a decisiveness that's surprising.

When we get in the store, he picks up one that has a bunch of flowers on the cover.

"You're sure?" I ask, though it does look like covers of books I've seen Emily reading. Of course, I have no idea what's inside the covers. Even though I can read now, I'm slow, and reading anything substantial still feels like a lot of work if I don't have to do it.

"It was definitely this one," he says.

"Okay. And you're sure she put it back?" I scan through my memory of the books I've seen lying around the house, and I don't think I've seen this one.

"Yes," Amir says, and there's a hint of impatience in the word.

The kids does have a memory like a steel trap. There's a good chance this is exactly the book she picked up.

I buy it, and I have them put it in a fancy bag. Then I buy a blank card, but when I get back to the house, I sit at the kitchen table forever trying to think of what I can say that gets across how much what she did means to me without going too far.

If we hadn't had sex a couple of weeks ago, if I could stop thinking about having sex with her again, whatever I wrote wouldn't feel so loaded. In the end, I settle for something way more relaxed than what I feel, and I seal it up.

When Em gets home, I've fed Amir and I've left some food in the fridge for her. She heats it up and then calls to me in the living room.

"Trent, what's this?"

"Mom!" Amir yells from the top of the stairs, his hearing suddenly supersonic. "Wait! I'm coming." His little feet pound down the stairs, and he rushes past the living room door and into the kitchen.

I follow behind, and I lean against the kitchen door, watching as Amir practically buzzes with excitement over Emily opening a book. He's so her kid.

She misses the card and pulls out the book, a quizzical expression on her face. "What—"

"Trent said you did something extra nice for him today, so he wanted to do something extra nice for you too. I remembered that you almost bought that last week, so we bought it for you today." Amir says it all so fast that it's almost a blur of nonsense.

Emily's softened gaze meets mine. "You didn't have to."

"Neither did you. But it's appreciated."

Now that the excitement is over, Amir zips past me and back upstairs to his Lego set.

The air around us heats, and I wish I could close the space between us, lift her onto the kitchen table and show her just how grateful I really am.

"Just know," I say, "that if there were no rules, I'd be kissing you right now." Then I turn and go back into the living room.

Chapter Eighteen

Emily

Trent has already left for work, and Amir has just gone to school when the bleeding starts. Even though I didn't really expect to get pregnant the first month, I can't help the tears that form.

Rather than having to tell Trent in person, I send him a *not pregnant* text.

It takes a while, probably because the shop has been busier since Maggie, Grady, Mia, and Tyler stepped up for him on socials, but he replies.

Are you home at lunch? Or do you have some showing or closings to do? I'm here.

I don't add that I don't feel like talking to anyone or doing anything. Instead, because everything I could do can be put off until later or maybe even tomorrow, I crawl back into bed.

I wake to a knock on my bedroom door, and when I call for them to come in, Trent pushes it open gently.

"Came to check in on my favorite Emily," he says.

"Aren't I the only Emily you know?"

"I could know thousands, and you'd still be at the top of the pile. On a scale of one to ten, how upset are you?" He steps into the room, and he's got one hand behind his back.

"Like a five?" I say, though it's probably more like a seven. Though I'd never say it out loud, I'm worried that the longer Trent and I do this, the harder it'll be to re-establish normalcy. Already this new closeness feels normal, and I don't think it should.

"I thought it might be more like an eight, so I had my mom pick up cookies from Kathy's Café," he says, bringing the box around. "They're the double chocolate ones that you love."

"Trent!" I say, tears forming in my eyes. "It *is* more like an eight. God, you bought me cookies?" I hold out my hand, and he approaches the bed, opening the box.

After I take one, he plucks one out and perches on the edge of the bed, chewing with what feels like thoughtfulness.

"Redouble the efforts this month?" he suggests.

"What does that mean?" I ask.

"The internet has a lot of advice," he says, as though that explains what he means.

"And?"

"Sixteen hours might be too narrow of a window."

"What does the internet suggest?" Though I'm sure I already know.

"Try to prime the area before ovulation." He squints at me when he says it like he thinks I'll hate the idea.

"Have sex the day before I think I'll ovulate."

"And then hit it hard."

"Oh my god. Your phrasing."

"You're the one who thinks we need to keep it all clinical."

"There's clinical and then there's shop talk—prime the area, hit it hard."

"Baby, I'm going to grease those wheels so hard, you'll never recover."

He delivers the line with such false bravado that I can't help but laugh. He flashes the cookie box at me again, and I take another one.

"Okay," I say. "We have a deal. The day before I suspect it'll happen, and the day of."

"Yes!" He pumps his fist. "My shop talk worked."

I laugh again and sit up more in bed, pulling the covers around me. "I'm taking Amir to have his genetics tested next week. I still don't know if I'll be able to look at the results, but I think you were right before. It's hanging over me like it's true—like he has it. I might as well know for sure. And when I talked to the genetics counselor, they said even if he has the genetic mutations, it's not a guarantee that he'll get ALS. It's not one hundred percent, but more likely."

Which isn't soothing—it just feels like another thing that'll hang over my head. If he has the mutations, whether he gets full-blown ALS at some point will be a not-so-fun surprise. Letting myself think about that too long sends me on an emotional spiral, so I'm keeping all those thoughts buttoned up.

"What can I do?" Trent asks, plucking out another cookie.

"The counselor said the results are mailed from the genetics lab."

"Same with mine when I got it done," he says. "You want me with you when you open it?"

"Will you? If it's bad, I just…" I shake my head. "I think I'll be a mess."

"I'll hold your pieces if you fall apart," he says, his gaze earnest when it connects with mine. "Whatever you need, I'm there."

I absorb his words for a beat before I say, "I'm really glad that you're the guy. That you'll be the guy."

"It's an honor," Trent says, and he slides the box of cookies on my nightstand before heading for the door. "I'll see you after work."

The next day, I've recovered from my pity party, and I'm meeting a potential new client at their house to assess their property. It's on the outskirts of Little Falls, and it has huge acreage. Lorna and Robert are old money in the area, but they've decided to move to Florida to retire and be closer to their kids.

When I get there, Lorna gives me a tour of the house and all the outbuildings they have. I take photos and careful notes of everything.

Then we sit in their kitchen, and I pull up a few comparable listings on my tablet from memory. I go over what their place has or doesn't have in comparison to the other sales, and then I let them know that I'll have a firm number for them in a couple of days.

When we're done talking real estate, Lorna says, "I heard Trent Castillo took over Bruce Mullen's shop."

"He did," I say. "Are you looking to get some work done?"

"No," she says, glancing at her husband whose expression seems slightly perturbed. "I also heard he's living in your house. Are you with that man?"

The way she says "that man" as though he's a toxic substance gets my back up in a way that's never happened to me before. Well, maybe not never, but it's been a long time since I've felt such a strong desire to not just defend someone but flatten the person making the accusations.

"He's renting a spare room from me while he gets his business off the ground," I say, trying to maintain a polite façade for the sake of business. Their property, if I was able to list and sell it, would be a huge commission.

"So you two aren't dating?" Skepticism coats each word.

"No, we're not."

"I told you, Robert. These Sullivan girls aren't stupid enough to get mixed up with him twice."

"There's a lot of chatter about it round town," Robert says. "Your daddy'd be rolling over in his grave if you got mixed up in that like Maggie did."

"To be clear," I say, measuring my tone, "Maggie wasn't mixed up in anything the first time, and there's nothing to be mixed up in this time. Mullen Mechanics is a legitimate business."

"It *was*," Robert says, sliding a glance at his wife.

"You know," I say, rising to my feet. "I don't think I'm the right real estate person for you. I have no interest in working with or representing people who believe someone is exactly the same person at thirty-four that they were at nineteen. It's ludicrous, actually, and I think you should both be ashamed for being so gossipy. My father," I say, my rage barely controlled, "would be proud of me for keeping an open mind and giving people a chance to prove they've changed."

"It's a real shame," Lorna says, "that you're going to let Trent Castillo drag down your reputation like this."

"Florida seems like it'll be a really great fit for you both," I say, gathering my things and storming out of the house. I throw my car in reverse to turn around, and once I'm at the end of their long laneway, I pause to take a few deep breaths.

I should have said more, defended Trent more. But while I have dealt with a few thinly veiled comments since Trent moved in, no one has been that blunt.

No one has ever spoken to me like that at all. And I realize now that part of that was probably the buffer of my doctor father and my lawyer mother. The Sullivan name *did* mean a lot in Little Falls, and it makes me irrationally angry that Trent, who is such a good man, is being cast as a villain, someone who deceives the Sullivan women and drags them down.

The reality is that he's only ever lifted me and Maggie up.

Next time someone tries to confront me about Trent and his past, I won't hold back.

Chapter Nineteen
Trent

Bruce left last week, and this week, thanks to the social media posts and the article in the paper, we've had steady bookings. Even next week already has a number of slots taken with regular service appointments.

Overall, May isn't looking too terrible, and I'm feeling a tiny bit of hope about the future. There's a chance I can make a go of this.

It helps that I have Mia's endorsement tucked into my back pocket if things slow down or don't continue on a steady increase. She did warn me that if she told people she only uses me to look after her vehicles, that I'd probably draw a more national and international clientele. Lucrative, but not exactly the small-town experience I'm hoping to keep going here.

For now, I really want to keep my focus on establishing good relationships in town, making the locals feel like they can trust me.

Around town, it's been a mixed bag of reactions, with some people making shady comments to my face while others offer heartfelt congratulations about getting my life turned around. I figure anyone who hasn't said anything that's gotten back to me is reserving judgement, waiting to see if I'll fuck up or make a go of it.

Brett's working the late shift on Thursday, and my mom has left for the day. Brett's just tidying the shop before we close up when a BMW

X1 pulls into our lot. It's a flashy canary yellow, which isn't to my tastes, but my curiosity is piqued. I haven't seen the vehicle around town.

When the driver's door opens, it takes me a beat to clock who steps out. Dan Ramouli. I'd heard from Grady that he'd taken over the gas station across town, so I'd avoided filling up there or stopping in for any reason.

"Brett," I call into the shop. "I need you to be present for this conversation, if you don't mind."

My mother is still doing the booking, but whenever a client has a complaint or question, I'm the one who deals with it. Last week, an irate customer got me cornered outside my office and started throwing my past in my face after my mother left for the day, and Brett suggested that a second person floating around might make at least some people less likely to let loose. For those who are truly unhinged, I'd have backup.

In Utica, Earl handled all the forward-facing client relations, and I never really considered how people who weren't happy no matter what we did were appeased.

Brett saunters into the reception area, and he pretends to be organizing things along the wall when Dan comes in.

"Trent Castillo," he crows as though we're old friends rather than borderline enemies. He sold me out to the cops when we were kids to make sure he got away without jail time. "How's business?"

"It's been fine," I say. "I think Hutchinson across town can probably help you with whatever you need."

"He can't, actually," Dan says, strolling around the reception, looking at the artsy car paintings on the walls. "Is there somewhere we can talk in private?"

"If whatever you want to talk about can't be said in front of Brett, it's probably not worth saying," I say.

Brett gives up any pretense of organizing the front reception area and comes to stand at my shoulder.

"I heard business was slow," Dan says. "So I came to offer you a partnership, of a sort. I get people at the gas station asking for mechanic recs all the time. I could do that for you, and you could do something for me."

"We're good here," I say. "I'm not looking to create any partnerships with anyone."

"Doesn't seem very small-town neighborly," Dan says. "We all get better together, isn't that what you used to say?"

The fact he's brought that up—a phrase from another life—makes me certain that whatever partnership he wants to enter into isn't legal. No matter how slow business gets, I'd rather give up the shop than do something to land me in prison again.

Despite his lack of jail time, his level of success has never rang completely true to me. When Grady told me Dan managed to buy out the gas station, and now seeing him driving a flashy car, I have to wonder whether his brush with the law and his ability to get off only made him bolder.

"I don't know why you'd come here," I say.

"Tiger doesn't change his stripes," Dan says. "Just gets better at camouflage."

"That might be true for you," I say, "but our business with each other ended in a courtroom when I was nineteen."

"I think you'll find that a lot of the same rules still apply," Dan says. "If you don't play the game, you risk getting hit by a stray ball."

This fucking guy. His code isn't even particularly well done.

"That sounded like a verbal threat to me," Brett says beside me, picking up the receiver for the phone. "Want me to call that in?"

Dan puts up his hands and backs toward the door. "Didn't mean nothing by that. Just reminding Trent how this all works, in case he really has been out of the game all this time."

"You stay the fuck away from me and my shop," I say. "There isn't a game you could be running that I'd want a piece of."

Dan smirks and gives me a long look. Back when we were kids, I sort of understood why he played nice with the cops. It's possible if I'd been given the chance, I'd have done the same thing. But him showing up here, insinuating that we should have any kind of relationship, is a fucking joke.

As soon as he's out the door, Brett sets the receiver back down. "The past never stays buried, huh?"

"I keep shoveling more dirt on top of it," I say. "Surprises me, sometimes, the people trying to dig it up." It's another one of the reasons I hesitated to take Mia's offer. That much attention would be bound to bring some heat to my past, and I hate talking about it, addressing it.

"Think he'll be back?" Brett asks.

"If the shop isn't doing well, yes," I say.

Two things I can say for certain about Dan—he's excellent at smelling blood in the water, knowing when people are desperate to survive, and he's persistent. Back when we were dealing drugs, that combination made us both a lot of money, but now that I'm on the other side of it, it doesn't feel so good.

On Saturday morning, I get waylaid before I can get out the door by Amir, who's desperate for some breakfast. Rather than telling him to wake up Em, I text Brett that I'll be a few minutes late, and I make him a couple of pancakes with some extras for Emily when she wakes up. I put the leftovers in the oven, and I give Amir instructions to show Emily when she comes downstairs.

I'm in my truck on the way to the shop when Brett calls. "We've had a break-in," he says. "Judy and I are standing outside waiting for the police."

"Do you know what they took?"

"Place looks ransacked," Brett says. "I didn't want to touch anything. As soon as I saw the smashed front door, I called the police."

"I'll be there in a minute. You can go home, if you want. I'll handle whatever work we've got booked this morning. Tell Judy that I'll still pay you both for the morning."

On Saturdays, we are only open until noon—mostly last-minute bookings and emergencies—so it's a small crew that rotates out each week. I'm glad Brett's the one who discovered the break-in. Some of my greener employees might not have known to call the police right away.

"I'll send Judy on her way," Brett says. "But I'll stay until the police are done. After the other day, I wouldn't want anyone getting the wrong idea about you."

"Thanks, man," I say. "I appreciate that."

Brett's working on a car, and I'm matching inventory to our records when Emily arrives.

"Maggie called and said you'd had a break-in?" she says, coming straight into the shop where Brett and I are both working.

"I always forget how fast gossip tracks in this town," I say, checking off another item on my list. So far, I'm only missing two tools, and I can't even be sure if they're missing or someone didn't put them away where they belong. That'll be the next step.

"Maggie is the mayor," she says, looking around. "Other than the front door, was anything else taken or broken?"

"Not one hundred percent sure yet," I say. "Where's Amir?"

"Tyler's house. I dropped him off before coming here. I wasn't sure if I'd be able to help, and I wasn't sure either of us would have the patience for Amir's questions about what happened. Not to mention the fact that I'd rather not freak him out about a break-in."

"My money is on Dan trying to send a message," Brett says from under the car.

"Dan?" Emily says.

"Dan Ramouli," I say.

"The guy who helped send you to jail? Maggie was pissed when he came back to town, but she couldn't block his purchase of the gas station," Emily says.

"Mayor Maggie has good instincts," Brett says, stepping out from under the raised vehicle. "Are you telling Emily?" he asks me.

"I am now," I say, though I probably should have told her the other day when it happened. I just hate any reminders of who I used to be. "Dan stopped by to see whether I'd have an interest in working with him. When I said I did not, he said I might get hit with a 'stray ball.'"

"What does that mean?" Em asks.

"Trying to intimidate him," Brett says. "I was here, so I already told the cops about what happened. Said they should be monitoring Dan's gas station and people he's associating with."

"Why would Dan even come talk to you? That seems reckless," Emily says. "There's no love there after what he did."

"He heard the shop isn't doing well," I say, staring at the wrench in my hand before putting it back in its place. "And he knows what I'm like. How laser focused I can get."

"On doing well?" she asks.

"On doing whatever it takes to do well," I say, sparing her a quick glance before going back to my checklist. "But I don't do that anymore. I've taught myself to cut my losses."

"Almost," Brett says with a chuckle. "I'd wager that laser focus is just better applied now. When something is broken and there should be a fix, you're relentless."

"That's different," I say. "The only thing I'm losing is time, and people are helped, not hurt, when I fix those problems. You don't know what I used to be like—neither of you do."

"You're really hard on yourself sometimes," Emily says quietly. "Maggie wouldn't have gone to bat for you when you got out, wouldn't have maintained such a close friendship with you if she thought you weren't a good guy at heart, Trent."

"You and Maggie both have the same problem," I say, "you see more of the good in people than the reality."

"Trent," she says, and I hate the tone in her voice, scolding and disappointed.

"This is my mess to clean up," I say. "You should go spend time with Amir."

She stands there for a beat, and I can almost feel her censoring herself, coming up with replies and then casting them aside. If I look at her, she'll continue the conversation, probably wear me down to the point where she'll be trying to help me fix this mess, and it's not hers to fix. She's got enough to worry about in her own life.

So I keep focused on the tools until I feel her walk away, until I hear her car pull out of the lot.

"Nothing wrong with letting people who care help," Brett says as he tightens a bolt in the car he's working on.

"I'm not dragging Emily through the mud of my past," I say. "If even a spot of dirt got on her, I'd be so angry at myself for putting her in that situation. She's had enough tough moments. She doesn't need to be bathing in mine too."

"You know her better than me," Brett says.

Then we work in silence until just before lunch, when all the tools are accounted for, and I've decided to check the front reception and my office.

It's then that I discover someone tried to break into my laptop computer in the office but ran out of password attempts. The two computers are synced, but I got into the desktop earlier to check appointments and schedules without issue. It makes me nervous that whoever tried to get into this one actually got into the other.

Immediately, I go back to the desktop and check the activity. There was one login attempt at three in the morning that failed, but that's it. It's hard to know if whoever it was tried that before or after the laptop.

"I think I should get cameras," I say to Brett as we're boarding up the front door, securing the other areas as best we can. "Maybe a security system."

"I would," Brett says. "No way to know yet if this was Dan, but if you're right and he's going to try to force your hand, ruining your business so he can 'save' it is the best 'stray ball' he's got."

It is, and that makes me really fucking nervous.

Chapter Twenty

Since the break-in, Trent's been at the shop even longer hours than normal. Although he hasn't said much to me, I've overheard conversations with security companies about cameras and sensors, and I can almost sense a thread of worry sewing itself underneath Trent's tough exterior. I've always said he's the softest tough guy I've ever met, but he's been doing an impeccable job of putting up an impenetrable mental and emotional barrier between us the last couple of days.

Any other week, it might not bother me that he's pulling back, distancing himself a little. In some ways, it's a relief because we were becoming so close, and a tiny sign at the back of my brain has been flashing a bright yellow caution regarding my emotional attachment to him.

But the calendar doesn't lie, and with the way Trent's been behaving, I think there is a real chance today will go unnoticed.

So when I drop Amir off at jiu jitsu, I decide to pay Trent a visit at the shop. The front door is fixed, and when I open it, a doorbell goes off throughout the shop. That's new.

"Hello?" Trent calls from the garage area.

"It's just me," I say.

He comes out of the shop, cleaning his hands, and my heart kicks at his rugged, disheveled beauty. Every time he fixes something at the house—big or small—it's like my libido gets switched on. Change a lightbulb. Damp panties. Stop a toilet from running constantly. Clenched thighs. Fix Amir's favorite toy so it works like new again. One grazed fingertip short of an orgasm.

Seeing him come out of the shop, noticing the way his gaze drags along my body, as though the sight of me does the same thing to him, gives me a boost of confidence. The distance that he's stuck between us made me wonder whether I'd have the conviction to do what needs to be done.

"Everything okay?" he asks. "Amir at jiu jitsu?"

"He is," I say. "Can I talk to you in your office for a minute?"

Trent throws the cloth he was using toward a wash bin and leads the way to the back. Once we're in the office, I close the door, and I push in the lock.

He sits in his chair, rocking back and watching me.

On the wall is a bank of screens, and each camera seems to be pointed at a different part of the shop—the bays, the front desk, the parking lot. There's even one that seems to be recording in here, and I glance behind me to see one perched high in the corner.

"Isn't that overkill?" I ask.

"Whoever broke in tried to get into my laptop," he says. "Until the police know who did it, I've got eyes everywhere."

"How long does it keep the recording?"

"Each recording is saved for a month."

"Can anyone else see the footage?" I ask, a hint of nerves hitting me. What I had planned didn't account for this.

"Just me. Why?"

"Have you looked at the calendar lately?" I ask.

"I have," he says, steepling his fingers. He shifts in his chair, and I'm not sure I like the way his posture changes. "Listen, Em, after what happened here, I'm not sure we should be doing this."

"What do you mean?" I ask, my stomach dropping into my toes.

He rises from his chair to lean against the wall, and he crosses his arms, as though protecting himself. "I'm not having any part of my past touch you."

If he knew that it already had, he'd break this off for sure. Lorna and Robert haven't been the only clients to express some discomfort with my relationship—whatever they perceive it to be—with Trent.

"So you know that the person who broke in here was Dan?" I ask, heart pounding.

"No," he admits. "But it's the logical conclusion."

I cross the room and sit on the edge of his desk, and his eyes track the shift in my skirt, how it draws up my legs. He's not immune, which makes me feel a little better about how dirty I'm about to play.

"But you don't know that for sure," I say, and I wiggle, my skirt creeping up more.

"No," he admits, his voice rough.

"There could be any number of explanations," I say. "Right?" I let my knees fall apart, and I lean back on the desk, my hair cascading behind me.

"Today's the day before, isn't it?" He's holding still, but the air around us is crackling with tension.

"It is," I say. And it's obvious how much my antics are working. "But I wouldn't want to pressure you into doing something you didn't want to do. If you think there's a *chance* Dan was involved and that is enough to make you want to put a stop to this..."

"I don't want you dragged down," he says, his voice husky.

"No one is dragging me anywhere, Trent. My eyes are wide open." I increase the distance between my knees because my eyes aren't the only thing that's open.

"Fuck," Trent says, closing his eyes briefly before he eats up the distance between us. His lips are on mine, and he hauls me to my feet, hands in my hair. "How much I want you is so fucking irresponsible."

"Just the way you like it," I murmur, and he chuckles against my neck.

"This'll be recorded." His hands snake under my dress and up my thighs.

He's kneading the skin, his palms rough, and I long for him to inch his fingers higher, palm my most sensitive area. It's only been a month, but each day feels like one too many when he's this close. The dark, rich vanilla scent of his cologne is mixed with motor oil. Every inch of my skin is desperate for his touch, hyperaware of the journey his calloused hands are taking.

"But I promise I'm the only one who sees it," he says against my neck. "I can't promise I won't watch it again."

"I trust you," I say as I tug at his belt buckle. "I know you'd never hurt me."

He stills my hand for a minute and stops his assault on my senses to make eye contact. "I'll always protect you from anyone and anything, Em. I'd do anything to keep you safe. Anything to make you happy."

"That's really sweet, Trent," I say. "Now shut up and fuck me."

"Yes, ma'am," he says with a laugh. "By the time we're done with each other, you *will* be asking me to fuck you on the kitchen table. I guarantee it."

"Yeah, but if you're going to talk so much while you do it, I might change my mind." I push down his jeans and they pool at his ankles.

"You only like it when I talk dirty, huh?"

"You got anything I haven't already heard?" I ease my hand under the band of his boxer briefs to grip his length, and Trent lets out a hiss.

"I could talk about fucking you for days," he says, tugging my dress over my head.

"I have to be back in thirty minutes. Less is more today."

He flips me around, and I plant my hands on the desk. He runs the flat of his hand along my spine, and I shiver in anticipation.

"You're so beautiful. Look at you," he says, pointing to the screen on the wall. "I want you to watch while I take you, watch how I can make you come apart."

I barely recognize myself in the video. My hair is already wild, and I look almost drunk. Anticipation has eaten away my sanity.

He moves my panties to the side and slides his finger along my wetness, circling my clit. "I love how wet you get for me, how much you want me. Some days, this is all I can think about. Sliding into your wet heat."

Then he pushes in, and I moan at how full he makes me feel, how turned on I am with so little effort.

"You like that?" he asks in my ear. Then he pulls out and eases in again, slow and deliberate. "I love seeing myself enter you, knowing I'm the one who gets to do this."

One of his hands stays on my hip while his other comes around, playing a steady rhythm on my bundle of nerves, making it impossible for me to focus on anything but how it feels to be with him, to hear his ragged breathing in my ear, the consistent thrust of his hips.

"Look at yourself," he says, "look at how well you're taking me, how much you love it."

And I see it, how dazed I look, as though I can't get enough, can't believe he's making me feel so amazing. No one has ever had me like this—so bold and uninhibited.

The doorbell sounds, and I throw wide eyes over my shoulder at Trent.

"Did you lock the door?" Trent asks, his pace even and unhurried.

"Yes," I whisper. "We should stop."

"We're not stopping. You come, and then I come." He kisses my shoulder. "If you want a baby, you'd better get your head back in the game."

I close my eyes to block out the person at the front desk, whoever it is.

"Trent!" Grady calls out in the shop.

When I tense, Trent thrusts harder. "Concentrate, Em."

"I don't think I can," I say.

"You can." He applies a little more pressure, enters me with a bit more force.

"Oh, god," I mutter, my hands turning white on the desk. "Trent," I plead.

"Come for me, Em. I want to feel you milking every last drop out of me, taking it all for yourself."

Then he changes his angle slightly, and I see spots as I fall apart, shaking with the force of my orgasm, practically collapsing across the desk as he races toward his own finish, spilling himself inside me.

"Holy fuck," he whispers in my ear. "I would say that was worth the wait, but I actually hate the wait. If I could, I'd be doing this all the time."

I don't say anything, but I know what he means. The intensity between us is all consuming. I can't believe I just had an orgasm while Grady stood in the reception area.

"Grady," I mumble.

Trent slides out, sliding my panties back into place and then adjusting himself. He kisses my shoulder and sets my dress beside me on the desk.

I watch him open his office door and slip out. I'm still so completely spent I can barely move.

Even as all of my parts start to reassemble, I remember that Amir is going to my mom's tomorrow, that we'll be locked together like this over and over, and I'm surprised to find myself getting turned on again, that even that time period feels too far away.

I glance at my watch and realize that if I don't get moving, I'll be late to pick up Amir. When I put on my dress, my thighs are sticky, and I'm keenly aware of why as I adjust my hair and check my makeup in my phone camera.

In the reception area, Grady has just left, his back retreating toward his truck in the evening light.

"Did Grady hear us?" I ask, feeling self-conscious.

"No," Trent says. "When he asked what you were doing here, it wasn't a smart-ass question."

"Is everything okay?" I ask.

"Yeah, he just wanted to talk about what we were getting mom for her birthday, and I never responded to his texts." He shrugs. "Things have been a bit hectic."

"Yeah," I agree. "I guess they have."

His gaze trails over me, and he shakes his head. "Honestly, never in my life did I think I'd have a pregnancy kink, but I can't stop thinking about how I've filled you up, and how I really wish you didn't have to pick up Amir so I could do it again."

"Tomorrow," I say, my pulse thrumming at his words.

"Can't come soon enough," Trent calls after me as I open the door to go get Amir.

Chapter Twenty-One
Trent

I only rewatched my little session in the office with Em once when I was here alone one night, and then I deleted it. And for that, I'm quite proud of myself, because seeing it play back felt like a lifetime highlight. The video was the first time that it hit me full in the chest that I'm going to be the father of Emily Sullivan's kid. Me, Trent Castillo, and Emily Sullivan. And the way she so clearly wanted to be with me, wanted *me* when I watched the video, was a bit awe inspiring.

When I was serving time, if someone had told me that this is where I'd end up—running my own shop, trying to have a kid with Em, I'd have told them they'd done too many drugs.

Every part of me is glad to be where I am right now in life, but I definitely don't think I deserve it. Not any of it. Even if we're hiding our arrangement, Em and this life still feel like mine. Mine in a way that it shouldn't. She doesn't want another relationship, and with my past, I'd only drag her down. She'd be foolish to want anything more than what we're already doing. And I need to keep sight of that—that we're temporary. Enjoy every second, but don't turn our situationship into a relationship, not in my mind and definitely not out loud.

"Trent," my mom calls from the front reception. "Emily is on the phone."

My mom has decided that helping me out three days a week gives me a chance to be in the shop with the guys when she's here and learn the front office when she's not. Ever since Grady paid off her house and all her debts, she's been semiretired, only working when she feels like it. She's refused to take payment from me, but I've been trying to set money aside to give to her when I take over all the finances from Emily next year.

I clean my hands and head to the closest phone. "You okay, Em?" I ask when my mom patches Emily through.

"I'm sorry to call you at work," she says, her voice shaky, and immediately my hackles go up.

"What's happened? Are you okay? Is Amir okay?"

"There's an envelope from the genetic testing facility," she says. "I should have just waited until you got home. Sorry. It's just..." There's a thickness to her voice that makes my chest tighten in response. "I panicked."

"Do you want me to come home?" I'm already mentally shuffling work to other mechanics to be able to leave.

"No," she says, but there's a hitch in her voice. "That would be silly. Whatever's in there will be the same later."

A surge of protectiveness runs through me at how she's barely holding herself together. I'm ready to slay a fucking dragon, and all I need to do is open an envelope and read the response so I can either find an impossible way break the results to her gently or help her celebrate.

If I've told her I'll be the one to pick up the pieces or hold them or whatever she needs, I can't let her down today of all days.

"I'll be home in thirty minutes," I say.

"You don't—"

"I'll be home in thirty minutes," I reiterate firmly.

"Okay," she says, her voice quiet. "I'll see you when you get here."

I hang up and go to my mom to look over her shoulder as we check appointments. I'd love to reschedule some of them for later tonight, but if the results are bad news, Emily and I will be a fucking mess. Instead, I go to Brett, who's my most senior person and the one I trust the most.

"Do you mind working a bit late tonight?" I ask as he stands under a car removing the exhaust.

"Overtime?" he asks. "Got a last-minute booking?"

"Last minute family emergency," I say.

Brett glances toward my mom, Penny, in the front office, but he doesn't ask any more questions. "Yeah, I can handle whatever's left over at the end of the day. Just push people back, if you can."

"I'll let my mom know. Thanks, man. I appreciate it."

"I hope whatever's going on works out okay," Brett says.

"Me too." My heart is already feeling a bit heavy at the alternative.

When I get home, Emily is sitting at the kitchen table, hands in her lap, staring at the envelope on the table like it's a fucking viper ready to strike.

"Is someone picking Amir up from school?" I ask. Though it's just before noon, I don't know what kind of shape either of us will be in, and I remember Emily saying how she tried so hard to pretend to be fine for Amir, even when she's not.

"My mom," she says. "I didn't tell her why."

"Open it now?" I ask, running my hand across her back and dropping a kiss onto her temple.

"I don't think I'm ready," she whispers. "I'm really regretting even getting it done, to be honest."

I take the envelope off the table, and I fold it, stuffing it into my back pocket.

"What are you doing?" she asks, her eyes rising to face me.

"We're going to get out of here. I've got somewhere in mind, and when you're ready for me to open it and take about ten years to read it, you can let me know."

"It won't take you ten years."

"You clearly have no idea how slow I read. There's a reason I do most of my learning through hands-on experimentation." I trail my gaze down her off-the-shoulder summer dress. "There are some benefits to that method."

Her cheeks turn pink.

"Did you cancel all your work for the rest of the day?" I ask, taking her hand and leading her toward the door.

"I moved everything around to tomorrow and the rest of the week. Though I honestly..." She shakes her head, and I know what she's going to say because I feel the same way. If the results aren't what we want, tomorrow will come too soon for a lot of things.

"Take it as it comes, right?" I suggest as she slides her feet into her sandals.

"Am I dressed okay for wherever we're going?"

Her anxiety in the question, in what we're prolonging, is so obvious that I stop just before the door and turn to examine her. I slide my hands into her hair, and I press my lips to her forehead. She sighs and leans into me, her hands resting lightly on my sides.

"I don't know what I'd do without you," she whispers.

"And you're never going to find out," I murmur before drawing her into a tight hug.

"We're going in that?" Emily asks, her tone brimming with disbelief.

We're facing a battered red rowboat while standing on a dock on Lake Speers. It's a small inland lake not far from Little Falls that stocks fish and has little rowboats, paddleboats, and other small watercraft. Since it's a weekday, it's not too busy.

The sun is shining, and there's a gentle breeze rustling the leaves on the older trees that circle the lake while fluffy white clouds roll overhead. Under other circumstances, it'd be the perfect day.

"I'm going to flash everyone when I get in," she says, holding onto the bottom of her skirt while I grip her elbow to help her step down into the boat.

When she sits down on the triangle seat at the back, the whole thing shudders and shakes, and she turns wide eyes up to me.

"Don't tell me that Emily Sullivan hasn't been in a rowboat before?" I say, stepping into the boat where the paddles sit, getting comfortable. Truthfully, I've only been in the boat once before with Amir, and my reaction was much like hers just was. A total "what the fuck am I doing?" when the thing swayed with wild abandon.

This one is bigger than the one I rented with Amir, and though it's rocking a little, it doesn't feel quite so much like we might tip in. I learned that lesson last time as Amir and I tried to fish and I kept a hand on the head loop of his life jacket, terrified he'd fall in.

"What's the plan here, Castillo?" she asks, gripping the sides of the boat as though we're all about to go down with the ship.

"We're going to row out to the middle, and then we're going to lie in the boat and watch the clouds."

Her earlier tone of disbelief is now followed by a look to accompany it. "You're kidding."

"No. It'll be relaxing. You'll see." Or at least it seems relaxing in my head. I even grabbed one of the blankets I keep stashed in the back of my truck so we wouldn't be lying on the cold steel.

Once we seem to be close enough to the middle that we won't drift quickly to the shore, I lock in the paddles and lay down the blanket. The lake doesn't allow any motorized boats, so we aren't in danger of being hit by anything fast moving. I shift onto the blanket, the boat rocking, and I gesture to Emily to come down with me.

"Couldn't we have done this in a field?" she asks with a hint of a laugh as she carefully wobbles down to lay beside me.

"Probably," I admit, but the truth is that I wanted us to be somewhere we'd never been before together so that nothing we know and love becomes tarnished with a bad memory if the result isn't good.

I don't want to remember sitting in her kitchen or being at my favorite thinking spot or the best coffee shop—I want to be somewhere that we'll never have to go again, somewhere we'd have to actively choose to go again, if I open the envelope and her world falls apart.

The middle of the lake is also pretty private for whatever might come.

She lies beside me, and we stare up at the cloud-filled sky. As one particularly large cloud passes by, I point to it and declare, "Elephant."

She turns her head slightly. "More like a hippo." With her index finger, she points to another, "That's a cat."

"Clearly a dog," I say with a chuckle.

Then we're off, debating cloud shapes and combinations, drawing what we see with our fingers on the clouds as they pass us by. Emily's laughter over some of my claims makes the tightness in my chest loosen a little. The envelope in my back pocket still feels stiff and heavier than it should. I want to open it, and I want to leave it tucked in there forever.

"That's weird," Emily says, pointing to a cloud. "That one looks kind of like it's on fire with the way the sun is coming through."

I don't say anything, but she's right. It does look strange, almost otherworldly. "The aliens are sending a message," I say, my tone teasing.

"And that one," Emily says, pointing behind it. "That looks like an ax."

And again, it does. I can't even pretend like it's something else. "Yeah," I murmur, not following how or why her voice has changed to a tone tinged with confused excitement.

"Oh my god," she says with a baffled laugh. "That's a fire hydrant and a fireman's hat. You can't convince me otherwise."

I wouldn't even try. It's like someone placed them in the sky, perfectly formed, as though made from a cookie cutter.

She curls into me, burying her face into my chest, and I hold her close, surprised for a beat.

"Open the envelope," she says. "Can you open it? I don't want to look, but I need you to open it."

I shift, keeping her close, and I awkwardly dig it out, rip off the top, and tug out the letter. My heart is hammering, but I'm trying to pretend it's not. She keeps her face buried, and her palm rests on my chest. She can probably feel and hear the rapid beat of my heart.

It really does take me forever to read and comprehend something, so I read it very carefully the first time, and then I read it a second time to be sure I've really understood it. I can't get this wrong.

"It says," I say, my voice rough with emotion, "that he doesn't have any of the gene mutations known to cause ALS. He's at no greater risk of developing ALS than the rest of the general population."

Emily doesn't say anything, but she clutches onto me, her hand on my chest clenching my shirt into a fist. She releases a sob so strong that I wonder if she's been holding it in for years. I drop the letter into the boat, and I hold her tight, trying to keep my own tears of relief at bay. The weight that rises off me is probably nothing compared to the one that's been laying on her since Omar died, since she realized there might be a genetic component.

I don't even know what I would have done if the result had gone the other way. I run my hand along her back in a soothing motion, kissing the top of her head every once in a while. She cries and cries, and I don't try to stop her or convince her she doesn't need to.

I can't help but think she's crying about more than the relief over Amir, but also about her dad and maybe even about Omar still. She's held onto a lot of grief and uncertainty the last few years. She deserves to let it out.

When her crying quiets and she pulls back, she sniffs and stares up at the sky. I'm not sure what to say, so I don't say anything. The silence between us is comfortable.

"I ruined your shirt."

"It'll wash, and if it's going to be covered with any kind of tears, tears of relief are the best ones."

We're both quiet for a beat before I say, "What made you decide to open it all of a sudden?"

"Omar was a firefighter," she says.

Holy shit. All those shapes in the clouds. It hits me like a blow to the chest, and I turn my head to look at her, but she's still staring up.

"And I just knew," she says, "that no matter what was in the envelope, it would be okay."

Chapter Twenty-Two

Emily

We get deeper into June, and I'm still not pregnant, but after getting the news about Amir, I'm not sure anything can bring me down. I hadn't realized what an unconscious heavy burden the uncertainty about his medical future was until it was gone.

"Mom," Amir says, climbing into my car from the after-school program, "I made something for Father's Day at school, and then we made something in the after-school program today, too."

My heart seizes for a beat, and I'm at a loss for words. Are we taking those things to the cemetery?

"Oh?" I say, hoping he'll expand on what he's thinking before I make any wild suggestions.

"Yeah," he says, buckling his seatbelt. "I think Trent will like them."

Speech has definitely lost me. He knows his father died when he was a baby, but since Trent lives with us now, maybe he's gotten confused.

"And some of the other kids were talking about how they make their dads breakfast in bed and stuff, and I want to do that too."

When I still don't say anything, he says, "It's this weekend. On Sunday, I think? Yeah, Sunday. I'm pretty sure."

Trent did help Amir in May to deliver me breakfast in bed for Mother's Day, but I'm stumped about the best way to approach this. Trent doesn't even want to be a true father to the baby *we're* trying to have, so asking him or making him take on that role for Amir seems unfair.

"You know," I say, carefully. "Trent and I might need to talk about this before we do anything."

"But I want it to be a surprise."

"But honey," I say, struggling to find the words, "Trent isn't your dad."

"Right, but he's *like* a dad."

He did make him breakfast, take him to do fun things, occasionally correct him when he was doing something wrong, and so I could see how all of that added up to "Dad-like" to Amir, but I have no idea how Trent would see it.

Even bringing it up to him makes my pulse jump with anxiety. Since I haven't gotten pregnant yet, we haven't had to revisit our earlier conversations around how involved he'd be, around who we'd tell, and letting Trent slip into such an important position in Amir's life seems like it warrants another discussion.

"I don't think this is something we can just spring on him," I say. "I won't tell Trent what you've made or anything, but I think I should check with him. That's he's okay for you to treat him that way."

"Who else would I treat that way?" Amir asks. "My dad died. Grandpa died. Uncle Tyler is someone else's dad. Uncle Grady is nice, but he's not Trent. I want Trent."

His matter-of-fact statements hit me square in the chest. "I understand that," I say, carefully, my throat tight with emotion. "I just need to talk to Trent first."

"Don't spoil my surprise," Amir says, a hint of stubbornness entering his tone.

"I won't spoil your surprise," I say, but inside I wonder what part of this whole thing Trent is going to find most surprising and what the hell I'm going to tell Amir if Trent doesn't want to be seen in this sort of light.

That night, Amir asks Trent to put him to bed, which only delays the "dad" discussion that has my guts twisted in knots. I have no idea how Trent is going to take it.

The bedtime request has happened often enough, either because I'm showing clients a house or Amir wants the bonding time. Trent and Amir have a system. Instead of Trent reading the bedtime story, Amir has to pick one he can read to Trent.

Any time I've walked past the room while they've been doing their routine, it's made my chest glow with warmth. Trent is always lying on the single bed, wedged in beside Amir, his hand under his head, staring at the ceiling while Amir hunches over a picture book, sounding out words and trying to make sense of the story he selected. They chat back and forth about characters and plot as though the storyline is riveting to both of them.

If I wasn't already eager to have Trent's baby, that probably would have been enough to seal the deal. I love the way he loves my son.

But I'm also very aware of how Trent's past casts a long shadow over what he thinks he deserves, what he's capable of having, who he can allow to push that shadow away, even for a moment. Since we've been living together, I've become more conscious of how he sees his past than I ever was before. He won't let the weight of his past mistakes go.

When Trent comes down the stairs and into the kitchen, my breath catches at how good rumpled and a little tired looks on him. His jeans hang just right, and the T-shirt he's wearing hugs his chest and accentuates his impressive biceps. He's in the gym at least three times a week—sometimes in the early morning, sometimes late at night. He told me once that working out is the best way to keep any stress in check, which was something he discovered in prison. I certainly appreciate the results of that anti-stress routine.

"You're not watching TV?" Trent asks, grabbing a Gatorade from the fridge and twisting off the lid.

"I was feeling a little anxious about something, so I couldn't focus," I admit, fiddling with a piece of stray paper on the counter.

He comes over so our shoulders brush and rests against the counter beside me. Maybe the proximity should bother me, but I love that he likes to be close to me, that any chance he has to touch me, he does. And it amazes me how he can ramp up the sexual tension between us from casual friendship to "I want to rip off your clothes" only when required.

Sometimes it makes me question whether he really does think about me in that way throughout the month, or if he just flicks a switch, makes himself feel a certain way.

Ever since that first kiss, it feels like I have a pilot light inside, lit just for him, waiting to be turned to full strength. I notice things about him in a way I never did before.

He takes a long drink from the bottle, his throat working, before screwing on the top and setting it beside him. "What's going on? How can I help?"

"I've been wracking my brain trying to think about how to approach this," I say.

"Are you cutting me from the baby making team because I can't hit the target?" Trent asks.

"No," I say, and I let out a startled laugh. At this point, I like having sex with him far too much to be cutting him from the team, even if the results have been slow to come. "It's about Amir."

"Okay," Trent says, clearly waiting for more.

"He would like to celebrate Father's Day this year," I say.

Trent nods slowly, and it looks like he's trying to process what this would mean. "Sounds kinda morbid, but do you mean at the cemetery?"

"No," I say, taking a deep breath. "I mean with you."

"Me?" He sounds genuinely surprised.

I don't say anything, I just give Trent a beat to work through the implications of that.

"Oh, I don't know, Em," he says, running a hand along the top of his head. "I wouldn't want to let the kid down."

Even though he doesn't elaborate, I understand both ways he means it. Saying "no" would let Amir down, but saying "yes" leaves Amir open to criticism from people around town. While Trent and I are adults who can deal with people's old perceptions of him, Amir might be hurt or confused by them.

"What does he want to do?" he asks.

"Cook you breakfast. Give you a few things he's made."

"That's it?" he asks.

"Yes, but..." I struggle to find the right words. "We'd be setting a precedent. I don't know if he'd want to do that next year and the year after—assuming you're still in our life." I say the last part quietly, almost afraid to put it out into the universe.

"I'll be here," he says firmly and quickly. "I'll be here, right?" There's a hint of panic in the second question. "We made a promise."

"And I'm planning to keep it, but I also know life doesn't always go how we expect, how we want it to."

Trent is quiet for a beat, and his hands flex on the counter as he leans back into them. I have no idea what's going through his head, but the expression on his face makes me think it's a lot. I knew Amir's request wasn't a light, easy one, and I'm glad he's taking it seriously, but I'm worried I'll have to tell Amir that his plans will have to change.

"One of the reasons I wasn't sure I could say 'yes' to this whole baby making thing was him, you know? He's lost his dad, and he lost his grandfather, and we've gotten close. Like, I can't deny that." He glances at me, as though checking to see if I'm following along. "And I'd never want to put anything in place that would make my relationship with him harder." Trent swallows and looks away. "Like what if you got remarried at some point? I don't have a legal or biological claim to Amir at all."

I want to tell him that I'm never going to get remarried, but the truth is that having Trent around, the support he's given me, has been nicer than I expected. I'd forgotten what it was like to be with a partner who was truly an equal, and he is. There's no task too big or too small for him around the house, with me, with Amir. *That's* what I'd want, if I were to ever do it again. And I understand how rare it is to have this. Even admitting all that in my head makes me a bit queasy.

"If we have a baby," I say, "you'd be around no matter what. Right? You said you'd be involved in the baby's life, even if we never really tell anyone the biological connection. I want you involved. It would be easy enough for Amir to have a relationship with you too, if you want."

"Do you really think this is a good idea, Em?"

"I think he already sees you as a dad figure, and I think this is proof of it. Whether we let him celebrate you or not, he already feels that connection. Maybe already wants that bond with you..." I watch him carefully while I say the next bit. "But if *you* don't want that, then I think we need to consider setting more boundaries so that Amir doesn't get confused."

I can almost see the two versions of Trent mentally wrestling for control—the nineteen-year-old kid who made a lot of mistakes and went to jail, and the man he's worked so hard to become since he got out.

Despite what he believes about himself, he's not a bad role model for Amir, and if I believed that, I never would have let them get so close, I never would have wanted him to father a baby with me.

That's the reasonable, rational way to look at the situation, but I know that's not Trent. He's all raw emotions and gut feelings.

"It wouldn't bother you for him to put me in that role?" he asks, finally.

"My only concern is that, no matter what happens between us, you don't disappear on him. He's lost Omar, and he's lost my dad. I'd never forgive myself if I put another man in his path that got ripped away." And I think, in some ways, that's also been my problem with dating. When I know I might bring a man into our lives who won't stay, it's hard to commit.

"I won't disappear on him," he says, and his voice is rough with emotion. "But I really don't know that I should be the one guiding him."

"Your past is in your past, Trent. None of that is happening right now. It's done. And look what you've accomplished since you got out? If you ask me, you're exactly the kind of person I'd want him to learn from. You're kind, patient, and you treat others with respect."

"I'll trust your judgment, Em. If you think it's okay, then I think it's okay too."

I just wish getting that response was that easy for our potential baby, but maybe it will be by the time I get pregnant and have our child. Maybe by then he'll have been able to let his past go, tuck it firmly behind him, and embrace the notion that he's changed. That he can be a good person who once made some bad choices.

"Brace yourself then," I say with a small smile. "I have no idea what he has planned."

"I consider myself warned." A hint of an answering smile touches Trent's lips.

Chapter Twenty-Three

Trent

Before I knew what it was like to sleep with Emily, I never had to worry about my behavior around her. Casual touches and close proximity made me think dirty thoughts, but I had those under control—mostly. None of it was ever going to go anywhere, or so I thought.

Now, though, it's like my whole body *knows* when she's in a room, when she's close enough for me to catch a hint of lemon or peaches, and there's some subconscious part of me that's become aware of the rhythm of her, beyond the calendar and her technical cycle.

Some nights, I can tell when she's feeling *me* a little too much. Most of the time, I work really hard to ignore any impulse to push her buttons. I know I could, but doing that is wrong.

Right?

Except, sometimes wrong feels a little too good. That's always been my problem.

So when I get home from the gym a week before anything physical should happen between us, I notice how she moves through the kitchen, tidying up, as though she's also hyperaware of me, where I am, what I'm doing.

And I should let that sensation go. That's the responsible thing to do. She doesn't want things to get out of hand between us, and I want us to be able to return to friends once my duty is done.

Or I think I do.

I will admit to myself, usually when I've had a drink or two, that the idea of this *not* ending when my duty is done isn't out of the question. At least for me. On those rare days when it feels like what I did in this town is fading into the past, being buried in people's memories, the idea of keeping Emily is more appealing than it should be.

No matter what happens, I definitely get I should be savoring what we have right now. Emily Sullivan is *mine*.

And I swear to god, or all the aliens in outer space, Emily's sundresses were put on this planet to torture me. When she's in sweats, I can almost pretend we're just friends, but when she's still wearing one of the dresses she wore to show a house or film a promo, I hold on to my sanity by a thread.

Not only is she wearing a dress tonight, she's wearing my favorite yellow one with these little purple flowers on it. I don't know how she wears it for work because it barely reaches mid-thigh, and it's a wispy material, the kind that would be soft and silky to the touch.

The air around us has heated, in a way I normally only let it when I know it's go-time, but I don't feel like fighting it tonight.

In fact, I might be feeling a little bit of an urge to break the rules.

"There's food in the fridge, if you want it." She's at the sink doing the last of the dishes from dinner, I presume.

"I'm definitely hungry." I let my gaze drag over her, not hiding what I'm thinking about eating at all.

A flush rises to her chest and into her cheeks. "Help yourself," she says.

Instead of going to the fridge, I approach her at the sink, and I trail my fingers along her exposed leg, stopping at the hem of her dress, and then I put my palm on her hip, kiss her on the temple.

"I'll definitely help myself," I say.

I heat up the leftover casserole, and I sit at the table. When she goes to walk past, to head into the living room, I catch her wrist, and I tug her between my spread legs. She cups the back of my head, and she doesn't make any noises of surprise or dissent.

"Is this okay?" I murmur, looking up. If she tells me to keep my hands off, I'll rein myself back in.

"Yes," she says, her voice hushed.

I drag my palms up her outer thighs, under the hem of her dress to cup her ass. She leans into me, into the contact, and I hear the smallest sigh of contentment. She likes having my hands on her. I lift up her dress, and I kiss a line along the top of her panties. Her fingers dig into my scalp, and I think she'd let me do more, if I pushed.

Instead, with superhuman self-control, I remove myself and tug her dress back down.

"I'd have you for dessert, if you'd let me," I say.

"One more week."

That just means one more week of self-gratification and cold showers for me.

When I get out of the shower and hear swearing coming from behind Emily's door, I knock lightly, mindful of waking Amir up.

"Can I come in?" I call softly.

There's an obvious commotion, more swearing, and something thuds on the floor before she calls for me to come in.

"You okay?" I ask when I push the door open gently. "Sounded like you were having trouble with something."

"No," she says, her voice high pitched and strained. "Everything is fine."

I step closer because Em's version of fine and most people's aren't always aligned. And then I see the lube on the nightstand. Then I focus on her face, and I see what I should have noticed the minute I walked in. She was clearly in the middle of something.

"Are you having fun without me?" I ask, a little surprised.

Her cheeks turn pink, and she seems momentarily at a loss for words. "One more week."

"I am very aware of our timeline," I say, closing the distance to the bed. "But if you need some satisfaction in between, I'd love to be the one to take care of you."

"My batteries died," she whispers.

"I'm good at changing batteries," I say, "but I'm even better at eating pussy."

And I swear, she melts, turns to absolute liquid in the bed.

"Lock the door," she says.

She doesn't have to ask me twice, and I'm back at her side of the bed, drawing back the covers to see her nightgown around her waist, and she's bare. I get on my knees, and I tug her toward me, turning her on the bed. She comes willingly.

"I could not love this view more," I say. "Fuck one more week. I'd do this every day if you let me." Then I lick a line up her, and she shudders, clutching the blankets.

"You got me so turned on downstairs, I could hardly stand it," she says, moaning when I cover her with my mouth.

"Don't worry," I say, "I'll make it all feel better."

I love the taste and feel of her on my tongue, and the way she lets out panty moans and throaty noises of pleasure when she starts to get close to reaching her orgasm. We might only do this once a month, but they are marathon sessions, and I feel like I know every sigh, every pitch and tone she makes when she's turned on, ready to rocket off the bed when I get her to the finish line.

When I slide two fingers into her as I work her over, she cries out and then covers her mouth, letting out a loud groan of pleasure. She can be loud, so doing this with Amir sleeping a few rooms over is probably irresponsible.

That's the tricky part about wanting her, though. I have no self-control once I start.

"Maybe put a pillow over your face," I say.

"Oh, god," she says, but she grabs one and presses it to her face.

She must be close, and I keep licking, sucking, and swirling in the rhythm that I know doesn't just get her there, but gets her there in a way that drives her a little insane before she tips over. She told me once that she can never decide what she wants more when I do this—for me to keep going or for her to hit the peak.

"You're right there, Em. You're right there. You're doing so good," I murmur against her thigh as my fingers and thumb keep up the tension.

She lets out an audible whimper, and I go back in one more time. With a tiny bit more pressure, her hips shoot off the bed, and she cries out.

"Oh my god," she says. "I've been thinking about you doing that all day."

"You only need to ask," I say, rising over her to make eye contact. "I'll do anything you want."

"I want you to fuck me," she says without even a hint of self-consciousness.

I search her expression, trying to figure out if this is post-orgasm talk or she's serious. "Right now?"

"Right now." She hooks her ankles around my waist.

"The timing..." I can't even believe I'm not already sliding into her, but this feels like a slippery slope. It's one thing for me to get her off whenever she wants, but it's another to have sex become a free for all.

"Maybe that's what we've been doing wrong. Too rigid. Maybe we should just do what feels good."

"Em, are you—"

Her hand on the back of my neck, dragging me into a kiss kills the last of my protest. Maybe this is a bad idea. Maybe the slope will be slippery and dangerous. Maybe I'll lose sight of the goal. Maybe this will blow up our friendship.

And it's that last thought that gives me the tiniest hesitation until her hand is in my box-briefs, shoving them down, gripping me, guiding me to where she wants me.

Who am I to deny her what she wants when she wants it this badly?

"Fuck, Em," I mutter as I slide in.

"I don't think I've ever wanted anyone this badly," she says into my ear as I move inside her.

That comment, coming from her, is the biggest aphrodisiac of my life. I may not have much to offer, but I can give her this. I can give it to her whenever, wherever, and however she wants.

"I love when you're inside me," she whispers, clutching onto me. "I love it so much."

If she keeps saying shit like that to me, I'm only going to last another two or three thrusts, but I can't deny how much my chest swells to hear it, how good it is to know that I matter in some way to her.

Because we've been together so many times now, I recognize the signs that she could hit a second orgasm. It's rare, but it seems like tonight she's extra keyed up, which is good because it gives me something else to focus on. With each thrust, each brush of our bodies, I watch her reactions shift until I'm driving us both toward the height of pleasure.

And when she cries out my name, I kiss her deeply, and I follow right behind.

Chapter Twenty-Four

Father's Day morning arrives in the house like Christmas. Amir is up before the sun, knocking on my door and asking if it's time to make breakfast for Trent. I convince him to come into my bed for more sleep, and I send a text to Trent telling him not to go downstairs if we're still sleeping when he wakes up.

When Amir wakes up again, it's ten in the morning, and I'm sure Trent's been cursing my instruction to stay in bed. He's often up and gone to the gym early on Sundays.

My son is frantic, convinced Trent wouldn't have followed instructions and his Father's Day dream of delivering breakfast in bed will be ruined. When he goes into Trent's room to take his order, he's happy he has to wake Trent up. But I wonder if Trent was faking sleep after hearing Amir's distraught rambling in the hallway.

Either way, I'm grateful to him for playing along.

Amir skips down the stairs with Trent's breakfast order of bacon, eggs, toast, and coffee in his head. Trent and I talked about the food we had in the house last night because I knew Amir wanted to play waiter.

Amir puts on his superhero apron, and he shows me how he learned to crack an egg with one hand from some online chef he watched. It's impressive. Some days I can barely crack an egg with two hands without ending up with some stray shell.

Since breakfast isn't anything fancy, we're done in no time, and Amir is carefully balancing the plate in his hands on the way up the stairs. I follow behind with the scalding hot coffee. Trent can drink it straight out of the pot without cream or sugar like some sort of unhinged person.

As soon as we get to the top of the stairs, Amir whips around, almost sending the breakfast flying off the plate. "I forgot the presents in my school bag," he says.

"That's okay," I say. "We can drop off breakfast and then you can go down and get the stuff to deliver to him."

"It's already wrapped," Amir says, and then he waits for me to open Trent's door.

I give a light tap with my knuckles before we enter. Trent is sitting up in bed, on his phone, and when he glances up, Amir yells, "Happy stepdad day!"

"Uh," I say, shocked by what's come out of his mouth.

"Here," Amir says, passing Trent the plate before dashing back out the door.

"I have no idea what that's about," I say as soon as he's gone.

"Not exactly what we talked about," Trent says with a strained chuckle. "He must not know what it means."

Amir comes shooting back into the room, two decorated brown paper bags in his hands. He puts one out to Trent then draws it back and puts out the other, as though he can't decide which to deliver first.

"Which one do you like best, bud? Give me that one first."

"This one," he says, passing Trent the longer one.

Trent carefully removes the tape from the top of the bag. And he pulls out a long, thick piece of cardboard in a makeshift frame. I can't see what it says, but I can tell from Trent's face that it's made him emotional.

"Do you want me to read it for you?" Amir asks, all innocent helpfulness.

"Nah, bud. I'm just taking it in. You did a good job on this." He glances up at me and turns it around. I move closer, and I see where the stepdad comment came from.

On the top of the list are the words *To the World's Best Stepped-Up Dad,* and under it are all the things Trent has done over the last year and half that have meant something to Amir. The list is long and detailed—exactly what I'd expect from Amir—but it makes my throat clog up. While I'd known the time they spent together was important to Amir, I'm not sure I fully realized all the things they'd done together, all the ways Trent had left an impact.

"That's amazing," I whisper, and I can't keep the tears from forming in my eyes, so I turn away in case they spill.

"And this one," Amir says, passing him a shorter bag.

Trent sets the first gift on the nightstand, propped up so it's easy to read. Then he takes the second bag and opens it just as carefully, the paper crinkling as he tries to open it without ripping anything.

He pulls out what looks like a series of wide popsicle sticks with some paper attached. Trent grins and turns this one toward me. Pictures of Amir and Trent are in each "frame," and there's a sentence under each to say what they were doing. The center of the piece says *World's Best Stepped-Up Dad* again.

"Where'd you get the photos?" I ask.

"I think I know," Trent says. "Joanna asked me for some photos of me and Amir a few weeks ago for the family photo albums. I sent her a bunch. Is that right?"

Amir nods. "Grandma helped me get the pictures. I knew Mom would ask a million questions."

He's not wrong. Part of me is glad for their connection, and part of me is wary of it, especially given what Trent and I are doing that he knows nothing about. Trent has promised he won't abandon Amir, and I have to trust that, but it's hard to know I'm putting my son's heart on the line with the choices I've made.

But when Trent reaches over and ruffles Amir's hair, drawing him into a hug, I realize it's not just Amir's heart I've put on the line. It's pretty clear Trent loves him just as much.

The boat sways when I get in, and I hold out a hand for Amir to step down after me. Trent is trying to hold the rowboat steady from shore, with all the fishing equipment clasped in his other hand.

Trent had given Amir the choice of activity today, and this is what he'd picked. It felt a bit bittersweet that he picked this place. It's where the weight of his potential illness was released, and it's also where I last felt Omar's presence.

Without knowing it, he probably picked the perfect thing for us to do, even if I really *hate* this boat.

I triple check Amir's life jacket as Trent gets into the boat, and it wobbles quickly and uncontrollably.

"Someone is going to fall in," I mutter, gripping the side while Amir laughs with delight.

"No one will fall in," Trent says with a lot more confidence than I feel. Of course, he was right about it all last time—coming here, renting the boat, releasing my anxiety into the clouds.

Amir moves around the boat with confidence, not at all concerned about the rocking, to get to the front. I sit at the back, facing Trent, and he's got the fishing stuff at his feet and the oars in his hands.

Then the worker at the dock pushes us away, and Trent begins to row.

Last time, I was too keyed up to take in the view, but every time Trent rows, his muscles flex in the most appealing way. Watching Trent makes me wish Amir wasn't here. Sex in a boat might not be the best experience, but it's one I find myself craving the longer Trent rows.

Last week in my room, having sex without a clear purpose, the floodgates of my desire opened. Not that I'd been keeping a particularly good cap on it—the vibrator had been getting a solid workout for weeks, hence the dead batteries—but it's insane how much I want him now. All the time. Everywhere. It's like he gave me a pill that said, "Trent," in bold, and I've been unable to break the habit since.

In the house, if he moves past me, I've got a hand on him somewhere. Before, it was Trent with the casual touches that I took to mean nothing. Now, they mean everything, and I'm doing them too. Physical foreplay that goes somewhere if we can be quiet enough. If we can find the time and space to be together in some way.

Last week, while Amir was at jiu jitsu, I was so starved for alone time with Trent that I showed up at his office, and within minutes, he had me bent over his desk, watching myself on the security screen getting completely lost in the moment.

"Seems like a good spot," Trent says, clicking in the oars and getting the fishing poles rigged up. "You fishing?" he asks me.

"No," I say with a little laugh. "I'm going to enjoy the view." And I rake my gaze over him, in case he doesn't understand what I'm talking about.

His focus slides over me in the same way, and then he says, "Would have been too rocky."

"Might have to try it sometime."

"Would you?" He seems genuinely surprised.

"With how I feel right now, I definitely would."

"What are you talking about?" Amir asks from the front of the boat.

"Getting wet," Trent says, winking at me. "You mom thinks she'd go for a swim in this water if it got too hot."

I laugh a little at how he's turned what we were really talking about into a private joke only we can understand.

"Cooling off might be necessary, that is true," I say.

Amir stands and looks into the water. "Too much gross stuff in there."

"You're right," I say. "I might not enjoy it, but I'm willing to try."

Trent leans forward so his lips are close to my ear. "You're a naughty one."

"Surprised?" I murmur.

He leans back and searches my face. "Actually, not really. But I like it. A lot." He lets out a self-conscious laugh. "Probably too much."

And that feels like the crux of our developing problem. Before, when we were keeping strict lines and boundaries, I was confident we'd be able to return to friends. Sure, it might have taken a period of adjustment, but I was certain we'd get there.

Now that the lines are blurring, that I'm practically erasing them at times, I don't know what'll happen when I get pregnant.

I know what I'm starting to want, but it feels scary to consider it, to even allow the idea to fully form. Trent was clear before this all started, with Lila first and then me, that he doesn't want a relationship. This path, the one I won't let myself consider in any detail, could lead to heartbreak, a broken friendship, a heartbroken little boy—the kind of outcome with Trent and for Trent that I'd never want. It's not an outcome I'd want for myself and Amir either.

But to stop this slow descent into madness, I'd need more willpower than I currently possess. There's nothing rational about what we've set in motion, but I can't seem to find the motivation to draw those clear lines again, to back us up and away from danger.

"Watch the edge of the boat there, bud," Trent says as he passes Amir a pole ready to go. "You don't want to fall over the edge. The water looks murky and deep."

"Yes," I agree, staring at Trent. "Yes, it does."

Chapter Twenty-Five

Trent

We spend the Fourth of July together at the parade and fireworks, then we come home, and I make fireworks go off for Emily in a different way after Amir is asleep.

I don't know what made Emily relax the rules between us, but I'm not questioning it. For however long this arrangement lasts, I'm savoring every moment.

But the length of this arrangement is weighing heavily on my mind when I make an appointment to see Doctor Rigilotto.

"Trent! It's wonderful to see you again," Doctor Rigilotto says as he enters the examination room. "What can I help you with today?"

I checked the internet before making this appointment, but my reading is slow and laborious, and I wasn't completely sure I understood what was being said in all those blog posts and medical journals. Beyond that, I probably could have asked Emily, but I didn't want to make it seem like I was putting pressure on her or to imply in any way that I wanted our arrangement to have an expiry date.

"How long does it normally take couples to get pregnant?" I ask.

"You and your partner are trying to get pregnant?" he asks, tapping the keys to get into his computer.

I wince at the partner comment, but there's no way to correct him without making it awkward. He'll already see and remember the tests I asked for months ago once he's in there.

"We've been trying since April," I say, "and we haven't had any luck."

"Your sperm count was good," he says, scanning the results on the computer. He leans back in the chair and steeples his fingers. "We tell teenagers that the chance of getting pregnant is a hundred percent every month to prevent risky behavior. But the truth is that the chance is more like twenty percent. Even once a pregnancy has occurred, there's roughly a twenty percent chance of miscarriage."

"At what point do doctors step in if a couple has been trying for a while and is not getting pregnant?"

"We usually suggest a year," he says.

"A year!" I sit forward in my chair, and I don't know why I'm so shocked, but I never considered this deal with Emily going on for that long. I thought a month or two, maybe. Now that we're well beyond that, and we're becoming more and more comfortable in ways I'm not sure we *should* be comfortable with each other, I was hoping he'd tell me it would happen any day now. Instead, he's told me we're not even at the halfway point yet.

"A year," he confirms with a chuckle. "At that point, I'd suggest that your partner has some tests run to see whether there are any problems on her end."

"She's had a baby before," I say.

"Well," the doctor says, his brow furrowed. "That doesn't always mean there are *no* problems, but it should give you hope that you'll be pregnant within the year."

"Okay," I say, taking a deep breath and standing up.

"That's all you came in for?" he asks.

"I wasn't sure if there was something we were doing wrong."

"Assuming you're tracking her cycle, using ovulation kits, and so forth, that's the best you can do. When you get close to the egg's release, having sex every other day or even every day can give you better odds."

"Right, yeah," I say, thinking of Emily's calendar that she hasn't filled in for July yet. "We're doing all that."

Having enough sex isn't the problem—at least not since mid-June. We're all over each other any chance we get. I've never physically needed anyone, ached for them, the way I do with Em.

"Then it's just patience and persistence. You'll get there." He rises and escorts me out of the room. "Tell Emily she can come in to have some tests ordered, if she's worried."

"Thanks," I say, lost in my own thoughts.

It's not until I get into my truck and am staring at the steering wheel, wondering whether I can handle another seven or eight months of casual fucking without it feeling not so casual, that I realize the doctor mentioned Emily.

My heart sinks. If the doctor said her name as though it was no big deal, without me having confirmed in any way that "my partner" was Emily, it means the town must be rife with gossip about us. That *should* bother me, and it does, but not nearly enough to consider putting a stop to whatever is happening.

In the end, I want Emily to have the baby she longs for, and she and I can deal with any fallout in Little Falls or with each other, if it comes to that. I still believe we're good enough friends that we can figure out what "after" looks like without it becoming painful for either of us. We had a deal, and neither of us is the type of person to go back on our word.

Tyler sends me a text while I'm at work, telling me he just had a reminder on his phone that today is the anniversary of Omar's death.

Emily might be off today, Tyler writes. *Today has been a tough day every year so far.*

For the rest of the day, Tyler's warning is at the back of my mind, and I can't seem to let it go. Rather than working late like I normally would, I ask Brett if he'll take some overtime to finish everything and then close up. He agrees.

When I get to my truck, though, I still haven't made a plan. Emily seems like someone who'd want the day acknowledged in some way, so I drive to Amir's day camp, and I pick him up rather than leaving him there for the after-care hours.

He climbs into the truck, bubbling with stories about his day. Once he's strapped in, I decide on a course of action.

"We're going to buy some flowers, bud," I say, starting the truck. "One set is for your dad, and the other is for your mom. Think you can help me with that?"

"For my dad?" Amir says.

"For his grave," I say.

"Mom and I used to do that," Amir says. "We used to take flowers to dad's grave and to Grandpa's, but we haven't done that in a long time."

"No?" I ask, and I make a mental note to get three bundles of flowers. While we're there, we might as well honor Jim too.

"No," Amir says, and then he seems lost in thought. "I think Christmas was the last time."

I want to ask him if he thinks doing this will upset Emily, if maybe she hasn't done it in so long because she decided it wasn't the best thing to do. But he's a five-year-old kid, and I don't want to put him in a weird position.

I'll stick to my plan, and I'll brace myself for Emily telling me I've done it all wrong, if it comes to that.

At the flower shop, Amir looks around, picking up bundles of flowers and then putting them back.

"Having trouble deciding?" I ask.

"Well," Amir says, gesturing to the premade bundles, "I want red for my dad. Just red. And I want purple for Grandpa. But they're all mixed up."

"Ah," I say. "How about we tell Mrs. Maynard what we're after and see if she can get us what we want?"

"So we're not buying one of these?"

"We don't have to. She'll make special bundles for us if there are certain things we want."

"Yes," he says with finality. "Let's do that."

Sometimes his decisive personality makes me laugh a little on the inside. I try not to let it out in case he thinks I'm laughing *at* him. His personality quirks entertain me, and I'd never want him to take *who* he is to be a bad thing.

Amir points at the flowers he wants, and he's very specific about how they should look within the bundles. His dad gets red carnations and red roses. His grandfather gets lavender and some other flowers I don't recognize. When it's time to get his mom flowers, he turns to me.

"What do you think?" he asks.

"Maybe we use some of the flowers from your dad's and grandpa's arrangements and then add in some white with them?"

"Yes!" Amir says, his enthusiasm returning. "Just like Trent sent."

Mrs. Maynard sends me an amused look as she makes up the third bundle and then rings up the total. I take out my card and pay for them.

"Now we just need to get your mom," I say as I carry out two of the bundles and Amir carries the third.

"Maybe you can tell her to meet us there," Amir says.

In the truck, I take out my phone and text Em to ask if she's busy.

Just finished showing. Going to get Amir. You at work still?

Nope. I have Amir already, actually. Sorry. Should have told you. We're going to the cemetery. Want to meet us there?

There's a long pause before I receive another message, and then when I do, it's just one word.

Okay.

My heart hammers in my chest as I drive to the cemetery. I'm really not sure I've done the right thing here, but it was the best I could come up with.

When we get there, Emily is already parked near Omar's grave, which is helpful, because I didn't actually know which one it was. I put my vehicle in park, and Amir scrambles out, the two bundles in his arms. I leave Emily's on the passenger seat, suddenly self-conscious about the choice.

"Who told you?" Emily asks when I get close enough. Amir is already deep into trying to "plant" the flowers around Omar's grave in the dirt. Not exactly what I was expecting, but he's five.

"Tyler," I admit, staring at the dates on the headstone, how close together they are. Seeing them, it drives home how young he was, how surprising the whole thing must have been for Emily.

"We brought flowers for Grandpa too," Amir says, gesturing to the other bundle he's left on the ground.

Emily's soft gaze meets mine, and I know I did the right thing. My chest swells at the proof on her face, at that tender expression she normally has when she looks at Amir. To think that I inspired that kind of emotion is pretty amazing.

"Thank you," she says. "You didn't have to."

"I like taking care of you," I say, and it's true, in all the ways she's now letting me do it.

She draws me into a tight hug, and I hear her shaky intake of breath near my ear. Her peach scent swirls around me with the light breeze.

When she steps away, her hand seeks mine, and she threads our fingers together. We've never held hands before, and I try not to read anything into it. If she needs some of my strength today, she's got it.

Instead of cooking, I ask if Omar's favorite restaurant is still open in town and if I can take them both there. She tells me that Bontaine Burgers is his favorite—him and three-quarters of the town. I've never tasted a burger like it anywhere else.

After we eat, we head home, and we play board games with Amir at the kitchen table until it's time for bed. He asks me to put him to sleep, and so I trod up the stairs with him.

When I come back down, Emily has the game cleared off the table and she's rearranged her flowers in the vase at the center. I gave them to her when we got back here, and she got a little teary over it and tried to hide her reaction from me and Amir.

I haven't quite been able to pinpoint her mood tonight, just as Tyler predicted. A little rocky, but maybe it would have been that way no matter what I'd done.

"You okay?" I ask.

"I am," she says, tearing her gaze away from the flowers. She searches my face for a beat, and I can almost see the wheels turning, her deciding what she wants to say. "This is the first year since his death where I haven't died a little inside," she says, her voice thick with tears. "There's no way to thank—"

I close the gap between us, and I kiss her. I pour every ounce of my complex feelings into that kiss so that I don't voice any of them out loud. To know I've taken even an ounce of her pain away with my presence is a gift I didn't know I needed.

"I want you now," she says against my lips.

"Tell me where," I say, lifting her up. Her dress hitches up almost to her waist.

"Here," she says.

"Here?"

"On the table," she says.

I turn and shut the kitchen door, snapping the lock into place, Emily still in my arms. The benefits of an old house with smaller rooms and lots of doors.

"You're sure?" I ask.

"You're not really going to make me beg, are you?"

"I should," I say, laying her down on the wooden surface. "Full-circle moment." I push up her dress and tug down her panties. "But fuck me, I love the sight of you too much to wait." I run my calloused hands along her thighs, and she visibly shivers.

"You're taking too long." She rises to tug on the button of my jeans.

"I had to take a moment to admire what's mine." I kiss her deeply as she shoves my jeans off my ass, and they pool on the floor at my feet. She makes short work of my boxer briefs next.

Then I'm sliding into her, and she's clutching onto me. As I move inside her, my thumb rotating on her bundle of nerves in a way that I know she loves, I can recognize that there's something different about the vibe between us tonight. Every time we make eye contact, I see that affection I saw earlier mixed with desire, and I'm sure I'm looking at her the same way.

"I don't know why I love this so much, why I can't get enough of you." There's a hint of awe in her voice, as though it really is puzzling.

Instead of saying it back, which is what I should do because it's how I feel too, I kiss her. And I keep kissing her so that neither of us says anything we shouldn't.

She's never been just any woman to me, and sex with her has always meant something, but I can almost sense what we're doing slipping past meaning *something* to meaning *everything*.

And for the first time, I'm worried we'll *never* be the same when this is over.

Chapter Twenty-Six

Emily

Victoria's first birthday party is a weird mix of extravagant and down-to-earth. A lot of Mia's friends from the music industry have invaded Little Falls and my mom's house. Sarah Telling is the only one I know by sight, and her husband has been making the rounds to every woman in the room as though he's the true gift at this party. A relationship like that would not be for me.

Pasha isn't on duty today, but you'd never know it from how he's lingering by the door, constantly checking on those who are supposed to be standing watch. Since I'm trying to avoid Sarah's husband and not make it look like I'm so attached to Trent that I can't leave him alone, I wander over to him.

"Lot of people here," I say as I gaze up at him.

He nods. "Yes." He hesitates for a beat and then he says, "Mia told me it was the anniversary the other week. It's always a hard day."

"It is, yeah," I agree, searching for Trent in the crowd without meaning to. "Mia told me you lost your fiancée in Russia."

"Yes," he says. "Was a long time ago now."

"Time is weird like that, though, isn't it? What feels long in some respects is short in others."

"I talked to someone in Russia and here to figure out how to make it better in my heart," he says. "Was not easy."

"No," I say, "it's not easy. I never went to speak to anyone. I probably should have. Maybe it would have been easier for me to move through the grief. I don't know if we ever move past it, necessarily."

"What are you two talking about?" Mia asks, appearing at my shoulder.

"Grief," I say. "It's a really uplifting topic for a first birthday."

Pasha frowns. "I—"

"That wasn't directed at you," I say to Pasha. "I appreciated you saying something. Too often we don't because it feels awkward."

He nods.

"Your mom was just talking to me about grief too," Mia says.

"Oh, god," I say. "What was she on about now?"

"She thinks you need to go to counseling to be able to move into a new relationship."

I love Mia's directness. At first when she returned, it was a bit hard to know how to take her, but she says what she means and she means what she says. She never delivers a line, at least to anyone in the family, with the intention of wounding or making things awkward.

"That is also a great conversation for a first birthday," I say. "She's projecting. She hasn't gotten past Dad's death." And maybe six months ago, she might have been right about me too. But I don't feel like I can't move beyond Omar anymore. Whatever is happening between me and Trent has made me believe that it *is* possible to find what I once had, someday.

"Yeah," Mia says. "I kind of wondered. She hasn't seemed to have dealt with the loss much at all, and she really avoids talking about Tyler's dad."

"The memories are hard. Special but hard." And I'm the same way when it comes to my dad. When Amir casually mentions something he used to do with my dad, my heart seizes for a moment, and it's nothing for tears to form. "She just keeps herself extra busy," I say. "And I've done that, so I get it."

"Aww," Mia says, nodding at one of the couches in the living room. "Trent and Amir with Victoria. So f-ing cute, right?"

"If you'll excuse me," I say, my heart in my throat, "they aren't allowed to have baby cuddles without me."

By the time I get to the couch, Amir has scampered off with Grady to toss the ball for the dogs outside.

Victoria is on Trent's lap, and she keeps standing on his thighs to slobber kisses all over his face. Then she draws back to look at him as though she expects it in return, and he gives her a kiss on the cheek, and she giggles. Rinse and repeat. When she's not kissing him, she's got her fist in her mouth, drool running down.

I grab a cloth from the diaper bag and take a seat beside Trent, cleaning off Victoria's face.

"This kid is adorable," Trent says.

"She looks just like her mom probably did at that age. The resemblance is uncanny."

Trent searches my expression for a beat and then says in a voice pitched much lower than the din of conversation around us, "Who do you think ours will look like?"

We've never even stepped around this topic, much less addressed it. I don't know if he's thought about it before, but I have.

"I just hope they don't get saddled with red hair," I say. "Other than that, healthy is really the only thing I care a lot about." I already spent too many years worrying about the health of my first child.

"I like the Sullivan red," Trent says, gazing around the room at the various shades that exist in our family.

"It's just unusual, so people always have comments to make about whether they like it or you get teased for it."

"I hope they don't get my dyslexia," Trent says.

"But we know to watch for it, and we can get the right help as soon as possible."

"Times have changed, I guess, since I was a kid," Trent says. "People are a bit more aware of others struggling. That sometimes it's not that someone won't, but that they can't."

"Maybe getting Maggie to help you learn how to read in high school without telling anyone wasn't the best coping strategy," I say, "but you knew you needed help, and you sought it out."

"Definitely should have told my mom. She was really hurt that I kept it from her. Just felt like too much to put on her after my dad died and she was working so much just to keep our life stable."

"I sometimes wonder how Amir perceives me," I say. "It's been a tough couple of years, and I just now feel like I'm coming back into myself. That this version of me is who I should have been all along."

"Feels good?" Trent asks as Victoria gives me another slobbery kiss and then giggles at the one he gives in return.

"It does," I say. "The fog is lifting."

"If I've had even an inch of influence on that, I'll take it."

"How about seven inches?"

"Six on a good day." His grin is cocky and knowing.

"We'll compromise. Six and a half."

"What are you two over here grinning about?" Maggie asks, collapsing into the seat beside me.

I pray that my cheeks have not gone as red as I suspect they have.

"We were just talking about how quickly things grow," Trent says, and he wiggles Victoria a little. She laughs. "Like little humans."

Maggie slides me a look as though she can smell Trent's brand of bullshit from a mile away. She probably can. They've been friends for a long time.

"I'm going to go grab a drink," I say. "Trent, do you need anything?"

"I'm good," Trent says, his focus back on Victoria as though we weren't just sitting there flirting over the length of his penis.

God, what has gotten into me? Aliens must have brought the wrong version of me back to earth. This one is becoming far too obsessed with Trent Castillo.

Maggie leans back in her chair behind her giant desk in the mayor's office. We've met in here once a week for years now. Maggie's first term was rocky, and when Grady came back to town and tried to run against Maggie to foil her reelection, I wasn't sure we'd have another four years in this place. As it is, Maggie is a year and a half into her second term.

"So you think rezoning those areas makes sense from a real estate point of view? I don't want to go into the council meeting without having thought through all the angles."

"Yes," I say. "We need more building lots."

"Tyler and Mia are talking about building on the outskirts of town. There's some acreage for sale right now. Given how popular the recording studio has become with singers from all over the world, paps come from New York City far too often."

"It hasn't been bad for the town," I say. "It's increased tourism, and I saw a Mia Malone shop opened in town the other day. Completely dedicated to her."

"Yeah," Maggie says. "That's Allison Ruttledge and her daughter who've put that together. Mia offered to sign some things and let them sell some exclusives to get off the ground, which I thought was really nice. She's protective of her brand—which she should be. I think Allison and her daughter are hoping to become a hub for anyone who records at Grady's studio to buy some merch."

"Not a business plan I'd want," I say. "Everything all set for the October wedding?"

"On track," Maggie says. "Grady has the time blocked off, and so do I. Slightly concerned about Lila being the maid of honor and Trent as the best man, but we'll build that bridge when we have to."

"I'm sure it's not Trent you're really worried about in that scenario." When Maggie had broached asking Lila to be her maid of honor instead of me, I hadn't been offended. She and Lila have been like two peas in a pod since they met as kids. Lila's been as much of a sister to both of us as we've been to each other.

"He is not," Maggie agrees with a little laugh. "Lila is an excellent grudge holder."

"Well, if that's it." I gather my stuff.

"No luck with the fertility treatments?" Maggie asks, her tone light. "I haven't wanted to ask too much because I can understand it's a frustrating process at this point."

"No luck," I say. "But I'm taking it in stride." In fact, I haven't been too bothered the last few months when my period arrived at all.

"Have you thought about moving into IVF?"

"No," I say, trying to feign nonchalance. "It's only been a few months." The reminder that I didn't even fill out the calendar for July springs to the front of my mind. Trent must be wondering what I'm even doing.

"How's living with Trent going?"

"Oh," I say, and I can feel the heat creeping into my cheeks. "Good."

"You know, it's weird. Grady says Trent hasn't even been dating anyone since he moved into your house."

"It would be a bit awkward for him to bring someone home," I say, my heart tap dancing in my chest. "He's just trying to be a good role model for Amir."

"He could always go to the woman's place for some alone time. *Amir* would never know."

"Yeah, well, I guess you'd have to ask Trent about that then."

"Anything you want to get off your chest about your living arrangement with Trent? About these supposed fertility treatments?"

"We're friends. The treatments are going well." I rise and press my purse against my stomach like a shield, trying not to appear defensive, even though that's exactly how I feel.

"You know, it's funny," Maggie says, and I can tell nothing is actually funny. "At the birthday party, Trent couldn't take his eyes off you. He looked at *you* like you were the present he couldn't wait to unwrap.

Weird, right? And then when I came to sit beside you on the couch, whatever you and Trent were talking about was not PG. You turned bright red before Trent spewed some bullshit to cover it up."

I slump down in the chair across from Maggie again and give her a pained look. "We made a deal."

"You bought Mullen's Mechanics for him, and he's going to father your baby," Maggie says, tapping a pen on her desk, her expression triumphant. "I *knew* I was right."

"It's a temporary arrangement."

"So you two are only having sex when you're ovulating, and the sex is actually really terrible. Is that what I'm supposed to take from that comment?"

"No," I say, carefully. "That's sort of the opposite of what's happening."

"The sex is amazing and you're having it all the time?! Emily!" Maggie cackles. "I love this and hate it all at the same time."

"Why would you hate it?"

Maggie's smile fades and she takes a deep breath. "Em, I love Trent like a brother, but he's commitment-phobic. And you are the opposite. Maybe both of you are in a moment of change. Who am I to say? I just don't want you to get hurt. Or him either. Shit fell apart with Lila pretty quickly, and they didn't even sleep together."

"It'll be fine," I say. "We have a deal. No matter what, our friendship comes first. Neither of us is going to do anything to screw that up."

"Which, if you'd kept clear lines—only having sex when you were ovulating, making the sex transactional—then I'd say maybe you stood a chance. But I saw with my own eyes the way you two were ogling each other on the couch. Those were not *friendship* eyes."

"Maybe the lines are blurred a little," I admit. "But it's still sex with a purpose, and once that purpose is served, we'll go back to how we were."

Maggie takes a deep breath and purses her lips, but she doesn't contradict me.

When I get home, I fill in the calendar on the wall with the dates for July and then I fill in the potential dates for August too.

Chapter Twenty-Seven

Trent

Once a week when my mother is manning the reception desk, I go get coffee and pastries for the crew. Today, all three bays are booked solid, and it feels like a gigantic win. Looking at the rest of this week and next, there are hardly any spots unfilled. That might mean a lot of overtime after hours for me and, possibly, Brett because I've committed to not turning anyone away. When people in Little Falls think of getting their vehicle repaired, their oil changed, or troubleshooting a tricky electrical problem, I want my shop to be at the forefront of their minds.

Each week I've picked up coffee and pastries, I've avoided Kathy's Café. Everyone says it's the best, but I went to high school with Kathy, and I've heard through the Little Falls gossip grapevine that she's not my biggest fan.

So it's with a fair bit of trepidation that I enter her packed café this morning. People who've been to the shop or who remember me from high school call out a "hello" as they collect their orders and breeze past me. It helps that Grady is so popular in town. His bid for mayor a couple of years ago helped restore the Castillo name.

The shop has large, curved windows at the front, and there are people dotted at the tables all around. The line is substantial, but if I want local people to support me, I need to do the same for them. The big-box stores and the chain restaurants aren't as small-town minded as the grassroots ones like Kathy's Café, where she and Sabrina know everyone who enters.

"What can I get for you?" Kathy asks when I get to the till.

The drink orders are memorized after so many weeks of coffee runs, and I rattle them off with ease. Then I scan the rows of pastries behind clear glass.

"Just an assortment, I guess," I say, unsure of what's even any good. I probably should have asked everyone before I left the shop, but I wasn't sure I'd actually get up the guts to come in here. "A dozen or so." My mom will give the rest to customers who stick around while we work on their vehicle.

"Sure," Kathy says, ringing up the order and then grabbing a strip of wax paper to put pastries into two large boxes. "Anything else?" she says when she returns.

"No," I say. "That'll be all."

She clicks through the total, and as the machine to pay loads, Kathy's gaze rakes over me. I brace myself for some snide comment. I do have slightly more respect for people who can say shitty things to my face and not just behind my back.

"Heard a lot of good things about your shop," she says as I dig out my credit card. "Bit of a buzz in the café about how good *you* are, specifically."

"Oh," I say, completely taken aback by her compliments. "That's—that's good to hear."

"I'm just glad you're not dragging another Sullivan into some shit-show."

Ah, *there* it is.

"Em and I are just friends." It irks me to say the words.

"Still," she says, "what you do impacts her, since you're living in her house, spending time with her kid. I'm just glad you've turned into a positive influence. Couldn't have said that in high school."

"People *can* change," I say, paying for my order and tucking my card back in my pocket before sweeping the boxes off the counter.

"It appears so," she says. "Collect your coffees from Sabrina over there." She nods toward the back and left where a chest-high counter sits and Sabrina seems to be frantically making drinks.

When I get to Sabrina, she passes over the drinks stacked in some fancy carrier thing. I'd been a bit worried about how I'd handle everything when I had to park a couple of blocks away, but it appears Kathy's Café is used to big orders from the local crowd.

"How are you, Trent?" Sabrina asks as she reads the order screen and starts mixing more drinks.

"I'm good, and you?"

"I heard your shop's doing really well, and Grady's studio is booked solid for months. Look at you Castillo boys, huh? Who'd have thought?"

"Who'd have thought…" I say, and I don't add anything more as I turn to head out the door. As I go, other people stop me to say "hello" or to talk about some issue they're having with their vehicle.

"Sounds like a fuel pump," I say to Mike McGregor. "Bring it by, and we'll get it fixed for you."

"Glad I ran into you," he says just before I squeeze out the front door and breathe a sigh of relief. I've always liked talking to people—more of an extravert than an introvert—but coming back to live in this town has been harder than I expected. I just never know what people are going to say to me, and I hate the uncertainty of not knowing where I stand.

At least in Utica, coming out of jail, my life had felt like a clean slate. In a lot of ways, it feels like I took a giant step forward in my career, and a massive step backward in my personal interactions by coming back here.

I just have to keep reminding myself that the personal will catch up with the professional if I just keep myself moving forward, doing what I know I'm good at, making a difference for people in the community.

When I get back to the shop, everyone cheers as I bring in the coffee and pastries. We take a communal fifteen-minute break to chat, eat, and drink coffee, and it fills my soul back up a little from my interactions in town. Seeing how much they all enjoy the pastries and coffee makes the stop at Kathy's worth it.

At the end of the day, just as people are leaving to go home, a Lexus arrives on the back of a tow truck. With a frown, I go into the lot to greet the driver.

"Trent?" the driver asks, hopping down out of the front seat. "Earl Runions paid to have this brought here. Some sort of electrical and mechanical issue."

"Where's the owner?" I ask. While I appreciate Earl sending me clients, I prefer a head's up rather than receiving a car on a tow truck just before closing.

"You'll have to call Earl," he says. "Where do you want this?"

"Load it off in one of the bays," I say. No matter what, I can't leave a car this expensive sitting on the lot when I don't know what's going on.

I step away from the driver as he reverses to get it off-loaded.

"What's going on?" Brett asks.

"Referral from Earl, except he didn't tell me it was coming."

"Want me to stay late?" Brett asks.

"Won't be straightforward if Earl sent it," I say. "I don't know if I'll *need* the help. Up to you."

"If you don't need it, no need to pay me the overtime," Brett says. "I just want to see you work through the problem."

"You're welcome to stay," I say.

Then I call Earl to find out what he knows about the car. Once I have all the details jotted down from him, I text Emily to let her know I won't be home in time for dinner and not to wait up. She texts back a thumbs up, and then I take Brett over to the car.

"Here's what I know," I say, giving him the starting place for our troubleshooting project.

By the time I get home, it's close to midnight, and I'm worn out. Brett and I managed to get to the root of the problem, but we had to rush-order some parts. I sent Earl an update to pass along to the owner.

I root around in the fridge to find a covered plate of food with my name on top. I'm not sure why Emily puts my name on a sticky note, but she always does. Maybe I wouldn't be as inclined to eat it, worried she'd made it for her own lunch tomorrow.

While the pasta and chicken heats in the microwave, I peer at the calendar. I don't know when she filled it out, but she's not crossing off the days like she normally does.

Honestly, I'm not even sure what to think about what's happening between us. Most of the time, I deliberately avoid thinking about it. Telling Kathy today that we're friends didn't feel right, but I also wouldn't want to put any *other* label on it.

After I eat, I head up the stairs, and when I get to Emily's door, it's propped open. That's been Emily's unspoken symbol that I'm welcome in her room for the last few weeks. I hesitate because it's so late, and I can tell she's already sleeping. The house is dead quiet.

I brush my teeth and get changed into my pajama pants, and then I stand in the hallway again. What I *want* to do is *right there*, but I'm not sure if it's the *right* thing to do.

Fuck it. All of this means whatever we say it means, nothing more.

I enter her room and I shut the door, locking it. My phone is in my hand, and I set an alarm for stupid early to make sure I'm out of here before Amir is awake.

When I slide under the covers beside her and rest my hand on her hip, she rotates into me, curling up against me, all of her soft parts molding to me.

"The door was open," I whisper.

"I know," she says, "I left it open for you."

Neither of us makes any move to turn this sexual, and I don't bring up that we're not just tiptoeing over the line, but rather leaving it so far behind that I'm not even sure it exists.

The things happening between us, the rhythms we're establishing, I've never done any of them with another woman. Couldn't even imagine being this close, this content, with someone else.

Instead of analyzing it, I tuck her a little tighter into my side, kiss the top of her head, and I relish the soft sigh of contentment that escapes her. Maybe that sound isn't because of me, but at this moment, it sure feels like it is.

Chapter Twenty-Eight

"Think about it," I say as I close and lock the front door of the house in the downtown core that I'm showing. "It has a lot of what you're looking for, but only you two know if that's enough."

"I really liked it," Leah says. "We'll talk it over." She smiles at her boyfriend, Donny.

"You know Trent Castillo, don't you?" Donny asks.

"I do."

"Do you know if he's hiring? We're just moving to the area. Leah got a teaching job in Little Falls, and I'm an auto mechanic. Everyone I talk to says that Trent would be the best guy to work for around here."

Warmth spreads across my chest. For the first few months that Trent took over, it felt like I faced resistance, both spoken and unspoken, about my perceived relationship with Trent. I definitely lost clients, and I'm certain people have said some not-nice things behind my back. A few outright told me they suspected Trent only took over the mechanic shop to run drugs or launder money. Those comments made my blood boil because they clearly didn't know Trent at all if they thought he still had or wanted any of those connections.

"I don't know," I say. "He only took over Mullen Mechanics a few months ago. But I can let him know you're looking for work, and if you're okay with it, I can have him reach out to you, if he thinks he has any hours to offer."

"That'd be great," Donny says with a broad grin. "I love how friendly everyone is."

"We're always happy when people choose to settle here," I say. "I'll keep an eye out for that perfect house for you within your budget."

"Thanks, Emily," Leah says, waving to me as the two of them head toward their vehicle.

Just as I get into my car, a text from Maggie pings on my phone.

You still good for next week's trip to New York? Long weekend, baby!

I still can't believe Lila's engaged. To say her relationship with Henry had been a whirlwind would be completely accurate.

Right? At least she's not beating me to the wedding.

Saturday night is your bachelorette?

Yes, but I told Lila to keep it low key. I probably won't drink. No need to go splashy. Plus, we have to keep Mia in mind.

Maggie hadn't been a big drinker in years, so it wasn't surprising that she'd opt not to drink even at her bachelorette. It was really a matter of whether Lila would listen. As for Mia, her hit album has caused a lot of fanatical fans to come out of the woodwork. Her security concerns are huge, which is also why she and Tyler are thinking about creating a high security property just out of town and building a new house there.

Trent's taking Amir? Maggie texts when I don't keep the thread going.

Yep. He has big plans for them. He's taking the time off work to take Amir fishing and to build some kind of giant Lego set that Trent got off a guy at work.

He'll be a good dad.

Maggie's message makes me flex my hands on the steering wheel. Even with how well things are going with his shop, how well they're going between us, I don't know if he's changed his stance on telling people if we get pregnant. He was so adamant about not being known as the baby's father that I'm not sure exactly what it would take to alter his beliefs.

Part of me wonders if I should broach it with him. Though I've tried not to think about our relationship too much or put much stake into how we are with each other, even the illusion of separate bedrooms has disappeared. For the last week, no matter what time he gets home, whether we're having sex or not, I leave my door open, and he's in my bed.

And I love it a little too much.

As soon as his hand is on my hip under the covers, it's like any worries from the day dissipate into thin air. "Come here," he'll say, his voice gruff, and I never hesitate.

It took me years to get completely over my high school boyfriend, but then I met Omar, and that connection felt magical, in a way. We didn't get nearly enough time together in the end.

But what I have with Trent is different again. He feels like *home,* but also like *desire* embodied. Being with him is the deepest, most solid thing I've ever felt in my life on every level.

It's hard for me to believe I'm the only one who feels those things so fully. What's built between us is real, and it doesn't have to be temporary. Or at least, that's how I'm starting to feel.

Saying that to him goes against everything we agreed to in the beginning. I don't know if we *can* go back to being friends if I declare my feelings. Despite what he said, I could see him withdrawing if he wasn't either on the same page as me or ready to admit he was. Trent's past weighs so heavily on him, and it's difficult to know if the success of these past few months with the shop, with me, has made that weight heavier or lighter.

At this point, I think I could survive us going back to being just friends. It would be hard—so, so hard—but I would rather that than not have him in my life at all.

Given where we're at, it's hard to imagine not leaving my door open, having him slip under the covers, curling around him, breathing in the scent of his vanilla-based cologne with a hint of motor oil.

If anyone had told me I'd one day find motor oil to be an aphrodisiac, I'd have been mortified. But here we are.

My phone rings as I'm driving toward my real estate office, and I see Maggie's name on my dash display. I hit Answer, and I say, "I wasn't avoiding you after your little comment."

"Can you pull over?" Maggie says, and I can hear the tension in her voice.

"I'm almost at the office. Is everyone okay?"

"No one is in imminent danger," Maggie says. "Call me back when you get to the office."

Ever since our dad died, we've both been twitchy about calls with this sort of vibe, so I know Maggie understands how seriously I take her tone. The minute I'm in the real estate parking lot, I call her back.

"What's going on?" I ask as soon as she answers. From the buzz in the background, she must be at town hall in the mayor's office.

"I just heard that the police raided Trent's shop. He's been taken in for questioning."

"What?" I breathe out the word, shock hitting me like a wave of ice-cold water. "What?" I say again.

"Dan Ramouli was arrested a few days ago on suspicion of running a drug ring in Utica that's spilled into Little Falls."

"Oh no," I say. "He came to Trent's shop and threatened him."

"Did he?" Maggie sounds surprised. "Dan was always such a dick. You don't think Trent—"

"No, absolutely not." I have zero doubts about Trent's culpability. He's so paranoid about his past coating him that he's probably dying inside right now.

"If I go to the station, do you think they'll let me see him?"

"He's not arrested," Maggie says. "I'm being told he was brought in for questioning. I sent Mom down, just to see. I'd go home and wait. He should be released. I just..." I can almost hear Maggie shaking her head. "I can't believe he'd get involved in *any* of that again."

I *know* he hasn't. I have zero doubts. But the other thing I know, the thing that's causing my stomach to sink with dread, is that Trent isn't going to take any of this well.

Chapter Twenty-Nine
Trent

My head is so fucking mixed up that I don't know what I'm thinking or feeling. After vowing I'd never end up here again—obeying the speed limit, always getting a designated driver, ignoring Dan's threats to my business—I still somehow ended up under suspicion.

My lawyer, Thomas Rodriguez, came as soon as I called. We're in a separate room to meet before I get questioned, which I suspect means he thinks I actually could be mixed up in this. I've got nothing to hide.

"Alright," Thomas says, consulting his notes. "The police traced a drug ring from Utica to Little Falls. The problem is that it appears to have started in Little Falls around the time you took over Mullen Mechanics. Or at least, that's when the police have been able to trace it back to."

"Nobody can be saying I'm part of this," I say. "I didn't do shit."

"Dan has said he approached you, and you agreed to run some drugs."

"What?" I practically yell the word. "That slimy motherfucker. That's not true. It's not true. They won't be able to find one ounce of evidence to link us."

But then I remember the break-in, how we all assumed it was Dan, but we never got a clear answer about who did it. We cleaned up the shop after that, but what if Dan planted something. That'd be just like him.

Whoever had been in there had tried to break into my computer system, so they were clearly aiming to do more than steal a few tools.

"Are they arresting me?" I ask.

"You're correct in that they don't have any evidence, other than Dan's comments, to link you two." He takes a deep breath. "Yet. They have the warrant to search your shop, your computers, and your security system."

"If they find anything," I say, clenching and unclenching my hands under the table, "it was planted. I swear to you that I've got nothing to do with this."

"When we go in there to speak to the police, check with me before you answer any question. Just a visual check-in is fine. They're feeling you out, but they have no evidence. We don't want to inadvertently give them something they feel the need to pursue."

"Thomas, I'm clean." A hint of frustration has crept into my voice.

"Trent, I told you this last time, my job is to defend you to the best of my ability, make sure the rule of law is followed."

Unlike last time, that response is maddening. I just want him to know that I didn't do it. Last time I did, and I was prepared to pay whatever price the law required. The injustice of it all just makes me want to fucking cry, but getting emotional isn't going to get me out of here.

"Let's get this over with," I say, rising from my seat.

Together, we head into the police interrogation room, and I tell them everything I know.

When I pull into the driveway, Emily's car is already there. My heart thumps in my chest at what I know I have to do. No part of me wants to go in there, but I can't hide from her forever. It's bad enough that I drove around town for an hour, went to the lake and sat staring at the water for a while, too. I wouldn't be surprised to look down and find my boots made of concrete.

With a deep breath, I open the door into the kitchen. Emily turns from the sink, and relief is clearly written across her face. She closes the distance between us and envelopes me into a hug, clutching onto me like I'm a lifeline in a storm. But I'm no hero today.

I let my arms circle her loosely, but I don't sink into her like I normally would. I'm not sinking into anything anymore. Surface level is so much safer for everyone.

"Are you okay?" she asks.

"Is Amir here?" That was the other thing weighing on my mind as I sat at the lake. If things got messy between me and Emily, I didn't want him to see any of it. But he should be home by now. I left it too late. Somehow, I'm never quite making the right choices.

"He's with Mia and Tyler."

"I'm going to go stay with my mom," I say, stepping past her. "I just came here to grab my stuff."

"For tonight?"

"No," I say, "I'm staying there until I'm allowed back in the shop, and then I'll stay there until I can find someone to rent to me."

"Trent."

I close my eyes at the way she says my name because it sounds like heartbreak, and that's not what either of us signed up for.

"I can't stay here," I say, but I don't leave the kitchen to pack my things.

"I understand if you want some space tonight, and how pulling away might seem like the right choice. But none of what's happened today was your fault."

"You're sure about that?" I ask. "You don't wonder if maybe I did do it?"

"No," she says. "Not for a second."

"Probably half the town right now feels pretty damn good about how they resisted giving me a chance."

"I don't care how the rest of the town feels. I know the truth."

I rub my face and brace myself to ask the question I've avoided these past few months. In the back of my mind, I knew if I asked and she gave me the answer I expected, I'd have to cut things off. And honestly, I just really wanted this chance with the shop, with her.

"Tell me," I say, taking a deep breath. "Tell me you haven't lost one client because of your association with me? Tell me that no one has said they won't use your real estate company because of me."

Emily stares at me and her jaw tightens, but she doesn't admit what I've known subconsciously for months. There are people in this town who will *never* forgive me, and that makes Emily guilty by association.

"I'll see myself out," I say, moving toward the stairs to pack my stuff.

"Trent." My name is more of a sob than a word, but I can't turn around, can't hold her, because I'll only drag her down.

After I've finished shoving everything into my two suitcases, I stand staring at the two pieces Amir made me for Father's Day, and my lungs feel tight, like I can't quite breathe. The life I could have had is just there—out of reach. I slide open the nightstand drawer, and I put both pieces inside. I can't bear to take them with me.

Downstairs, Emily is still in the kitchen, standing at the counter, and it's pretty clear she's been crying.

Anger and sadness keep hitting me in waves, and I don't even know what to do with all these pent-up emotions.

"Go tonight," Emily says, "but come back."

"You know that's not going to happen. I'm not having my choices, my past, reflect poorly on you. That's not fair."

"I'll stand beside you. I know you didn't do this. You went to jail for god's sake. You paid for your mistake. Who cares about the people who can't see that?"

"Both of our jobs are dependent on people wanting to trust us, work with us. I'm not tanking your business when I'm already doing that to my own."

"People will come around."

"How many times do they have to come around, Em? How many times do I have to win them over?"

Tears are trickling down her cheeks, and it's making my heart feel like it's going to leave my chest to comfort her because my feet won't move.

"Back in October, I felt like a shell of a person," she says, her voice cracking. "And I don't feel that way anymore, and that's because of you. So I don't care what the rest of the town thinks. I don't care. They could all hate you, and I would still love you."

I close my eyes and rock back on my heels. The truth is, I've seen the change in her, and I wanted it to be because of me, because of us, but in this moment, I don't want that at all. But I also can't lie to her—won't.

"I love you too," I say. "So fucking much. And that's why I can't stay. What's happening to my life, I won't have it happen to yours too. I can't. It's so much worse that I'm dragging you down too." Then I push out the door and carry my bags to the truck.

Emily is still standing at the back door, and I can see her crying. It takes every ounce of self-control, every ounce of certainty that I can't allow her to be coated with the mud of these accusations, to put my car in reverse and leave this life behind.

My mom comes out of her two-story house when I pull in the driveway. When she tries to take one of the suitcases, I shoo her away. I'm barely holding my shit together.

Last time when this happened, I knew I'd fucked up, and while it was devastating, it didn't feel like this. A punch to the gut so hard that I'm almost doubled over with it.

I'm innocent. Haven't done a single shady thing since I got out of jail. But the fact is that I don't know for sure they won't find anything in the shop because I know what a snake Dan is.

In my old bedroom, I dump my stuff, and my mom has followed me and is hovering at the door when I really, really need to be alone.

"I'm fine, Mom," I say, trying to keep my voice even.

"You're not fine," she says. "I wouldn't be fine if I was you, either. And there's no shame in admitting that, in admitting that this situation is awful."

"I'm not involved in any of this," I say.

"I know that," she says. "I work there. You think I wouldn't know?"

I don't bring up the fact that I did a lot of shit right in front of her nose when I was a teenager, and she didn't have a clue.

"You know," my mom says, wagging a finger, "I do wonder about Judy, though."

"Judy?" I rub my face, not following.

"She works part-time for you, but she's always flashing money around, talking about expensive things she's bought, trips she's planning. No second job that I know of." She leans against the doorframe. "And someone tipped Dan off in the first place that the shop had lost business when you took over."

"Doesn't take a rocket scientist to make that leap, Mom. A lot of people in this town don't like me."

"From my experience, most people actually *do* like you, Trent. People didn't know if they could trust you because you fooled so many of us last time."

It's not lost on me that she includes herself in that statement. And my past is exactly what makes this situation hard. Proving myself innocent when people are already suspicious is like trying to walk up a vertical wall.

"How was Emily?" Her voice is gentle, and when I glance at her, she must see something in my face because she tugs me into a hug. "Oh, baby," she says. "It's okay to let people in."

"My reputation impacts her," I say, my voice thick. "And I already fucked up with Maggie all those years ago. I can't let that happen to another Sullivan. I *won't* let it happen to Emily."

"Maggie was a kid, but Emily is an adult. I think it's fair to let her decide what she can handle."

I step away from her, and I shake my head. "I didn't do anything bad, but if your instincts about Judy are right, that doesn't mean I won't get knocked down in the fallout. Desperate people do desperate things."

From prior experience, I am well aware of what Dan is capable of, how he'll do anything to keep himself afloat and sink everyone else to the bottom. I just have to hope like hell he hasn't put weights on me that I never saw him attaching.

Chapter Thirty

Emily

The shop is closed, and I'm not sure what I expected, but seeing all the police tape grabs me by the throat. It *looks* like a crime scene, even though I know Trent didn't do anything wrong. Seeing what they've done to the place causes a spike of irrational anger.

Of course Trent would get cold feet and throw up barriers when the place he's poured so much into is now a sign of potential illegal activity.

Dan might not have been able to lure Trent back into drug dealing, but he's certainly making sure Trent's punished for his unwillingness to go along with Dan's plans.

To make things worse, as Trent predicted, some factions of the town are already *tsking* and buzzing about how they knew something was fishy when Trent was doing so well. When the truth comes out, it won't reverberate as loud as the lie, it never does, and there will always be people who'll look at what's happening now with side-eyes, convinced Trent got lucky and not that he's innocent.

If I could strangle Dan with my bare hands, I think I'd have it in me to do it. At least then Trent and I'd both have criminal records and he could stop throwing his past up like an insurmountable barrier.

I drive away, and I head to Kathy's Café to get Maggie and myself coffees before I stop by the pharmacy. While I stand in line, I can hear people whispering, gossip flying around me like arrows, narrowing, missing their mark.

"Oh, Emily," Kathy says when I get to the front. "I was so sorry to hear Trent let you down."

"He didn't let me down," I say, bristling. "He hasn't done anything wrong."

She lets out a deep sigh and shakes her head. "Maggie said that in high school too, you know. That Trent couldn't have been doing what he was doing. We all know how that turned out."

"For what it's worth," Sabrina says at Kathy's shoulder, "I don't think Trent did anything wrong this time."

"What can I get you?" Kathy asks, shooing Sabrina back to mixing drinks.

I give her the coffee orders, even though I might become like Maggie and stop coming here. Judgmental bullshit is not what I want to be sipping. When it becomes clear that the chatter behind me has a lot to do with Trent, I rotate on my heel after I've paid, and I survey all the familiar faces. If this costs me a client or two, I can't even be mad about it. I don't want to represent them anyway.

"Trent is going to be cleared. I can guarantee you that he's not involved in this in any way."

A couple of people shake their heads, like I'm deluded, and that same anger surfaces, threatening violence.

I go to the counter, and I grab my coffees from Sabrina. I try not to storm out of the café. I don't want to give a single person a reason to believe I don't have total faith in Trent's innocence, and how I act matters.

Maggie's pharmacy is quiet when I enter, and Maggie glances up from the back counter, where she's filling prescriptions.

"Slow day?" I ask, approaching with the coffees.

She takes the one I offer, and she comes around the retail counter to lean against it with me. "I probably shouldn't say this out loud, but I suspect it's slow because of what's going on with Trent. I never distanced myself from him, and that was easy to say and do when he lived in Utica." Maggie takes a long sip. "It'll be back to normal tomorrow."

"I loudly declared Trent innocent in Kathy's today, so I'm sure I'm also on people's shit lists."

Maggie holds her hand up and I high-five it. "Honestly, if I was going to root around in shit for anyone, it'd be a Castillo man," Maggie says.

"He moved out," I say, staring at my cup.

"I wondered if he would. He's always been really hard on himself about what he did, and I get it, but I still wish he could move past it."

"Hard to move past when it's being shoved back in your face by the man who contributed to your jail sentence the first time."

"Fair point," Maggie says.

Silence sits between us as we sip our coffees.

"I'm in love with him," I whisper, "and this whole thing is making me so angry and so sad, and I just..." My voice catches on a sob.

Maggie sets down her coffee and draws me into a tight hug. "Does he know?"

I nod against her shoulder, but I can't get any words out. Last night, I tried so hard not to cry too much while I was talking to Trent. If he was going to stay, I didn't want it to be because he felt sorry for me.

"Did he say it back?" Maggie asks, her voice gentle.

"Yeah," I say, my voice thick as I step away, wiping my tears. *I love you too. So fucking much. And that's why I can't stay.*

Maggie grabs a tissue box from her counter and passes it to me. "That's huge for him."

Part of me knows his admission is a big step. The problem is that he brandished the feeling like a shield, as though it justified pushing me away rather than drawing me closer.

"He loves me, so he can't drag me into this," I say.

"Oh," Maggie says, and she kneads the middle of her forehead with her index fingers. "And he's really stubborn."

"I am aware," I say, releasing a shaky breath.

"If this gets resolved, do you want to be with him—like permanently?"

"I haven't felt anything close to this since Omar died. Trent's my person. Like, soul deep. And I know that seems over the top, but it's true. I love everything about him, and I'm so...I can't believe this is happening."

Maggie picks back up her coffee, and she takes long sips, clearly thinking. "I don't know how much headway you'll make with him until the police confirm he had nothing to do with Dan's drug bust."

"You think I should just leave it alone?" I say, and my heart is already launching a protest in my chest.

"No," Maggie says, carefully. "He's going to try to push you away, and it'll have to be up to you to make sure he doesn't, that he can't."

"Oh, is that all?" I say, tears brimming.

"The reason Trent and I stayed friends through everything is because I didn't give up on him. Maybe someone else would have let our friendship go, but what he did for me in high school—it meant more to me than the mistakes he made. So when he pushed, I pushed back. And yeah, it's going to be harder to do that in this town with half of them being assholes right now, but if what you want more than anything is him, then you don't give up."

"But you were never in love with him," I say. "What if he never wants what we had again? What if I push back but I never get what I want from my persistence?"

Maggie sucks in a deep breath. "What's the alternative, Em?"

That I never get any part of him, ever, at all. I set down my coffee on the counter, and I cover my face, another sob rising. "How did I get here?" I cry.

"You were brave enough to put your heart on the line again," Maggie says, enveloping me in another hug. "Honestly, I've never seen Trent with another woman the way he is with you. If you give him time and don't let him go too far, he'll figure it out. I think he'll figure it out."

Except I know from the way she says it that, like me, she is not completely sure of that, that it's entirely possible that Trent's version of "figuring it out" has already happened. He'll spare my reputation, but he'll sacrifice both our hearts.

Chapter Thirty-One
Trent

Thomas calls to tell me the police need to speak to me again about something they discovered. He tells me he doesn't believe it's a big deal, but they have implicated Judy in Dan's drug ring. They didn't find anything at the shop, but they got a warrant for her house, and they located enough to charge her too.

Even though it's not, it feels like everything is collapsing on my head. Maybe I wasn't dealing drugs, but apparently, I was employing a drug dealer. Tell me that's not going to rub people in Little Falls the wrong way, and I'll call you a liar. Guilty by association.

My mom has gone for a grocery run because she's braver than me, and for better or worse, she's faced this kind of fall out before. Except this time, I didn't do anything wrong, and I'm not sure if that makes facing people's scrutiny better or worse.

Worse, I think. To be falsely accused is worse.

Emily's car pulls into my mom's driveway, and I take a deep breath before heading to the front door. I'd hoped she'd understand and stay away, but she's stubborn, so I should have known better.

"Em, you shouldn't be here," I say as she gets out of her car.

Emily doesn't even answer me. She just comes up the front walkway, steps around me, and enters the house.

She's got guts—I'll give her that.

With a sigh, I turn and enter the house behind her.

We stand in the living room, a face-off, and if she thinks I'm going to be the first one to talk, she'll be waiting a long time. I said everything I needed to say yesterday.

"I just wanted to make sure you're not cutting Amir out too," she says.

I hate that I can see, can recognize all the little tells in the way she speaks and moves that tell me how hard it is for her to be here. Having been behind the curtain of her life, I can't pretend I don't know how the show goes on.

"I'd still like to see him a bit," I admit, "not as publicly, but I made a promise to you and him that I'd honor."

"You made a promise to me too," she says, and her voice cracks.

"I'm not doing this to hurt you."

"But the hurt isn't nothing. The choices you've made impact me. A lot."

"I know that, which is why I'm putting some distance between us. You don't deserve to be impacted by them." I run my hand along the top of my head. "And I think we should sell the shop, before it loses too much value. I can't recover from this."

"Absolutely not," Emily says, her spine straightening. "I'm not selling."

"You'll lose money. It'll take *years* for me to build back the trust I just lost. Judy's been arrested for dealing. She worked at my shop. People will think they just couldn't get enough on me and Judy took the fall."

"I'm not selling."

"Then you should find someone better to run it."

"There is no one better."

"Brett could do it, if he wanted."

"You're not listening to me."

"Funny, I was just thinking the same thing."

We stare at each other, and the tears in her eyes almost undo me. Fuck, I hate this. I hate how much it hurts, and how hard I'm trying to hide the hurt. The ache to be close to her, to breach the gap between us, is a physical pain and so strong that it's distracting. But I won't let my emotions win out. She doesn't deserve any of this backlash, and I brought it right to her door.

"I'm just glad this all came out when it did," I say. "That you haven't ended up tied to me and my reputation permanently."

"You promised me that no matter what happened between us, we'd still be friends."

"When a friendship becomes more harmful than helpful, I gotta draw the line. There was no way for me to know this is where life would take us, but here we are." My words might be matter of fact and confident, but inside I'm struggling to keep it together. The last thirty-six hours have drastically changed the course of my life, and I can't quite find stable emotional footing. I want things I shouldn't. Things I can't have anymore.

"I understand how disorienting the last day and a half has been for you. You've worked really hard to regain people's trust, to make the business run properly. Seeing that at risk must be really difficult." Her voice is thick with tears. "But just like you didn't abandon me when I was having a tough time, I'm not abandoning you now. Maybe you think you don't want me here, but I'm going to be here. It's taken me four years to feel like myself again, and this Emily," she says, pointing to her chest, "is a *fighter*, not a quitter."

God, I fucking love her. My whole chest is filled with it, and it's pushing out into the rest of me, begging me to go to her, tug her into my embrace, tell her I don't care about anything but her and Amir.

That's the irresponsible version of me struggling to break free. Damn the consequences, I'll take what I want. And I'm not that guy anymore.

Maybe it hurts right now, but someday it won't. I won't have to hear people talking shit about Emily because she's with me. They'll know she cut ties with me, and they'll go back to seeing Emily as she is—untainted by me.

"I'm not even in the fight, Em. I've tapped out."

"Lucky for you," Emily says, hitching her purse onto her shoulder, "I've got enough fight in me for both of us."

Before I can tell her it's futile, that I'll never let her get that close again for fear of the impact it'd have on her life, she's out the door and halfway to her car. I watch her go, my heart sinking at how much I want her and how sure I am that I can't have her.

If there's one place I never want to go again in my life, it's here, the police station. Everything about it sends chills down my spine, and now, knowing they've pinned something on Judy and have questions about my business, I have no idea what exactly I'm walking into.

"We should talk," Thomas says, greeting me when I walk in the door. We duck into an empty room reserved for lawyers and their clients, and he shuts the door behind him.

I don't sit down, preferring to stand, and Thomas leans against the wall too.

"What do they think they have?" I ask.

"You installed security cameras in your office and around the shop, correct?"

"Yeah, after the break-in."

"That probably saved you from Judy dealing there. One of the people associated with Dan admitted he broke into the shop. The purpose of the break-in is a bit hazy, but I don't think they anticipated you responding with so many cameras." He lets out a little chuckle.

None of this is funny to me.

"So, great—the cameras saved me. Why am I here?"

"There are several hours, and sometimes whole days, that are deleted from the security footage archive. A few times where it appears you turned *off* the cameras in your office. They can't pin anything on you, but they want those holes filled in. Judy hasn't implicated you, but Dan keeps trying to say you were part of it. Judy hasn't really said definitively either way."

The deleted footage. My stomach drops when I realize what footage I deleted. *Fuck.* I even called the company and made sure any cached files were also deleted. There was no way I was leaving Emily exposed.

"They need me to confirm why I did that?" I ask. As long as it's what and not who, I can take the heat for that.

"A logical explanation, yes."

"I have one," I say.

"Do you want to tell me now? Will it create more complications?"

"I doubt it," I say.

"Alright," Thomas says. "Let's go explain it to them so we can get all this cleared up."

In the small room next door, we sit and wait until two officers enter. They sit across from us, and then they slide a piece of paper to me. On the paper are dates and times when the security in the office was turned off or deleted.

"We're hesitant to believe you're involved in all this, Trent, but this missing information is a giant question mark. You could have been doing anything in the office."

I want to ask whether they traced who entered my shop on those days and nights, but I really want to leave Emily out of this—any of this. Besides, that doesn't account for the times I deleted whole days instead of just isolating the timeframe she was in the office. My laziness has consequences.

"I had a woman in the office, and we were doing things I would rather not have recorded."

The two officers exchange glances and the older one says, "We'll need the name of the woman or women to confirm dates and timeframes."

"Why would you delete a whole day?" the other officer asks.

"Laziness. To delete a specific section, you have to watch it back, isolate the timeframe, and then delete that specific section. Then you have to go into the deleted files and delete it there."

"But you also called the company and had them delete any version saved on their backend."

"Right. Privacy is an illusion when it comes to a digital footprint, right? I did the best I could to make sure the woman I was with wouldn't suffer any embarrassing consequences."

"We'll just verify this with her," the older man says again. "Name and contact?"

"I'm not giving that out," I say.

Thomas glares at me from the side. I can feel it penetrating my head.

"You understand that we can't close this until we verify that the missing footage isn't somehow connected to the drug ring—some elements of which Dan Ramouli is trying very hard to pin on you."

I'm almost afraid to ask, given Judy's involvement, but I do anyway. "Did you find anything—even one scrap of evidence—that links me to what Dan and Judy were doing?"

Neither of them answers, and it feels a lot like their refusal to close the claim has more to do with preconceived notions about me—the ex-con—than a real need to verify who I was having sex with in the office.

"Now, if you're not arresting me, I think we're done here." I rise, and when they don't stop me, I walk out the door.

Thomas follows fast on my heels. "Trent!"

But I don't stop until I'm out the door of the station and it feels like my lungs can take in a full breath again.

"Trent!" he calls again, and I stop near my truck. "Look," he says, out of breath, "whoever is on the deleted footage—their name won't go beyond the station."

"Bullshit," I say. "The small-town gossip network is sneaky and persistent. Someone will hear something, and it'll spin out. There are no secrets, so I'm keeping this one close to my chest." Locked in my fucking heart.

"They won't close this line of questioning—your shop will stay closed—until they can be sure you're not involved."

"They *are* sure," I say. "They're prejudiced against me because of what I did last time. And I never lied about it then. I got caught, and I put up my hands and said I did it."

"The loophole—"

"I'm not dragging her into this mess. Next time you talk to them, tell them they just need to be satisfied with the truth *I* gave them."

"Your stubbornness is going to cause your life to be fucked up longer than it needs to be," Thomas says with a frustrated sigh. "And maybe you're okay with that, but I'm not."

In the last two days, my whole life has been turned upside down, and I'm just doing my best to protect the people who matter to me. I don't care what happens to me, but I care a lot about what happens to them.

Chapter Thirty-Two
Emily

At breakfast, Amir stares thoughtfully into his cereal. "Trent's not going to watch me while you're on your trip?"

"No," I say. "Grandma has planned some fun things for you two. Trent has a lot going on with work right now."

"That's why he moved out..." Amir stirs his cereal, but I can tell he's still processing the sudden change in his life.

Trent had been here since April, and while I always considered the impact my relationship with Trent would have on Amir, I never expected everything to blow up so spectacularly. Trent is being so stubborn in a way I'd never anticipated.

It also means that I'm back to barely holding my life together. All the threads are clenched so hard in my hands that I've been in tears almost every night. Trent has been right about people around town—many of them haven't been nice. Some of them have treated me as though I'm some poor, wounded thing, and others have treated me as though I should have known better—but in every case, those people are assuming Trent is guilty.

And it makes me so, so angry.

"Someone at camp said Trent was arrested. Is he in jail again?"

Amir's comment makes my heart stop.

"How was Trent in jail before?" Amir sets down his spoon and focuses on me.

"When Trent was a teenager," I say, carefully, "he made some bad choices, and the police caught him making those bad choices."

"This time too?"

"Some people Trent knows made some bad choices, and the police wanted to know whether Trent knew about those bad choices."

"Did he?"

"No."

"So Trent's not in trouble?"

I turn away from him to stare into the sink. "He shouldn't be." The truth is, I don't know the status of the investigation. He hasn't been charged with anything, but I don't know if that means he's been cleared yet either. Last Maggie heard, there were still some lingering questions, but she didn't know exactly what those were.

"So I can tell Marcus he's a liar?" Amir says.

"You're probably better not to talk about it at all," I say.

"I can't let them tell lies. That's wrong."

"You can tell them it's not true, but I wouldn't sink to calling other people names in response."

"But it *is* a lie."

"He was misinformed, and he told you the information someone else probably told him."

Amir slumps back in his chair, and I can see the same sadness reflected in him that I feel in myself. Part of me resents Trent for leaving me to explain all of this to Amir, but I also understand he's got a lot on his plate right now. It's a silly way to feel, but I can't help myself.

"Can I call Trent later?" Amir asks. "When I get back from camp?"

"Sure," I say, and I vow to text Trent at some point today to tell him it'll be Amir calling and not me calling to fight. I've always been more of an in-person fighter than one to do it over the phone anyway. "Now, if you're done with your cereal, go get dressed and pack your bag for camp. I've got your lunch in the fridge when you're all set."

"Okay," he says, and he scrambles up the stairs.

"Knock, knock," my mother says as she enters the kitchen door.

"What are you doing here?" I ask, grabbing Amir's bowl and dumping the leftovers before slotting it into the dishwasher.

"Lovely to see you, too, dear," my mother says, sliding into one of the kitchen chairs.

"You know I didn't mean it like that. But it's really early. I didn't ask you to take Amir to camp, did I?"

"No, you didn't. But I think that'll probably be what will happen."

"What do you mean?"

"You should sit down."

I slide into the seat across from her, and she reaches out and scoops up my hands, bracing them with hers.

"What I'm about to talk to you about is highly confidential, and it would get quite a few people in trouble if it were to leave this kitchen."

"Okay," I say slowly, my pulse jumping into gear.

"Trent's lawyer came to see me last night."

"Oh no."

"Trent is okay, but he's being a very silly boy. Perhaps noble is a better word."

"What do you mean?"

"The holdup to closing their investigation into Trent revolves around security footage in his shop."

Immediately, I can feel heat rising into my cheeks, and I'm tempted to tug my hands out of my mom's. But this is a familiar pose, one she uses to deliver tough news that she thinks one of us will struggle with. She already knows.

"He deleted some footage?" I'm guessing. Trent never told me, but I can't imagine him keeping it, letting anyone else see it.

"That's right," my mother says, her tone gentle. "But he's refusing to give the name of the person he deleted that footage for."

I tug my hands out from hers, and I cover my face, tears springing to my eyes. "It was me. It was us."

"That's what I thought," my mother says. "I saw the way he was looking at you near the end of Victoria's birthday, and I wondered why I hadn't seen it before. But I think that's the first time we'd all been together in a while." She leans back in her chair. "I was a little surprised, though. I thought something had happened between him and Lila."

"That was a misunderstanding," I say.

"And this?" she asks.

"I love him," I whisper. "Like really, really love him."

"Oh, sweetheart," she says, and she rounds the table to draw me into a tight hug. "What is it about these Castillo men?"

I let out a watery laugh into her shoulder.

When I think I've got myself together, I step away, and my mom rubs my back in comforting strokes.

"I can take Amir to camp," she says, "but if you want to help Trent, I would go down to the police station and out yourself. He won't do it. His lawyer said Trent would rather let the unresolved footage hang over his head for months than tell them who he was with."

"His stubbornness was cute when it was helpful to me," I say.

"It's a bit self-destructive, which is a little concerning for my gentle-hearted girl." She searches my expression for a beat. "You're not worried?"

"He's cut ties with me right now," I say. "He's convinced that his reputation is damaging to my career."

"But I get the sense that his presence buoyed up every other aspect of your life the last few months."

"Yeah," I say, wiping away tears. "I feel like myself again."

"Do you think you two will get back together?"

"I want to."

"This is my motherly advice, which you'll probably ignore. He needs to go talk to someone about how heavily his past is impacting his perception of the future. Is what's going on now bad for him professionally? Yes. Challenging for you professionally? Probably. Does it mean he needs to abandon you and Amir to protect you from that? My personal opinion is that he doesn't, and that what he's done is damaging in a different way than if he'd stayed. We can't protect the people we love from *everything*. As much as we might try."

"We pick our battles."

"We do."

"I want to fight for him," I say.

"Then your first step is going to the station and brandishing the sword of your knowledge." She mocks pulling out a sword and swooshing it around like a lightsaber.

"You're ridiculous."

"Grandma," Amir says from the doorway, "are you pretending to be in Star Wars again?"

"It's our favorite way to battle, my little Obi Wan."

Amir giggles and goes to the fridge to get his lunch. He stuffs it into his backpack and then looks back and forth between me and my mom. "Who's taking me?"

"It is I," my mother says, bowing to him. "I hear we're spending a few days together when your mom goes on a trip." She ushers him toward the door.

"Yeah, but I wish I was still hanging out with Trent. We were going to build my Lego set."

As he goes out the door, my mom turns to blow me a kiss, and then they're gone, chatting. At least I know that Mom can handle Amir's curiosity and confusion about Trent. It's not the first time she's had to explain the unexplainable to Amir's curious mind.

Gathering myself together, I brace myself for the visit to the police station. I'm going to be unbelievably embarrassed, but if it gets the police to close their investigation into Trent, then I can handle the heat.

Chapter Thirty-Three

Emily

The limo ride to New York City to see Lila is almost surreal. Mia's renewed and increased level of fame since the album release means that Pasha and one other bodyguard are in the front, and we're being followed by a second security vehicle that'll be with us all weekend. We had to preselect where we were going to go for the bachelorette gathering—I can't even call it a party—so that Mia's team could secure a VIP area for security and privacy.

The whole thing is mind boggling. I don't understand how she lives like this or even that my brother really enjoys all of it. But he seems to. Guess it all happened to the right person.

"When does the tour start?" I ask, though I have a vague recollection of something about the fall after Maggie's wedding.

"November," Mia says. "We're mostly skirting the edges of the country, staying several days in each place, with a few stops in Missouri for the hometown fans."

"I can't imagine the planning for that," Maggie says.

"It's mostly Taryn and Rebecca who handle those details, and I just hired an HR company to deal with onboarding staff for the tour."

"Do you work with the same people a lot?" I ask.

"My mom had a rule about changing people out every tour, but I wonder now whether that was to keep me isolated and dependent on her. If I didn't have many friends, there wasn't much of a chance I'd figure out Laura was more my manager than my mother, you know? She was all I knew. Sarah's been my best friend forever, but even she was someone my mom approved of—a workaholic like me." She lets out a laugh. "All that to say that I might have a couple dancers back who've toured with me before."

"I think I'd be lonely on tour," I admit.

"It can be lonely and disorienting if you're in a different city every night. It's part of the reason we're booking multiple dates in each place and hoping fans come to us. It's exhausting to pack up and move along constantly."

"Given how big the album has blown up, I can't imagine you'll struggle to fill the stadiums," Maggie says.

"Ticket sales have been going really well so far," Mia says. "No complaints from me." She grins and then digs into an armrest to bring out a bottle of sparkling water. "Anyone else want one?"

"There's water in the armrests?" I ask, lifting up mine. And sure enough, there's a selection of beverages. When I stick my hand in, it's surprisingly cold.

"How's Trent?" Mia asks, her voice quiet.

"My mom says the police have closed their investigation on him and Mullen Mechanics, but I haven't talked to him much." My stomach clenches at how little we've spoken. We've exchanged a few texts about Amir, especially since he was originally going to watch him while I was on this trip. Now that he's cleared, he agreed to stop by my mom's to do the Lego set with Amir.

It's a start. We're rebuilding a relationship from the ground up, and I keep reminding myself that I have to be patient and not despair. The connection is there, and the love is there. I know he loves me, and the fact he admitted that is huge. It's huge, and I need to hold onto the hope that at some point the love will matter more than any issues with his reputation.

The inquiry into his business, into him, was an earthquake, flattening the life we'd established. We hadn't been earthquake-proofed yet, and I'm not sure I really believed we needed to be, that anything could dismantle things so completely. We felt so solid in that house together that I was starting to believe nothing would shake us.

"You two aren't back to normal then," Mia says, more a statement than a question. "I don't know what I would have done if Tyler had ever pulled away. I can be a spiteful bitch."

The way she says it makes me laugh a little. "Key his car? Slash his tires?"

Mia's smile looks practically devious. "I would have enjoyed trying to come up with something, that's for sure." Then her smile fades, and she squeezes my hand. "But I wouldn't have enjoyed the heartache. It's the worst. Feels so hopeless, so helpless."

It's funny to me that Trent and I never confirmed anything to anyone, and yet everyone just seems to have assumed something was going on. Back when we were really just friends, their disbelief over our friendship frustrated me. But now—I don't know—maybe they were just seeing something I was too stubborn to acknowledge, too afraid to let it be true.

"I definitely feel a little helpless," I admit. "It's hard when you know what you want, but you can't make the other person see that it could work, would work."

"Trent is ridiculously stubborn," Maggie says.

"So am I," I say.

"I can get Grady to talk to him," Maggie says. "I won't interfere if you tell me to stay out of it."

"No," I say. "Trent probably needs to talk to someone, and Grady understands the whole picture—mine and Trent's." Whether or not he'll listen to Grady is a whole other discussion. Their relationship is complicated, but if Trent won't talk to me, speaking to Grady or Maggie is likely the next best thing.

"I'll ask him when we get back," Maggie says.

For the last few days leading up to our trip to New York City, I've been queasy. Food hasn't appealed to me, no matter what I've tried to eat. It's like my stomach has gone on strike since Trent got arrested.

When we get to Lila's apartment, her new fiancé, Henry, is already there. He's slightly taller than Lila, with a wiry build. Lila already told us all that they'd bonded immediately over similar experiences in emigrating from China to America as little kids.

Lila's glowing. Absolutely lit from the inside, and I couldn't be happier for her. Henry matches Lila's energy, cracking jokes and mixing drinks. If I could have imagined someone for her, that person would have been like Henry.

"Alright," Maggie says as we're all eating pizza in the apartment.

Well, they're eating pizza. I'm picking at my slice as though it's a toxic substance I'm being forced to consume.

"I have some news, and I wasn't sure when the right time would be to tell everyone, but since we're all together, I thought now?" Maggie keeps glancing at me, and I wonder what she hasn't told me that's clearly making her nervous.

"No vague posts," Lila says, digging out another slice from the box on the coffee table.

"I'm pregnant."

"Ahh!" Lila cries, dropping her slice back into the box and tugging Maggie out of her seat, practically spilling Maggie's pizza onto the floor.

Maggie laughs and keeps her plate of pizza in one hand while she hugs Lila with the other. Mia is next to embrace Maggie, and I pull up the rear.

When Maggie and I embrace, she whispers in my ear, "I'm sorry."

"Do *not* be sorry," I whisper back. "I'm so happy for you, and if I start crying later, those are *happy* tears."

Maggie steps back, and there are already tears pooling in her eyes.

"Don't!" I point at her, my throat tightening. "Don't you dare."

"I can't help it," Maggie says, scooping up the tears as they fall.

"No!" Mia cries. "Ever since I had Victoria, something's been unlocked in me, and I can't see people cry alone."

I look over and tears are streaming down her face.

"Oh, fuck," Lila says, her voice thick with tears too. "Look what you've done."

And then we're all crying, and Henry seems at a bit of a loss.

"We're happy?" he asks, uncertain.

"Yes," I say. "Happy tears." And maybe a bit sad, but I'd never admit that out loud.

The next night at the fancy restaurant Mia booked, we're in a special VIP room for privacy. Pasha, as per usual, is at the door, but it's closed, so we can't see him.

Lila is on my left, and there's no Henry tonight—it's just the four of us. Maggie and Mia are deep in a conversation about town limits and figuring out whether the property Mia and Tyler bought should be absorbed by Little Falls.

"I heard about what happened to Trent," Lila says, keeping her voice low. "He must have been devastated."

"He was," I say. "He is."

"Are you doing okay?" Lila asks.

"Yeah, of course," I say, my smile tight on my face.

"I thought with him living there..."

Part of me wants to tell her the truth, but I have no idea where her head is at when it comes to Trent.

"I was really harsh with him," Lila says. "Meeting Henry made me realize I was trying to fit a square peg into a round hole."

"Are you going to talk to Trent?" I ask.

"Oh, I don't know," Lila says. "I said some pretty shitty things to him." She hesitates for a beat and slides me a sheepish look. "About him."

"Admitting it to me is one thing," I say, "but I know the loss of your friendship, the iciness between you two, bothers him. I think it would mean a lot if you talked to him next time you're home."

Lila swallows and then takes a sip of her drink. She and Mia are the only two drinking. I'm still picking at my food, barely eating, feeling shitty and run down. I must be getting sick, or the stress is knocking me down more pegs than normal.

"He'd want to talk to me?" she asks.

"If you're not going to call him an asshole, I think he'd probably love to talk to you."

Lila gives a light laugh and shakes her head. "Turns out, I was the asshole."

"Sometimes that happens."

A comfortable silence sits between us for a beat while I cut a tiny piece of meat off my chicken and then don't eat it, letting it sit on my fork.

"Are you doing okay?" Lila nods at my plate. "Yesterday, you basically ripped apart the one piece of pizza you took without eating it. Today, you're eating like a bird. This is *not* the Emily I know."

"I'm wondering if I'm coming down with something," I say to cover the fact that this might just be heartbreak showing up in my stomach.

"Oh," Lila says, seeming surprised. "I wondered if there was going to be a double announcement. You were doing those fertility treatments weren't you?"

I can actually feel the color drain from my face as realization sets in. *Oh, shit.* From my purse, I dig out my phone, and I frantically check dates.

I can't be. I can't be. I can't be.

Except if my calculations on my phone are correct, I *could* be.

I sit back in my chair and stare at the wall, trying to decide the best course of action. Logically, I need to take a pregnancy test. But the idea of seeing two lines makes the queasiness in my stomach go into overdrive. The timing could *not* be worse.

At Trent's house, he basically told me he was glad I hadn't gotten pregnant. I'd ignored his comment because it had felt like a moot point.

I wasn't pregnant, so there was no need to get offended that he was glad it hadn't happened. He was right that it would have made everything happening a thousand times more complicated.

But fuck me. Of course it had to happen now.

Maybe I'm not, though. Maybe it's just stress. It could just be stress. And heartbreak. When Omar died, I had trouble eating for weeks, and when Dad died, I went through the same thing. While Trent hasn't died, something between us feels like it's withered.

"Earth to Em," Maggie says. "You okay over there?"

"On the way back to Lila's, I need to make a stop," I say.

Lila squeezes my leg under the table, and when she looks at me, there's excitement in her gaze. But I can't match it, and I really wish I could.

At the pharmacy, Maggie helps me pick the best test to buy, and when we're in the aisle alone, she hugs me tight.

"No matter what happens," she says into my ear, "I love you, and I'm here for you."

When we get back to the apartment, the only one who seems excited is Lila, and she keeps looking around at the rest of us like we're silly for not being hopeful.

After I pee on the stick and we're waiting for the results to show—I refuse to look before the timer goes off—Lila lets out a huff.

"What is going on? Why is everyone acting like this result is a death sentence instead of exactly what Emily wants?" She stares at each one of us, bewildered.

Mia shifts uncomfortably, and Maggie rubs her temples with her index fingers.

"If I'm pregnant," I say, feeling the full weight of reality settle over me, "the baby is Trent's."

Lila's eyes go very wide, and she stares at me for a beat before she says, "Oh my god, I knew it. He's always looked at you like you were this precious, adorable gift. It used to make me so mad. This makes perfect fucking sense. Did he finally tell you?"

"Things are really complicated between us right now," I say. "I just…" Can't find the words to say any more than that.

The timer goes off, and I go into the bathroom. There, two pink lines are on the viewer of the pregnancy test, and I burst into tears.

Maggie, Mia, and Lila pile into the bathroom behind me, and they envelope me into a group hug.

"Life has a terrible sense of humor sometimes, doesn't it?" Mia says.

"I thought this would be such a happy moment," I say through my tears. "But I'm dreading telling him."

Maggie's hand is on my back, rubbing up and down. "If you need someone with you when you do that, I can be there."

That sounds worse—a witness to how I'm sure Trent will take the news.

"No," I say, my words garbled. "I can do it."

Chapter Thirty-Four

Trent

The police tape is gone, Judy has been fired, and some guy named Donny dropped off his resume this morning. It's hard to have any enthusiasm when it feels like my life is a dumpster fire.

Last night, I went over to Joanna's house with my mom as a buffer. Which is fucking ridiculous—that I asked my mom to come with me, afraid Joanna would say something to me about Emily.

It's like I can't even think about her without it feeling like I'm being cracked in half. When the police were all over me, keeping her away from it, out of it, was exactly what I thought I needed to do.

Now that's all receding, the reality of what I've done is sinking in. It's still the right thing to do—ease their life in Little Falls by not having them so closely associated with me—but fuck if it doesn't hurt like hell.

As I sat with Amir last night building the Lego set, I realized I'd probably never be doing this on Emily's living room floor again. That all the things we'd done together—the trips to the fall fairs, the movie nights, the dinners we cooked together—all of it was over.

Emily still ended up going to the station to confess she was the one on the footage. When Thomas told me, I'd lost my shit, but he'd promised he hadn't been the one to talk to her. But I can't imagine how embarrassing it was for her to sit there and confirm all those dates and times.

It just solidifies my belief that she didn't benefit from being with me at all. A damaged reputation. Embarrassment. If I could go back to January me, I'd sit there listening to Grady and Kelvin explain how my relationship with Emily would fall apart eventually when she met someone, and I'd agree and tell myself she was better off instead of being consumed with jealousy over some nameless person she hadn't even met yet—a future I wouldn't be part of.

"You alright over there?" Brett asks from the bay beside me.

"Fine," I mutter.

"At least Dan's going to jail this time. Sounds like the police have a lot on him."

"He got cocky," I say. "I've been there." I stare out into the empty parking lot. Other than a couple oil changes, there's been no work today. It's the first day we've been open again.

"People will come back," Brett says. "Most probably don't even know we're open again."

I don't bother contradicting him, though I know our opinions don't align.

"Dan sold you out last time, and he tried to bring you down this time. Anyone in this town with even a hint of common sense will see the link is Dan, not you."

"Maybe," I say, grabbing another tool to clean. I'm not holding my breath. I'm going to give it a couple more weeks and then suggest selling again to Emily.

"I'm pissed I didn't see the signs in Judy," Brett says. "Should have."

"Sometimes we see what we want to see." For a while, I'd thought I could see a future with Emily—glimmery and distant and not fully formed. Turned out to be a mirage. "Listen," I say, "there's a good chance

I'll be selling this place. I already called Earl about maybe going back there."

"What?" Brett leaves where he's been working through cleaning tools too. "You've got to be shitting me. One little scare and you're out?"

"I wondered if you'd thought about taking over?" I ask.

"You mean if Emily won't sell this place?" Brett is eyeing me in a way I don't like. "She doesn't strike me as the type to back down from a fight."

"How do you know Emily's the investor?" I ask, my voice gruff.

"Came out during the police questioning," Brett says.

"They asked questions about her?" My heart feels like it's in my throat.

"You didn't do anything wrong," Brett says. "You've still got such a chip on your shoulder about what you did at nineteen. And sure, there are some people in town that'll hold that over your head forever, but you don't need to be holding it over your own." He takes a deep breath. "Yeah, they asked questions about Emily and her involvement in this place. But again, and I want you to really fucking hear me, you didn't do anything wrong."

"I dragged her name through the mud."

"*Dan* tried to drag your name and hers through the mud."

"Dan is only a factor because of what I did at nineteen."

Brett shakes his head and lets out a frustrated laugh. "You're so intent on putting yourself on the cross, man. Dan is a viper, and he does what any snake will do when they're backed in a corner—strike out at anyone they can. It's not your fault he's a viper. It's not your fault that his strike grazed her when it was aiming for you. It's not even your fault he was *aiming* for you. When he came here, you made the *right* choice."

"Coming back to Little Falls was a mistake," I say. "I can't build a life here."

Brett lets out a huff of frustration and throws up his hands. "I'm going to go get a coffee. You want anything?"

"Nah," I say, replacing one tool and taking another to wrap in the cloth in my hand. "I'm good."

The roar of Brett's truck reverberates through the silence, and then I hear him drive away. For a beat, the quiet feels good, but then all my thoughts start getting loud, telling me things I don't want to listen to.

"Hey," Emily says from outside the bay.

I whip around, startled, and I drop the tool in my hand. "Hi," I say, and I breathe out the word, conscious of the weight it holds in the air.

"Can we talk?"

I scoop up the tool off the ground, polish it up, and put it back. "There's nothing to say that hasn't been said." Mentally, I'm bricking up my heart, shoring up any leak in my emotions.

"There is, actually."

"Brett's gone on a coffee run, and no one else is here today." I gesture to the empty bays. "Business is shit."

"It'll pick back up. As soon as people realize it was a mistake."

"There will be people who'll never believe it."

"They were probably the ones who were never going to give you a shot no matter what. Not everyone in this town is a good, decent person who believes in second chances. We both know that."

"Is that what you came to talk about?"

"No," she says, and she releases a breath, as though she was holding it in, even as we were talking. "God, this is so hard. I really thought this would be different."

She's got my attention now, and I let myself scan her figure, search her expression. There's a grayish pallor to her skin, and I feel like the worst person in the world. She's obviously unwell.

My heart constricts at why she'd be here to talk to me when she was feeling sick. What if she's really, really ill? Dangerously ill. I take a step toward her, all my defenses starting to crumble.

"Em?" I ask, almost afraid to voice the rest.

"I'm pregnant," she says. "I just found out I'm pregnant."

Chapter Thirty-Five

Emily

"**O**h Jesus." Trent breathes out the words, and the shock on his face is clear. "You're pregnant?"

"I took a test when I was in New York City. I haven't been to the doctor to confirm, but Maggie said it's rare to get a false positive."

"Maggie knows?"

"Trent, *everyone* is going to know."

He stares at me for a beat, and I can see the wheels turning, as though he's picking his words carefully. "Congratulations."

"Trent." I close my eyes at the ridiculousness of that word. "I know the timing—"

"Obviously, you can't tell anyone now that I'm the father."

"And you think people won't be able to put two and two together? You were living in my house. I went to the station and told the police why the footage was deleted. People talk."

He runs his hands along his face. "I'll leave Little Falls and go back to Utica."

"You've got to be kidding me," I say, anxiety sloshing around in my stomach. "That's your solution."

"Have you seen the shop?" He gestures around him. "There's no one here, Em. What am I clinging onto?"

"Clinging on?" I scoff. "You're not clinging onto anything. You're letting it all slip through your fingers like you don't care about any of it." I shut my mouth before the rest of what I'm thinking and feeling spills out.

"I've learned when to cut my losses," he says. "There's a difference."

"There is, and it's not the one you've created. Cutting your losses when going after something is doing more harm than good. When you were a kid, you went after something with your whole chest, and it blew up in your face. You chose wrong. But this situation and that situation couldn't be further apart."

"I hurt people then," he says, "and I'm hurting people now. I can't keep going after something that hurts people."

"You think leaving doesn't hurt? That leaving isn't harmful? What about the people who've come to depend on this shop in Little Falls? The people who took a chance on you and your ability to fix things that were broken?" My voice catches, and I try to steady myself. I won't cry my way through this conversation. "What about Amir?" My voice is so thick with unshed tears that I almost don't recognize it. "What about *me*?"

"People in this town aren't going to be nice about me being questioned, about the shop being under suspicion. Tell me people haven't already said shitty things to you?"

"You know what made those shitty things people were saying worse?" I ask, stepping toward him. "Knowing that I didn't have you standing behind me. You were *nowhere*. I couldn't go home and tell you about the stupid thing someone said to me, or the terrible way someone made me feel. I was alone. I was alone when I had to explain to Amir why kids at camp were asking him about you going to jail."

"You're proving my point, Em. If I wasn't in your life, none of this would be happening. Those comments are exactly why it won't work."

"No, you're framing all of this in some warped way that only makes sense to you. I don't *care* what those people are saying if I've got you. I'll face those questions and comments, and I'll defend you with everything I've got. You have this—I don't know—idea that you're saving me and Amir, but you're *not*. You're just leaving us to face it alone."

"If I'm in Utica, you'll get it a lot less. Just ask Maggie."

He says it with such certainty that I wonder if he and Maggie talked about it one time. And it reminds me how I once suggested that Maggie could use Trent and his past as a way to tank Grady's bid for mayor. I close my eyes, and I try to breathe through that memory. My heart is squeezing so hard in my chest that I almost can't catch my breath. The realization that I did that, suggested that, stings.

"I'm not good enough for you," he says, and his jaw is set.

"Who says?" I ask, my eyes snapping open.

"Come on," Trent says. "You think no one has made a snide comment to me about sinking the reputation of another Sullivan woman?"

"Okay, fine," I say, feeling desperation creeping up my throat. "Are their opinions more important than mine? Who gets to decide whether you're good enough? Because if it's me—which is who it should be—then I call bullshit."

Everything I say is true—I mean it with my whole heart—but it also feels like I'm scrambling for footing in this conversation. He seems so set in his stance that we can't work, his opinion of what this looks like, what it should be.

"Who holds all the pieces when you're not around anymore, Trent?" I can barely get the words out of the tightness in my throat.

"You're killing me, Em," he rasps, and his hands cover his face, shoulders slumped.

"I don't want to kill you, Trent. I just want you to let me love you."

"I'm a marked man," he says, his voice rough with emotion.

He drags his hands down his face, and he looks as exhausted as I feel. I wonder if he's been having trouble sleeping too. Every night, I stare at his side of the bed, and I wish him there so hard. When I close my eyes, I can almost feel his rough palm sliding along my waist, feel the dip in the mattress.

"Judy was dealing drugs on the side, and I didn't know. But she'd have known the risks she was putting on me, on my shop. I can't know that this won't ever be a problem again. And I just..." He shakes his head. "I need to keep you and Amir safe from all of it."

"*You're* not a danger, Trent." I take a risk and step closer to him. "Nothing that's happened in the last week is something you brought on."

"My past is always going to rear its head. I'm never going to escape the ex-con label."

I'm close enough that I can touch him, and so I run my hand from his shoulder to his bicep. Even that brief contact makes everything in my body liquid, as though every ounce of stress and anger that's been holding me up is seeping out of me. Trent closes his eyes, and his hands clench at his sides.

It's wrong, manipulative, even, but I curl into his side, resting my head on this chest. His hand sinks into my hair, but his eyes are still closed.

"You smell like lemons," he whispers.

"Stress cleaning," I say, keeping my voice quiet like his.

"Those chemicals can't be good for the baby."

"I hadn't thought of that," I admit. Part of me has been trying to pretend I'm not pregnant because the idea of facing Trent felt too big, too ominous.

He draws me into a tight hug, and I sink into it, making fists in his shirt at the back, desperate for the contact, the scent of vanilla and motor oil swirling around my senses.

He sighs across the top of my head. "I love you," he says it like it's been ripped out of him. "God, I love you so much. It's like, painful. And I'm sorry I can't do what you want. But I'd always feel like I was ruining your life, and I can't. I just can't."

I clutch onto him and push my face into his chest, willing myself not to cry. It doesn't seem to matter what I say, and it's the most painful and frustrating thing that's ever happened to me.

"You didn't ruin my life, Trent," I say, as the roar of a truck echoes down the quiet street. "You healed it. You healed my heart."

"I've never regretted what I did at nineteen more than I do right now."

But I don't need more of his regret and self-flagellation. He needs to learn to let his past decisions go, to see that those don't *have* to define this future. That he has some choice in that, some agency, despite what's happened this last week. That it's okay to want things in life and to move toward those desires with good intentions.

He's so stuck in this warped sense of himself, of what he can offer. But he can't see that the man he's become more than makes up for the mistakes he once made. And I don't know how to make him.

Brett climbs out of the truck with two coffees in his hands, and I step back from Trent.

"I want you in my life, and I want you in this baby's life," I say, making eye contact. "Maybe you should think about going to talk to someone."

"Like who?" he asks, running a hand over the top of his head.

"A therapist?" I suggest as Brett gives us space by going into the front reception.

Trent grips the back of his neck, but he avoids making eye contact. "You don't think I'm expressing myself very well?"

"I don't think you're *seeing* yourself very well."

"I know who I am."

"Do you?" I say, trying to get him to look at me. "Because to me, it seems like when you hold a mirror up to yourself, all you see are your mistakes and none of your accomplishments."

"I know who I am," he says again, his voice firmer.

I run my hands through my long hair in frustration, and I leave without another word. Right now, I'm not going to get through to him, and I don't know what it'll take to make him see reason.

Chapter Thirty-Six
Trent

I'm so rattled from Emily's visit and don't have enough work to distract me, so I roll up to Grady's studio at the old train station to decompress. When I enter the building, the receptionist, Lola, grins at me.

"Trent Castillo, are you following in your brother's footsteps now? Going to record a song or two?"

"Not much of a singer," I say, going to the fridge and grabbing a soft drink. "What are you still doing here?"

"Sarah Telling is coming tomorrow with one of her proteges from Center Stage to record some kind of demo track. I'm just getting everything in order before I head out. Grady's in the studio, if you want to head back. No one else is there."

"Thanks." I crack the can and wander down the hallway to where the recording studio is located. There's an apartment here for all the famous people who do fly-by-night visits to record something before going back to LA or NY or some other city. There always seems to be someone here.

Grady isn't in the booth. Instead, he's in the part where people normally record, his guitar resting on his knee, a pencil in his hand, and paper on the music stand, scribbling away as I pull open the door. He's a producer, songwriter, and an occasional recording artist. His last album blew up, but he had no interest in going on tour.

"Emily come to see you?" Grady asks without looking up.

I freeze in the doorway. "What do you know?"

"Just come talk to me," Grady says, setting the pen on the music stand and setting his guitar back on the stand.

"Who are you writing for?" I ask, avoiding the obvious topic of conversation.

"Sarah Telling," he says. "That's confidential, obviously. Not sure if what I'm writing will get used or not."

I slide into one of the few comfortable chairs in the room and sip my drink. Grady doesn't say anything, and I know he's going to outwait me.

"Em's pregnant," I say.

"Congratulations," Grady says. "Maggie's pregnant too."

"She is?"

"Yep. Castillo cousins growing up together."

"Emily was supposed to be telling everyone she used a donor," I say, somewhat resentful, even if it's not justified. She was right in the shop today—it doesn't take much to put two and two together. It's just that I don't know what to do with how Emily and I made four without fully realizing it.

"You were living with her, man. Did you really think when she announced she was pregnant that *no one* was going to raise their eyebrows?"

"I was renting a room."

"Were you? What'd you pay her with? Dick?"

"Fuck off."

"I'm going to guess that you're not taking the news as well as both of you might have hoped."

"Definitely not as well as she hoped," I admit. "I'm not sure what I expected. It's going to sound fucking ridiculous, but when I agreed to all this, all I knew was that I didn't want anyone else to have her. Saying that out loud makes me sound like a dick."

"Makes you sound like you've had some pretty significant feelings for her for a while."

I absorb his comment, and when I let it settle, I think he's probably right. Every time I went to pick Emily up from a date, I felt a little vindicated that she couldn't find anyone she wanted to be around more than me. That at the end of those nights, she was with me. Back then, I had no desire or interest in analyzing that feeling, but I can see now that it was there.

"I know some part of you thought you could keep the paternity of Emily's baby a secret, but all secrets come out in time. We both know that. Do you really want it to be a secret? You don't want that life with her?"

Grady and I poke fun at each other all the time, and the sincerity in his voice makes me realize he understands that nothing about what's happening is a joke. That it's very real and very overwhelming.

"The way I feel about Maggie," Grady continues, "I wouldn't let anything or anyone come between us. And I sure as hell wouldn't be okay with anyone else raising my kid."

"Yeah, but you're you."

"What does that mean?"

"Come on, Grady. Rockstar. Celebrity songwriter. Friend to the stars. There's nothing seedy or bad about being associated with you in this town, in the world. Even you fucking up your run for mayor didn't tarnish your shine in this town."

"Ah," he says, as though it's clicked for him. "This is about you going to jail."

"Of course it is. And it's about how my past just won't fucking let me go."

"It won't let *you* go, or you won't let *it* go."

"Now you sound like Emily."

"If everyone is saying the same thing, then maybe there's something to it."

"I got brought in for questioning last week. Em was brought in for questioning. They asked people who work for me questions about her and her relationship with me. Those things happened to her because of me."

"So you think the sum contribution that you've brought to her life is that negative experience?"

When he puts it like that, it seems stupid. Of course it hasn't *all* been bad. "No, I'm just saying that something bad happened to her because of me."

"Was *she* arrested?"

"No."

"I'm just trying to figure out your logic here," Grady says. "It seems to me like you're letting the cloud of your past self hang over you. And I've been there. Punishing myself for past mistakes at the expense of my future happiness. *I have been there.*"

"You just had to figure out you were being an idiot," I say.

Grady stares at me.

"It's not that simple."

Grady sighs and runs a hand down his face. "Have you thought about going to therapy?"

"No," I say, and then I swallow down my pride. "Em mentioned it to me earlier."

"Maggie and I went to couples therapy when we first got back together. I..." His voice cracks. "I did some serious damage, and we needed to figure out a way through it, beyond it. Going into a marriage, into a life together with any lingering resentment seemed foolish. I'm in this with Maggie for a lifetime." He takes a deep breath. "Mia went to a lot of therapy before she came back here to be with Tyler and Victoria. She still meets with her support group online or in person when she can. Pasha went to therapy when his fiancée in Russia died. It's okay to need other people to help you sort through complex emotions, through complex experiences."

I rub my face, but I don't say anything in response. "You and Maggie never told me you were going to therapy."

"We both knew we loved each other, but we also knew we had a lot to work out together. The way I treated her when we were kids was not okay. And the way I was when I first got back also wasn't okay. I had to acknowledge that, and we needed to figure out a way to move forward together. You know, I almost lost Maggie because I was trying to protect her from the job offer I had. I didn't want to put stress on her that she didn't need if I wasn't going to take the job. Now, she and I don't have any secrets. It's how I knew about Emily—honestly, probably before you—sorry, about that."

"I told Em that I might move back to Utica."

"Why?"

"I just can't see how I can make it work here."

"With her?"

"With this town."

"You're going to need to give me more than that. Wasn't the shop doing well?"

"It was until I got taken in for questioning. Might as well have been arrested with the way people have responded. Today was a graveyard."

"It was closed for a few days. It'll take a bit for word to get out—about everything."

"How often is the truth louder than a lie?"

"Good question. I think if you consistently show up, even those people who never heard the truth start to understand the truth. They can see it reflected in who you are. That's what you were doing before, and it was working, right?"

"I just don't know."

Grady picks up his pencil and twirls it across his knuckles a few times. "If this past week hadn't happened, if Dan the snake had never materialized, and I'd asked you what you wanted from your life, what would you have told me?"

Emily. Amir. A baby.

It's right there without me having to even consider it. What we'd had together in that house for the last few months had been the happiest, most content I'd ever been. I had the girl. A kid who looked up to me, and the potential to be better each day.

"I love her," I say, my voice cracking. "I've never loved anyone like I love her."

"Then you fight like hell to keep that. You don't throw it away. You don't set it aside. But the fact that we're sitting here, that you're not with her, means you've got work to do. Your fight isn't out there," he says, pointing to the door, "it's in here." He touches his chest and then his head. "You get those two things aligned, and you're good, man. 'Cause she loves you too."

I put my head in my hands, and I'm barely holding myself together. "You really think I can have that? You think I deserve that?"

Grady rises off his stool and comes to my chair, hauling me out of my seat and into his arms. I can't hold it in anymore, and a sob escapes.

"I love you, man," Grady says as he claps me on the back. "And I think you deserve Emily and Amir and your shop and a chance to be a good dad to this baby. What you don't deserve is to keep punishing yourself and letting other people punish you for a mistake you already paid for."

I squeeze him tight, and I wonder whether it's really possible to let go of the weight that I've been dragging behind me since I was nineteen and the police raided my house.

I've been seeing Amber, the therapist Grady recommended and offered to pay for, for the last few weeks, and I've been surprised at how I've been starting to see my life differently. It's been weird to reframe my experiences just by talking about them.

When I got out of jail years ago, I was offered some reintegration support, but I'd already made up my mind that I wasn't planning to be a husband and father. That bridge had been blown up and couldn't be repaired. Who'd want someone like me?

"Tell me about you and Emily," Amber says.

"What do you want to know?"

"When you first came, you stated that being 'good enough' for her was a goal. So today I'd like to explore what that relationship has been like up to this point."

I try to figure out where to even start, how to categorize her and us. "I fake dated her younger sister in high school."

"The one who helped you learn how to read."

"Yeah, but Em and I never really connected. We didn't really know each other. Not until we worked on a fundraiser together almost two years ago now."

"The one for Little Falls after the flood?"

"That's the one," I say. "She was helping to organize it, and even then, we hung out a bit. But the night of the concert, something just *clicked*." I snap my fingers. "We were standing on the side of the stage, and I made her laugh. Her dad had just died, and she was clearly struggling, but I got her to laugh. When I looked over at her and saw her smile, I just thought—that's it." It's the first time I've ever admitted to myself, let alone out loud, that the lightning strike happened in that moment. But looking back on it, I never saw Em the same after that.

Sure, we were still friends, but she was *the* friend for me. The one I'd show up for no matter what time or where she needed me.

"Was that connection mutual?"

"I don't know," I say. "We hung out a lot. She called me when she needed something—something fixed, Amir looked after, picked up from a date."

"Picked up from a date?"

"Yeah," I say, realizing that might seem weirder than it was. "She was doing this dating experiment thing, but the guys all sucked."

"And how'd that make you feel?"

"I was glad none of them held her interest."

"Why?"

"You know," I say with a little laugh, "I think it might have been because I was already half in love with her."

"And what are some things you think you've done to express that love?"

I sit back in my chair, surprised by the question. The obvious ones come easy. "I agreed to father her baby, and I did a bunch of tests so she wouldn't have to worry about that baby." Then I think about it some more. "When she got Amir's genetic tests back, I held her while she cried, and on the anniversary of her husband's death, I went to the cemetery with her."

"If I told you that those would be things most people would consider as adding value to someone's life—being that system of support—what would you say to that?"

I take a deep breath and then release it, really letting myself consider her words without getting defensive or looking for an alternate picture of things. My fingers are gripping my knees hard. "I could see that." My chin trembles, and I blink away tears. "It's just really important to me that I don't make her life worse."

"I understand that," Amber says, and her voice is gentle. "Let's explore that some more. Because, like we talked about before, how we frame our experiences makes a difference in how we respond to them, how we move forward from them. Tell me about some of the other experiences you've had with Emily."

And so I do. I lay it all bare. Every joy and sorrow over the last two years, and I don't sugarcoat what's happened, but I also try not to downplay any of it either. Maybe it's possible that I can make Emily's life easier in some ways and harder in others, and that eventually those two things *do* balance each other out. That I don't have to give the negative more value or weight, even if that's what I've grown accustomed to doing.

The truth is, if I can find a path forward, one that takes me to her doorstep, I'll put in the work to get there, carve the path from rock with my bare hands if I have to. Because I know that if I step back through her door again, I have to be ready to handle it all. I can't walk away a second time.

Chapter Thirty-Seven
Emily

Amir is back at school, and it's mid-September. Maggie gets married in a month, and it feels like I'm constantly on the phone with Lila about one wedding detail or another. If I ever get married again, I'm going small and low-key.

Except, I can't see a world in which I do marry again. I'm back to that place—heartbroken and in denial.

Trent collects Amir from Grady and Maggie's house or from my mom, but we've barely spoken. He's left a giant, gaping hole in my life, and in some ways, it's worse than when Omar died. Trent has chosen to remove himself, and he's still out in the world where I catch glimpses of him.

His mom has been keeping me updated on the shop, and it's rebounded a little since the investigation. The payments Trent was making keep appearing in my bank account each month.

Business is not back where it was before Trent was taken in for questioning, but Penny seems certain that business will keep climbing again. Word of mouth has started to spread to the surrounding areas about how good Trent and his shop are, and that's allowed their business to start increasing there. Maybe some parts of Little Falls will never let the past go, but there are many others who don't even know that past exists.

I've been to the doctor, and I'm due at the end of April. Part of me is still holding out hope that Trent will somehow understand that his past doesn't have to define him, but the way he's been behaving makes me think I'm hoping for a miracle rather than something that's likely.

Although Maggie told me I'd have to fight like hell to keep him, and I was determined to do that, our conversation at the shop made me realize that you can't convince someone of something they refuse to see. No amount of begging or inserting myself into his life is going to change his opinions about himself. The problem isn't that he doesn't love me. If anything, in his mind, he loves me *too* much.

I've just finished signing some closing papers in my real estate office with Donny, who is working part-time for Trent now, and Leah when I get a text from Trent.

I say goodbye to Leah and Donny at the door, and then I go back into my office to stare at the text again.

Can you meet me at the lake?

After weeks of silence, the message doesn't feel like a crack in the ice, but rather a sudden, massive thaw.

When? I can't even pretend I won't go, that I won't change all my plans for the rest of the day to be there. If he's reaching out, there has to be a reason, and hope is stirring in me so hard that I can't stay seated. I'm pacing, waiting for his reply text.

An hour? Or whenever you can make it. Just let me know.

I read each word over and over, probably analyzing what's behind it far harder than I should. An hour feels like forever from now.

I will meet you there in an hour.

Then I shuffle papers on my desk, scan through real estate pages, and mostly feel the stirrings of worry mixed with anxiety and hope. What could this mean?

When I get to the lake, Trent is already there. He climbs out of his truck to greet me. His jeans sit low on his hips, and the T-shirt he's wearing seems to cling to all his muscles. Seeing him is like being hit in the solar plexus, and the breath is knocked right out of me. I don't know when exactly he started having this effect on me, but it's been so long since I've felt it that I have to hold onto my car door for a beat before I step away.

Depending on what he says, I don't know how I'll survive this conversation.

"Hey," he says, his smile sheepish. "Thanks for coming."

"You thought I wouldn't?"

He searches my face, and I wonder if my expression looks like his—as though I'm soaking in every detail, comparing it to the last time I saw him.

"It's really good to see you," he says.

The truth—that he could have been seeing me this whole time—sits on my tongue, and I have to look away before the bitterness creeps out.

"Are you okay if we rent a boat?"

I frown slightly. I wore another dress, but it's loose fitting and down to my ankles. I follow him toward the rental near the dock. "As long as it doesn't tip."

"It's not gonna tip, Em." He gives me another little grin, and my heart constricts.

It would be so, so easy to sink back into how we used to be with each other. But there's a part of me that's wary, worried he's going to smash my heart instead of just causing a spiderweb of cracks.

Oh, god. If he brought me here to tell me he's dating again, I might vomit. And it won't be from seasickness.

"Can you give me a little hint about what this is about?" I ask as he pays for the boat and the attendant gets one of the larger ones set up for us.

"I'd rather we were out there so I don't get cold feet," he says.

That is not a helpful comment for my peace of mind, and I grip my hands together in front of me. Then I practice my deep breathing, the routine I've done with Amir when he's feeling emotionally over-whelmed.

Trent's hand lands on the small of my back, and the contact makes me want to rotate into his side, gather him close and never let him go. But the familiar gesture also settles my anxiety in a way I never would have predicted. He's put his hand there so many times for so many reasons. It's like my body knows with that single handprint that whatever he's going to say on the boat won't break my heart more.

We climb into the boat, and it rocks, but this time neither of us laughs about the motion. Nothing feels funny yet, and I miss that ease.

He rows us out into the middle of the lake and then he clicks the oars into place. He swallows and runs his hands down his face.

The swishing in my stomach returns.

"I, uh, I'm not sure where to start. Which, since I asked you here, probably seems like poor planning."

"I don't care where you start, Trent. But I have to be honest, all of this is making me really anxious. Are you—are you dating someone else?"

"Absolutely not," Trent says with a startled laugh. "Not a chance."

I release the pent-up breath, and my whole body quiets. Whatever this is, it's not that. Thank god.

"Some of this is hard for me to say out loud, but my therapist thinks—I think—it's important you know it all."

"Therapist?"

"Took your advice—well, your advice and Grady's. It's been good for me. You know? I was so in my head in ways that weren't helpful or maybe even true."

"Trent, I'm so proud of you," I whisper.

A hint of a smile almost appears, and he puts his elbows on his knees. "That means a lot, Em, but you don't even know the half of it."

"Tell me," I say. "Whatever you want to tell me, I want to hear it."

"Not all of it is good."

"That's okay."

"You know about the drug stuff in high school," he says, "but what I never really told anyone, what I rarely said out loud was that..." He takes a deep breath. "Part of me was proud of what I accomplished then—even though I got arrested and went to jail, even though what I did hurt people. For a long time, I felt really ashamed of being proud of that. And I guess, what I've figured out with Amber's help—that's my therapist—is that I wasn't so much proud of the drug part, but I was proud that I was able to build something. It was hard for me to pull those two ideas apart, and so I saw my success as something, subconsciously, that I was ashamed of."

Some of that makes sense. Trent was good at joking about being good at things, but genuine compliments made him uncomfortable, and he would divert attention to someone or something else. When he worked for Earl, he'd seemed better at taking people's kind comments, but maybe that was because he didn't own the business, wasn't responsible for everything.

"On top of that, when I moved back to Little Falls, it felt like people were only comfortable with me getting so far beyond what I'd done at nineteen before someone felt the need to remind me that I'd been that guy, and that guy had been a total piece of shit."

"Oh, Trent." Tears fill my eyes, and I really wish we weren't in a rowboat so I could hug him.

"But I've had to learn how to separate *what* I did from *who* I am. If I let people who don't know me create my value, then I'm always going to struggle to get beyond that. They know what I did, but not who I am."

"It's going to take time—"

"It might," he agrees. "I also have to be okay if it never happens. If there are people who will always identify me by what I did and not who I am. I have to know and believe in who I am, and I have to have faith that people who do know me, who love me, aren't bullshitting me when they say I'm a good man." His voice cracks.

I knew there was a lot to uncover, a lot going on under the surface, but I'm startled by how deep it goes, how far those roots crept, unseen.

"Honestly, I'm not quite there with all of that. When you believe things about yourself, it takes a long time to reprogram those lines."

"I can understand that," I say.

"One of the things I asked if we could focus on in therapy first was..." He takes a deep breath and swallows. "How I feel about you and Amir."

"Okay," I say, and his uncertain expression makes tears form.

"What I've come to realize is that..." He takes another deep breath, and I can see how hard this is for him, like he's pulling the words from somewhere deep. "That two things can be true. That my ex-con past and the repercussions of that can make your life and Amir's more difficult, but that it's still possible for me to add value to your lives too. That I don't have to...my mistakes don't have to be worth *more* than my successes."

"I love you," I say, and I risk the wobble to get on my knees. The metal of the boat is cold, but I can't stand being away from him anymore. Once I'm between his knees, I wrap my arms around his middle, and he brushes my hair away from my face.

"I love you too. So much. But I didn't want to come back into your life if I didn't think I could be what you need."

In this moment, I could tell him he is exactly what I need, but I also understand he had to believe it too.

"I've been so afraid to go after what I wanted because of what I did and how I did it the first time."

"What do you want?"

"You, this baby, your son. The shop. I want the life we had in your house before Dan set off a bomb in my life and blew up the stability I thought I'd found."

"I want all of that too," I say. "So much." I close my eyes as tears slip down my cheeks.

He kisses them away and draws me into his chest, his chin resting on the top of my head. "I don't have it all figured out yet, Em, but I didn't want to miss any more time with you, with our baby, with Amir. No matter what, I'm not walking out on you again, if you'll let me come back."

"No matter what?" My voice is thick with tears.

"I know I hurt you," he says, and his voice now has the same thickness as mine. "I get that now—that leaving didn't save you, maybe created more harm than if I'd stayed. And I'm so sorry, Em." His voice cracks, and he holds me tighter. "I love you with my whole fucking heart, and I've never felt this way about any woman, ever. But I didn't think I deserved it, and I thought you deserved more than what I could give."

"You're exactly who I want," I say, drawing back to frame his face. "I love every part of you, even the part that smells like motor oil."

He lets out a watery chuckle. "I'm committed to being the best version of myself for you, if you'll have me."

"I haven't met Amber, but she's my favorite person, ever."

"Funny you should say that," Trent says, wiping his eyes. "She suggested we might want some sessions together."

"I'd be honored to go with you. Truly." I stare up at him, and gratitude and love rush through me. Part of me wasn't sure we'd ever get this moment, that he'd ever be willing to see himself in the light I see him. To know he's on that road, that he's committed to feeling better, is huge. "I didn't go when Omar died, and maybe I should have. If we're having a baby, we should definitely make sure that our foundation together is rock solid. Unshakeable."

He rests his forehead against mine, and his hands slide into my hair. "Have I told you how much I love you? It's possible I might have to say it to you a hundred times a day. Now that I've named this feeling, it's like..." He presses his lips to my forehead. "Every time I look at you, it's all I can think. *I love you. I love you. I love you.*"

I breathe him in a for a beat, and then I say, "Why did you have to pick a boat for all this?"

"I knew if I had you out here, that I'd have no choice but to be honest."

"Can you come down here?" I ask, sliding back a little to give him room to sit on the bottom of the boat too. Thankfully, it's dry.

He scooches down, and I hitch up my dress to straddle him. His hands grip my hips, and we stare at each other for a beat.

"I missed you," he whispers. "I wish I'd gotten my head together two years ago when we first met, so I was ready for you."

"We went on the journey we were meant to," I say, planting a soft kiss on his lips. "Who knows what would have happened if we'd been different people when we started hanging out? You could play the 'what if' or 'if only' game forever." I rock against him, and his eyes snap to mine.

"Here?"

"You're not going to get me all wet, are you?" I ask, kissing him again.

"I sure hope so," he says, and he laughs against my ear before kissing a line down my throat. "Peaches. I could eat you all fucking day."

"That sounds like a promise," I murmur, arching into him.

In no time, things get even more heated between us, a familiar rhythm we both remember and understand. Before wiggling out of my panties, I glance around the lake, but there's no one else out here today.

Trent releases himself, and he guides me down, my dress billowing around us. We both groan with relief as we connect, and Trent frames my face, kissing me gently as I start to move.

"You know when you said in my shop that I healed your heart?" he says, his voice rough with emotion.

"I meant it," I say.

"You healed mine too in a way I didn't even know I needed."

"I love you."

"I love you too."

And then we're moving together, seeking connection and release, a dance I'm sure we'll be doing for the rest of our lives.

Epilogue

Trent

I've been back living with Emily and Amir for four weeks. While the shop is gradually getting back to pre-arrest business, it's not there yet. Once a week, I'm seeing Amber, which Grady is still paying for. As much as it hurts my pride to have Grady pay for the sessions, I'm keeping track of the cost, and I intend to pay him back. No matter what, I'm not stopping, because I can recognize how much of a difference it's making for me and for my relationship with Emily. Before, I kept a lot of it inside, happy to help her with her tough days, but unable to give her the same trust. Now, I don't hesitate as much to share my bad days with her.

I didn't think it would be possible for me to be happier, to be more content than I was before the arrest, but it turns out openness and honesty—knowing exactly where you stand with someone—breeds more positives.

"Trent," Emily calls from the bottom of the stairs. "We're going to be late for the rehearsal dinner."

"Sorry!" I call down, grabbing my belt and looping it through my pants as I hustle down the stairs. Technically, there's no rehearsal, but Maggie and Grady decided they wanted a pre-wedding dinner with everyone involved in the wedding. Which is good, because I had a last-minute client show up when we were closing.

Em's been really patient with my hours, since I've been trying not to turn away anyone willing to give my shop a chance. But that means sometimes I'm running a bit late for things.

I kiss her temple when I reach the kitchen, and I give Amir a high five. Then I take in Emily's dress—a new pale green one—and I can't help thinking about where it's going to land later.

"Hey, Em," I say when she's grabbing her purse off the table.

She glances back at me.

"Have I told you today that I love you?"

"You've told her like a million times," Amir says with a huff.

"Hey, you know I love you too, little buddy," I say.

"You love everyone." Amir throws up his hands in a dramatic fashion.

"But I love you two the most." I ruffle his hair.

Emily wraps her arm around my waist and leans into me. "I'll never get tired of hearing it," she says to me. "Don't listen to him."

I kiss the top of her head, and we climb into my truck together. On the way to the restaurant, I hold Em's hand in mine. There's still a little part of me that rears up sometimes. Tries to tell me I don't deserve this. That someday she'll realize she could do better. But then I just remind myself of all the ways Emily shows me I'm enough. All the ways I'm working to be the best version of myself.

At the restaurant, everyone is already there, mingling. We say "hello" to Pasha as we pass him at the front door.

Inside, I go to the bar to get Em some water, Amir some chocolate milk, and a beer for me. When I see who else is at the bar, I hesitate for a beat, but I can't avoid her forever.

"Lila," I say, when I step up beside her.

"Trent," she says, and then she turns toward me. "Guess we're stuck together tomorrow."

"For part of it, at least. You going to be okay?"

"I meant to talk to you, but I've been embarrassed to do it." She faces the bar again, avoiding eye contact. "I was too hard on you about what did or didn't happen between us."

"And I apologize too," I say, "for not taking what happened seriously enough. For not understanding that your feelings might not be the same as mine."

Then she rotates to face me, the drink that was just delivered in her hand. She scans me, and then she smiles. "I cannot believe you're the same guy from two years ago."

I let out a little laugh in response, and then I order my drinks with the bartender. "At the risk of hearing something I don't want, why's that?"

"I'm not going to be mean," Lila says. "You just seem so settled, but lighter. I don't know how else to describe it. You were fun and flirty, but some part of you felt held back. And I think that's what I was reaching for. But I was never the one meant to unlock that. I can see that now."

"Emily tells me you're engaged," I say as two of my drinks slide onto the counter in front of me. "Congratulations."

"Thank you," she says. "Meeting Henry made me totally realize why you and I weren't a good fit. He and I just make sense." She glances over my shoulder. "Like you and Emily. I'm really happy for you both. She deserves it, and so do you."

Her statement doesn't make me draw back, and I try to let those words land instead of slide off me. "That means a lot," I say, my voice rough.

"I'm just glad I can say it and mean it. That we're all back in a good place."

"Do you still have any connections to the theater in Utica?" I ask. An idea has been half-formed in my brain the last few weeks.

"I know how to book it, if that's what you mean," she says.

"Is it expensive?" I ask.

"Trent Castillo, are you planning to strip again?"

I chuckle and shake my head. "No, but I have something I want to do there. Thirty minutes to an hour, tops."

"You and…"

"One other person."

A slow grin spreads across Lila's face. "I spent a lot of time on the phone with the woman who does the booking. Assuming she remembers me, I'll see what I can do. Leave it with me."

"Thanks," I say, and then I juggle to get all three drinks into my hands. "And Lila?"

She smiles.

"I'm glad we're okay again."

"Me too," she says.

To pull this off, I utilized all my resources. Kelvin was here fifteen minutes ago, and he got the screen set up with everything I needed. Grady came and did a sound check, and Mia loaned me Pasha to get Emily here right on time.

I've got thirty minutes of free use before another group comes in to set up some sort of theater performance that'll be running in this building for weeks. I'm not sure how Lila talked them into giving me access for free, but my bank account is grateful. It took a hit a few weeks ago when Maggie went shopping with me.

"Hello?" Emily calls out from the edge of the audience.

"Over here," I call.

"What are you doing here? This has been the weirdest day. Pasha came to pick me up, and for the first time in forever, the English he was speaking made no sense. But I got in the car."

"I'm glad you did," I say. "This seat right here is reserved for you."

"What is going on?" she asks, but she's laughing. "Trent, are you going to strip for me?"

"Why does everyone think I'm going to take off my clothes?"

She eyes me.

"Fair. I take them off a lot with you. But not today. Or at least, not *right* this moment."

I gesture to the seat in the front row, and she sits down. I sit beside her, and then the screen lights up.

"Since we watch so many movies, I made one for you," I say.

"What?" She lets out another little laugh of disbelief. "What even is my life right now?"

But then she sees the first image. It's a selfie of her and me from the Small-Town Saviors show, and her breath audibly catches.

Then it's my voiceover, 'cause I didn't want to fuck this up.

"We'd been hanging out for a while before the show, but this was the night that I fell in love with you, I just didn't realize it then. We were standing on the side of the stage, and I said something—I don't even remember what—and it made you laugh. It had been such a sad, emotional time that when I looked over at you laughing, something just clicked for me. Like a puzzle piece slotting into place. From that moment on, there wasn't anything I wouldn't do for you."

And then more photos and videos play of the year we spent together—raising Amir, doing silly things together. They all came off my camera roll or hers. I emailed myself stuff when she wasn't paying attention.

It freezes again on a photo of the two of us from New Year's Eve.

"It wasn't until you asked me to be the father of your child that part of me thought maybe it might be possible to have something else, something even better with you. I didn't really know what that was, what it looked like, or even if I could handle it, but I knew I wanted it. I wanted to grab onto it with both hands and never let go."

Then it starts up again, more photos and videos of things we'd done together in the months after that, when we were living together—and though I didn't admit it at the time—being a family.

"And then, when we lost our footing." There's a photo of my shop with police tape. "You never gave up on me, on us, and I'm so fucking grateful you gave me a second chance because now this gets to be my life."

More photos and videos play from when we got back together to just the other day. It freezes on the selfie I took of Em, Amir, and me in the living room on the couch when we were watching a kids' movie together.

I turn to her in the seat, and she's crying, tears streaming down her face. She's on the verge of the ugly cry face she hates to make but that has become so frequent during her pregnancy.

"I brought you back to the place where I first knew I loved you to tell you that I want to love you forever." I get down on one knee, and I pop open the box.

She covers her face, and she cries. Instead of waiting for an answer, I tug her out of her seat and into my arms. Accepting the ring is a formality. I know she'll say "yes." That we're doing life together forever. The thing she needs most right now isn't a ring, it's a hug.

She clutches onto me, and she says, "It's a...It's a..." She turns her face to the side so her ear is pressed against my heart. "Yes. Yes."

"I love you, Em, and I'm going to do everything in my power to make sure you know that, you feel that, for the rest of our lives together."

When she steps back, I slide the ring onto her finger, and she brushes away her tears. Taking her hand, I lead her out into the lobby where we're met with more people than I expect—my mom, Em's mom, Maggie, Grady, Tyler, Mia, Victoria, Pasha, Kelvin, and Brett, and scooting out of the crowd, is Amir.

"Mom, did you say yes?" he asks, his eagerness clear.

"I did," she says, her voice still watery with emotion.

"Yes!" Amir cries, raising his fist in the air. "A brother or sister and a dad. This is like—it's like the best day ever."

He runs toward us, and I crouch down, catching him up into my arms. I set him on my hip, and Em leans into my side as I put my other arm around her, and the three of us—soon to be four—are ready to face the future together.

It's a future I never expected for myself, and I'll always be grateful I managed to heal in time to grasp it.

To see their wedding, the birth of their second child, and other bonus content sign up for my newsletter here: https://bookhip. com/GDDHQCQ

To get Guarded Hearts, Pasha's story, click here: https://myb ook.to/GuardedHearts2025

What else have I written?

Bellerive Royals Series – Interconnected standalones

Fake Crown

Scarred Crown

Heavy Crown

Fallen Crown

Tucker Billionaires – Interconnected standalones

Temporary Love

Fierce Love – *Coming soon*

Colliding Love – *TBA*

Reckless Love – *TBA*

New Adult Sports

Saving Us

Fake Crown

Donaghey Brothers Series – Romantic suspense

Retribution

Resurrection

Redemption

Little Falls Series – Small Town Romance

Rival Hearts

Mending Hearts

Healing Hearts

Guarded Hearts

First Date Challenge – loosely linked to the same world – for maximum enjoyment, read after Book 2

Adult Contemporary Romance

When Stars Fall

294

Miss Matched

Acknowledgements

As with any book, I'm thankful for such a supportive partner and my understanding children. Sometimes I'm lost in a book idea or writing a chapter when I'm sure they'd like my attention elsewhere. Hopefully, seeing my pursue my dreams has a net positive impact.

I'm really grateful to my proofreading team of Proof Positive (Angela) and Red Adept Editing, who do their best to catch my typos and inconsistencies.

Thanks to my cover designer Shannon Passmore who is so easy to work with and always manages to figure out what I'm aiming for, even when I can't quite articulate it.

Thanks to Ember Literary PR for doing their best to give this book a good launch out into the world. Releases are always a bit nerve wracking, but they're much easier with a good team of people.

About Wendy Million/W. Million

Wendy Million is a high school teacher whose award winning contemporary romances about strong women and troubled men have captivated her loyal readers.

Writing as Wendy Million, she is the author of the romantic suspense series *The Donaghey Brothers,* as well as the contemporary second chance romances, *When Stars Fall*, and *Miss Matched*.

Writing as W. Million, she's the author of the *Bellerive Royals* series, the *Little Falls* series, and the *Tucker Billionaires* series.

When not writing, Wendy enjoys spending time in or around the water. She lives in Ontario, Canada with two beautiful daughters, two cute pooches, and one handsome husband (who is grateful she doesn't need two of those).